STICKS

AND

STONES

ALSO BY EMMA SALISBURY

THE DS COUPLAND DETECTIVE SERIES
FRAGILE CORD (Book One)
A PLACE OF SAFETY (Book Two)
ONE BAD TURN (Book Three)
ABSENT (Book Four)
FLESH AND BLOOD (Book Five)

THE DAVY JOHNSON EDINBURGH GANGLAND SERIES
TRUTH LIES WAITING (Book One)
THE SILENCE BEFORE THE SCREAM (Book Two)

Sticks and Stones

Emma Salisbury

Copyright © 2020 Emma Salisbury

All rights reserved.

No part of this publication may be reproduced or transmitted in any form or by any means without permission of the author.

All the characters in this book are fictitious and any resemblance to actual persons living or dead is purely coincidental.

Although real place names and agencies and support services are referred to in this book the storyline relating to them is completely fictitious.

Cover design by Author Design Studio

Interior design by Coinlea Services

ACKNOWLEDGEMENTS

Although as a writer of fiction I tend to make things up as I go along, there are times when facts are required. The websites and reports referred to in my author notes were particularly helpful, and I found myself returning to Val McDermid, *Forensics, The Anatomy of Crime*, (London: Profile Books Ltd, Wellcome Collection) as a fascinating reference book.

I am enormously indebted to my early readers, in particular Lynn Osborne, whose feedback is always invaluable. Thank you for being so generous with your time. I hope you enjoy meeting your character!

As ever, thank you to my family and friends for putting up with my overactive imagination, which has been known to seep into reality at the most inopportune times. And, thanks, of course, to Stephen.

PART ONE

CHAPTER ONE

The sign above the main entrance said 'Visitor Centre,' though it was unlike any tourist attraction she'd ever been to before. There would be a certain amount of sitting and gawping involved, she supposed…and a hell of a lot of relief when it was time to go home. She presented the ID she'd been asked to bring to the woman behind the reception desk. A passport and utility bill. The passport had been easy. Finding a paper bill had proved a lot more troublesome. In the end she'd had to go online and download a statement from her energy supplier, she couldn't think of the last time she'd been sent a bill in the post. The receptionist tapped on the keyboard in front of her before pointing to a wall of lockers. The woman opened her purse and fished out the pound coin the website had warned her to bring before placing her bag and phone inside one of them and making sure it was secure.

The queue wasn't as long as she'd expected. Mainly women chatting in groups or clutching onto small children. A teenage girl waiting in front of her carried a baby asleep in a car seat. A little girl with a woman too old to be her mother stood patiently, chewing on a finger nail as they waited to go through security. It was a bit like going on holiday, she supposed, as she placed her jacket into an oblong tray then lifted it onto the x-ray machine's conveyor belt before stepping through the security scanner. The rub down was more than she'd had to endure at any airport though, as she followed instructions to lift her hair and open her mouth so they could look under her tongue. Security checks completed, they were ushered into a small room, the rear door of which was closed before the one at the front opened.

She gave her name to the uniformed man behind the desk. He consulted a list in front of him, his finger tracing down the page until he found what he was looking for, then told her which table she'd been allocated. She was the only person who went straight to her seat. The other women, and they were mainly women, headed to a kiosk in the corner manned by volunteers, before traipsing back with drinks and snacks which they laid out in front of the empty place on their table. One by one the visitors took their seats until the room resembled a speed dating venue where only half of the prospective partners had bothered turning up. In the minutes that followed, the woman sitting at the table beside her repositioned the crisps, chocolate and juice she'd bought so that they faced the same way round, like a market trader setting out her stall. Satisfied, she sipped at the drink she'd bought for herself, hands circling the paper cup as she blew across the top of it.

She found it hard not to stare, yet the last thing she wanted was to catch someone's eye. To actually be seen here. To have someone look at her quizzically because she didn't fit in. Or worse still, nod and smile at her because she did. *That* would make it real.

A door at the far side of the room opened and a line of men filed in. Some cocksure, others bewildered, they moved towards the women, returning their waves with raised hands or a nod, their steps measured but purposeful until they'd reached the designated table. Smiles broke onto their faces as they stooped to hug and kiss their partners, careful to keep hands in view at all times. A sign on each table stated drinks and snacks could not be shared.

Two small children ran past her table to get to the play area. She was distracted for a moment, surprised at how normal they found their surroundings, but then children were resilient. It was adults who struggled to accept change when it came. She saw him then. Standing back from the others. Eyes scanning the room as though doubtful she'd show. She raised her hand to wave. He nodded, moving in her direction slowly as though fearful he'd be called back. She wondered if onlookers could see this was the first time they'd found themselves in a place like this. That this was the first time she'd seen him since his incarceration. She rose from her seat as he leaned in to peck her on her cheek; touched her face where his stubble had grazed her. He stood awkwardly in front of her before dropping onto the seat opposite, as though self-conscious of his dishevelled state.

Prisoners weren't allowed out of their chairs once seated and she realised too late that he might have enjoyed a hot drink and a biscuit. If she went to the kiosk now she'd have less time to spend with him. They stared at each other. Even though his lawyer had moved heaven and earth to get her on today's visit list the relief she'd previously felt turned to anger. 'For Christ's sake,' she spat. 'How the hell did this happen?'

CHAPTER TWO

Eccles Police Station

'DS Coupland, I appreciate your co-operation in coming here today.'

'Did I have any choice?' DS Kevin Coupland's question went unanswered.

The DI introduced himself even though their paths had crossed several times over the years. 'Better to keep things above board,' he said, as though he suspected Coupland of being a mason and would at any moment be rolling up his trouser leg or performing funny handshakes. He led the way to an interview room, placing his notepad and pen on the table between them. He swept his arm wide to indicate Coupland take a seat.

The DI's name was Alan Sharpe, known throughout the station as Spike, though few called him that to his face. They'd attended the same courses every once in a while, bumped their gums in the bar afterwards about teaching old dogs new tricks. A decent enough fella, Coupland remembered. Amenable. Though he seemed a damn sight less amenable now he was sat opposite him in an interview room.

'This entirely necessary?' Coupland asked, holding out his arms to indicate the tired room that stank of sweat and squeaky backsides.

'You should have said you wanted preferential

treatment, DS Coupland, I'd have booked us a table at the Marriot.'

Coupland understood Sharpe's desire to do things properly, but surely there was a meeting room they could have used, a corner of the canteen even, just to differentiate him from the normal footfall that came through here. He huffed out a sigh. 'I wouldn't mind but no one's told me anything yet, other than Reedsy's dead. I'm assuming he was murdered?'

'All in good time.'

Coupland was already shaking his head. 'Don't "All in good time" me, I'm not some wet behind the ears balloon head you're trying to put the wind up.'

'And I'm not some DC you can intimidate into getting your own way. I don't expect you to doff your cap at me, detective sergeant, but I am your superior officer and expect to run this investigation as *I* see fit.' Coupland sighed, aware of the pulse beating in his neck.

He'd hoped after all that had happened, that Professional Standards would allow his career to limp on. That he'd had a close call but was on secure footing once more. He realized with a start that hope was now a pipe dream, that because of Reedsy's murder he was spiralling downwards once more. He took a breath as he tried to compose himself. He knew from experience that the way he responded to Sharpe's questions would determine whether he was seen as a good guy or a twat. Or worse still a murdering twat. He clenched his teeth. 'Fine! So what do you want to know?'

DI Sharpe settled back in his chair, relieved, as though he'd expected Coupland to play up more. 'Where were you earlier this afternoon?'

Coupland creased his brow. 'Well I wasn't scaling the walls of HMP Manchester with a razor between my teeth, if that's what you're wondering.'

'Do us both a favour and answer the bloody question, Kevin.'

Another sigh. 'I was at my Professional Standards hearing. The one investigating Reedsy's complaint about me. I'm sure they'll corroborate if you ring them, it's no bloody secret.'

DI Sharpe wrote this information down on the pad in front of him.

'The DCs you sent to pick me up, they said something about an anonymous call implicating me in all of this. I take it the phone it came from can't be traced?'

A sigh. 'You don't seem to have grasped the concept here. I'm the one asking the questions, not you.'

'It's obvious I'm being set up though!'

Sharpe's face remained impassive. 'It's also a damn good motive for conspiracy to murder. We have no choice but to investigate this.'

Coupland took a breath. 'You know what happened, right? Reedsy's complaint is valid, I *did* assault him...'

'We all saw the clip of him being led from the building with a busted nose after that raid; someone uploaded it onto the division intranet.'

Coupland wondered why this was the first time he was hearing about *that*. Wondered which of the tech boys he'd pissed off enough for them to have a laugh at his expense.

'My Professional Standards hearing went well,' Coupland countered, avoiding Sharpe's eye as he said this, hoping to Christ there wouldn't be a recording of *that* doing the rounds any time soon. 'So what reason would I have to kill him?'

'You're asking a question like that after all your years in the job?' Sharpe threw him a look. 'We all know what it's like having your chain jerked, when you can't do right for doing bloody wrong. Don't tell me there wasn't some tiny part of you that wanted him dead?'

'There was a bloody big part of me that wanted him dead along with all the other child abusers he drove those kids to, doesn't mean I'm ever going to do anything about it. Just a fantasy that's all, like some folk dream about winning the lottery, or, if they're like my missus, getting stuck in a lift with Bradley Cooper. You know fine well it isn't going to happen.'

'Yeah, but you're forgetting one important difference. Your new BFF is Salford's very own Mr Fixit.'

'Hang on a minute. I've been civil to him in the normal line of duty. You make it sound like we hang out together braiding each other's hair.'

'I've no idea what you do in your spare time, DS Coupland, but that's what I intend to find out.'

Coupland's eyes narrowed. 'You looking to move into the dark side or something?' he jeered. 'Paving your way into a cushy job in complaints by collecting as many scalps as you can find?'

Sharpe's eyes flashed though his tone remained neutral. 'In my experience it's the guilty ones who mouth off about being hard done to. Deflection, I suppose…'

There was a knock followed by a WPC who popped her head around the door. 'Have you a minute, sir?' she asked. DI Sharpe sighed before stepping outside to speak to her.

Coupland barely had time to try and skim read the

inspector's note pad upside down when he returned. 'Your DCI's turned up,' Spike announced. 'And just to show I'm not the wanker you think I am, I've asked the WPC to bring him through. I'm going to check my emails for half an hour, and I hope when I return you show me the same air of co-operation that I have extended to you.'

Coupland doubted it, but he smiled anyway. Just to keep it above board.

*

'I called in a favour from Spike's boss,' DCI Mallender told Coupland as he entered the room. 'They treating you OK?'

'As well as can be expected.'

Mallender took the seat occupied by the DI minutes earlier.

'What's going on boss? He's not telling me anything.'

'That's because they've got precious little to go on. An anonymous caller dialled 999 this afternoon stating you were behind Austin Smith's murder. No one even knew he was dead at that point. The control centre made a call to the prison requesting a welfare check and he was found in his cell with his throat slit.'

Coupland recalled the flippant comment he'd made earlier about slipping into the prison with a razor and his heart sank.

'The allegation by itself wouldn't have carried so much weight other than the Super saw you talking to Kieran Tunney this morning outside the station.' Kieran Tunney was one of Salford's most notorious gangsters. His sister had been a victim in an arson attack on a residential home. Coupland had tracked down her killer before saving the crime boss from an attempt on his life, which in Tunney's eyes made him indebted to Coupland.

'Does that strike you as something a guilty person would do? Conspire to commit murder with a gangster in plain sight, outside the bloody station I'm based at, no less.'

'Does that even need an answer?'

'Then why am I still here?'

Mallender threw his hands in the air. 'It's not my call. The investigation has to be conducted as it would for a member of the public.'

'Without any evidence other than a phone call from secret squirrel? Give me a break...'

'It's not just you under the microscope, Kevin. Once news of Reedsy's murder reached the Super he was compelled, given what he saw, to ensure the investigation was conducted independently.'

'Just so long as the pips on his tunic don't lose their shine,' Coupland muttered.

'Kevin, you're going to have to start reining in that attitude. You're being set up, I can see that. We need to work out by whom and why, which means letting others get on with their job. Being belligerent at a time like this won't help. Right now, you need people on your side. The DI here is conducting the initial enquiries but the investigation into Reedsy's murder is being run from Nexus House. It probably doesn't feel like it but you're being interviewed here as a courtesy to keep you off the press's radar.'

Coupland felt like a balloon starting to deflate. He was hacked off with nowhere to vent it. 'Look, has anyone even bothered speaking to Tunney? Spike here is keeping his mouth clamped shut.'

'A warrant has been issued today for his part in the execution of James McMahon. We will question him regarding Reedsy once he's been detained. Alex is arranging his collection with the armed response unit.' James McMahon had been mowed down in a hit and run attack outside his sons' school. His killer, Sean Bell, was on remand at Wakefield, where he was keeping his coathanger mouth well and truly shut. The kid was nothing more than a low rent executioner, mowing down a father of two for the price of a pair of trainers. Tunney had ordered the hit and his would-be assassin, Liam Roberts, was willing to give evidence to that effect. It was the reason Roberts had been remanded to another jail.

'We'll need to tighten security around Liam,' Coupland said. 'He'll definitely be on Tunney's Most Wanted list. He was a rising star in his team and his evidence is pivotal in gaining a conviction.' No deal was being done in terms of Liam's own pending trial for the fire at Cedar Falls. He stood more chance of staying alive in a high security prison than he did awaiting trial in a safe house. There was a limit to how much protection they could offer.

'His mother has been rehoused to an undisclosed location following the roof of her car being removed with a chainsaw by members of Tunney's gang,' Mallender told him. Liam's trial was already scheduled to take place down south. 'It's likely he'll serve his sentence moving around high security prisons in their segregation units,' added Mallender.

'Some life.'

'What's your lawyer saying?' Mallender asked.

'My lawyer? I didn't think it was necessary. I'm only

helping them with their enquiries, though I must admit their hospitality hasn't been up to much.'

The DCI's face grew serious. 'Get a bloody lawyer, Kevin. Preferably one you haven't heckled when they've walked into the station. Consider it an order if you have to.' He got to his feet. Reaching into his pocket he pulled out a pack of cigarettes and a lighter. Placed them onto the table in front of Coupland. 'Thought you might have worked your way through your own supply.'

Coupland held them appreciatively as he leaned back in his seat. The boss had a point. Many a law firm would be rejoicing at the position he now found himself in. It would be a rare defence lawyer that wouldn't like to see him locked up given the contempt he'd shown them at one time or another. He pursed his lips. Back pedalling wasn't something that sat well with him; besides, he wasn't sure his snarky comments over the years could be waved away as banter. The problem with lawyers was they couldn't hide the fact they thought police were dim, and saw getting their clients off as intellectual point scoring. Even if he found someone who felt obliged to advise him now, who could he trust to prepare a decent defence if things took a wrong turn?

The name when it came to him was obvious.

Mallender was halfway to the interview room door when Coupland returned his attention to him. 'Can you get hold of Lynn? Tell her not to worry.'

'You can tell her yourself,' Mallender said. 'She turned up here the same time as me. Told the desk sergeant she wasn't budging till she saw you. I promised her I'd report back. The thing is,' Mallender, said, hesitating. 'She's kind of set up camp.'

Coupland ran a hand through his hair, 'Oh, for the love of—'

DI Sharpe appeared in the doorway just as Mallender was leaving. 'You been standing out there all this time?' Coupland accused him, eyes narrowed.

Sharpe looked put out. 'I came back to tell you that your wife and daughter are here. And a very angry baby.'

Coupland got to his feet. 'Can you give me a couple of minutes?'

Spike studied him before nodding. 'You're a lucky guy, you know. The only reason my missus would show up would be to make sure they were throwing away the key. Look, I don't intend to make a song and dance out of you being here but this is a murder investigation and the sooner I can eliminate you as a suspect the sooner I can get on with my job.' 'Agreed,' Coupland said, taking the coffee Spike was nursing as he headed through the door.

Coupland found his way back to the reception area easily enough; Tonto's lungs were doing a great job of alerting everyone in the vicinity to his location, his cries carrying around the station like an Islamic call to prayer. Lynn and Amy had commandeered a row of visitors' chairs which were strewn with baby changing paraphernalia and several toys the baby showed no interest in. Lynn hurried towards him the moment he stepped into the public area.

'I've just spoken to your boss; he's told me what's going on. Are they for real?' she asked, leaning into the hug he gave her.

Coupland swigged from his coffee cup one handed before placing it on the reception counter. 'They have to follow procedure…'

'Even so, I needed to be here, to know you were OK.'

Coupland eased her away from him. 'I'm tickety bloody boo, love,' he said, turning his attention to Amy as she paced up and down trying to pacify her son. 'Which is more than can be said for this little fella. What the hell do you think you are doing?' he hissed. 'This is no place for a baby.'

Amy stopped her pacing and turned to face her father full on. 'You said we were a family, Dad. Where I go, he goes.'

Coupland swallowed down his deepest fears, hoped to Christ this was the only time Tonto would be brought into a police station. 'Do you think me sitting through there worrying about you lot is helping? Get him home,' he said. 'I'll be back soon enough.'

He turned to reason with Lynn who was already showing him the palm of her hand.

'Save it,' she said, the look on her face telling him he'd be pissing in the wind if he tried sending her away as well. 'I'll put Amy in a cab if that's what you want, but I'm going nowhere.'

Coupland inclined his head to show he accepted her terms, waiting while she lifted her phone from her bag to order a taxi. When she ended the call he placed a hand on her arm. 'I had nothing to do with this. It's just someone playing silly beggars. They'll be done with me before you know it,' he told her. 'Though I'm going to call Roddy Lewisham as a precaution.'

A look of relief flitted across her troubled face. 'Well if anyone'll watch your back, it's him,' she answered, satisfied.

*

When Coupland returned to the interview room DI Sharpe was sat waiting, his hands circling a new coffee. 'Ready?' he asked.

Coupland eyed him. 'I would like a lawyer, after all,' he stated.

CHAPTER THREE

The last time Coupland had seen Roddy Lewisham it'd been to help him pack up his daughter's clothes and take them to the local charity shop. A job the lawyer had been putting off since her kidnap and murder three years before. Coupland had heard through the grapevine he'd made partner at the Law firm where he practised, and the cases up at Nexus House, the serious crime hub for Greater Manchester Police, kept him up to the eyes in legal aid work. Even so, Roddy had sounded genuinely pleased to hear from him.

'I'm glad you called me. I've heard you've found yourself in quite a predicament.'

'Bad news travels fast.'

'Well, you know how lawyers like a good gossip.'

Forty minutes later he showed up at the station, as good as his word. 'It's been a long time,' Coupland said, embarrassed, when he clapped eyes on him. 'I'm not even sure I need a lawyer, there's been no suggestion of anything other than I'm helping with their enquiries.'

Roddy looked at him askance. 'You've been dragged into Eccles Station on conspiracy to murder, why in God's name would you not want legal advice?'

His words made Coupland sit up straight.

Already a widower by the time he'd turned forty, he'd channelled himself into his work building a fearsome reputation as a defender of the indefensible. Officers cringed when they heard he'd be representing their suspects, knowing that they'd be in for a rough ride. After his daughter's murder he seemed smaller somehow, a reduced version of his former self, barely going through the motions. Coupland had kept in touch, even though their paths didn't often cross professionally, but he realised now as he looked at Roddy how much time had passed since they'd last spoken. All that had happened in his own life: Tonto. His mother. The fractious relationship with his father. And now this.

'Let's save sitting round a campfire toasting marshmallows and singing Kumbaya for another time,' Roddy said, as perceptive as ever. 'We need to get down to business.' Roddy was a solid-framed man with broad shoulders and a misshapen nose honed from years on the rugby field. Dark, neatly-trimmed hair framed a face that was starting to fill out again. His eyes, though sad, had lost some of their shadow.

Coupland told him the scant information he'd gleaned from DI Sharpe, along with DCI Mallender's concern that it could spiral into something else. Roddy looked up at the ceiling when he heard about Kieran Tunney's offer to deal with Austin Smith. Coupland threw his arms wide in a 'What the fuck could I do?' gesture. 'I'm not shocked at the thought he's had someone executed on his say-so, that goes with the territory, but when he asked me if I wanted it to happen I genuinely believed if I said no it wouldn't be done. To do it anyway then hang me out to dry afterwards doesn't make sense.'

Roddy looked less than impressed. *'Dictatum meum pactum,'* he quoted, matter of fact.

'You're using words with more than one syllable again,

Roddy, you're going to have to enlighten me.'

'It means "My word is my bond." Your view of Kieran Tunney is that he wouldn't double cross you. How can you be so sure?'

Coupland thought about this, his head winning over what he felt in his gut. 'I can't,' he shrugged.

'OK,' said Roddy. 'Whoever made the call can't make themselves known to the police to substantiate it because that would mean exposing themselves.' The lawyer was already shaking his head. 'This allegation doesn't have legs. Your name's been put in the frame as an act of malice at worst or more likely a smokescreen.'

'Yeah, but for what reason?'

'Finding out the reason why is your job, not mine.' Roddy closed his file and pushed back his chair. 'I'll speak to DI Sharpe. You've helped him all that you can for the time being and I reckon he knows it.'

Coupland stared at Roddy's back as he stepped into the hall, thinking how daunting an interview room was when viewing it from the other side of the table. Kieran Tunney wasn't the only one who considered himself a man of his word. The thought of colleagues doubting him, of sidelong glances being sent in his direction whenever he turned his back… He couldn't live under a cloud like that.

The interview room door opened and Roddy walked back in, DI Sharpe in his wake. 'You're free to go, DS Coupland,' the inspector said, his tone amicable enough. 'But don't go booking any holidays any time soon.'

*

'Shall we pick something up for dinner on the way home?'

Lynn glanced at Coupland when he didn't answer but said nothing. Instead she turned up the radio; let it fill the silence that engulfed them. A song came on she liked and she drummed her fingers to the beat on the steering wheel, trying to show a nonchalance she didn't feel. She wasn't a confident driver; her insistence at taking him home was her way of showing she had his back. Even so, he hated being the cause of the anxiety she was trying so hard to hide. The way she gripped the steering wheel tighter than she needed to. The constant checking in her rear view mirror, as though harking back to a time when their life hadn't been so complicated. He knew that stress could impact her health, waited with dread each time an ache or pain emerged that sent her back to her consultant. Some folk lead charmed lives. Shiny people who went about their day as though happiness was their right. Did they know they'd lucked out, he wondered. Or did they not think about it at all?

The news came on and Coupland braced himself but there was no mention of Reedsy's murder or that Coupland had been taken in for questioning. Small mercies, he supposed.

"The doctor charged with killing two patients at Salford Royal hospital appeared in court this morning before being remanded to HMP Manchester pending his trial. Consultant anaesthetist Piers Bradley maintains a technical blunder is responsible for the deaths of Blake Peters and Belinda Adamson, who had attended the hospital for routine surgery. The Greater Manchester NHS Foundation Trust has declined to comment at this time."

Lynn nodded at the radio. 'He did a few stints in the neo natal unit; thank God he didn't try anything there.'

Coupland suspected it was more to do with whether

the opportunity arose rather than divine intervention, though he didn't say as much. 'What was he like?'

'Typical gas man.'

'What do you mean?'

'It's what we call the anaesthetists, though that's not the only name that gets used. They're incredible perfectionists, which goes with the job obviously, but it can come across as arrogant – and often does. Dr Bradley was completely up himself, I'm afraid. Spoke to the junior docs like they were stupid, though to be fair a lot of them are. Anyway, everyone's been calling him Dr Death since it happened.'

Coupland considered this. 'That's the problem with reputations. They take years to build and seconds to shatter.'

Lynn gave him a sidelong glance. 'The truth will come out at his trial.'

Coupland huffed out a breath in agreement. Even so, no matter the outcome he wasn't sure he'd want Bradley putting someone he cared about to sleep should the situation ever arise.

Coupland let his eyelids droop, returning his attention to the radio. A celebrity no one had heard of was being interviewed about their appearance on *Strictly*.

'I can turn it off if you like?' Lynn asked.

'Nah, it's not their fault their day hasn't turned to shite.'

Halfway through the interview Lynn tutted, but when she turned to him her mouth had formed a smile. 'Can you imagine what life would be like if all you had to worry about was your Pasodoble?'

Coupland coughed out a laugh. 'Ah, it's all relative. Luck comes and goes, it never takes up residence.'

'And to think it was your sunny disposition that attracted me,' she muttered.

'Yeah, but it was my sexual prowess that won you over,' he smiled, his face aching with the effort.

*

Visitor Centre, HMP Manchester
Roddy Lewisham showed his ID to the prison officer manning the remand wing visitor centre. 'How's he been?' he asked.

The officer shrugged. His white shirt and black trousers looked freshly ironed; he'd not long started his shift. 'From what I've heard he's kept himself to himself. Mind you, with the number of plums in his mouth it's probably a wise move.'

'He's no threat to anyone in here.'

'No, but a bit of light relief maybe. An easy target depending on boredom thresholds and what's on TV.' He pointed to a side room with 'Legal personnel only' on the door, though it was a familiar path to the lawyer.

Roddy nodded his thanks and took a seat inside as he waited for his client. Within a couple of minutes the door opened and Dr Piers Bradley entered, followed by a prison welfare officer. Roddy waited while his client took his seat, then nodded to the officer who stated he would be back within half an hour.

'Apologies for being later than I said,' Roddy began. 'I had an unexpected client appointment that couldn't be postponed.'

'It's not like I'm going anywhere,' Piers shrugged, though it was clear he wasn't used to being kept waiting.

'There's always video-link, if there's something pressing you want to discuss. It'd save you money in the long run.'

Piers laughed. 'A lawyer offering ways to reduce his fee, now that's something I never thought I'd hear.' He fell silent, as though putting his rag bag of thoughts in order. 'I'm craving decent company, to tell you the truth. I've only been here a day and I'm climbing the walls already. Let's face it, I'm surrounded by brawn rather than brain, I'm hardly going to fit in.'

It wasn't the first time Roddy had heard this. Most folk who found themselves in prison thought they were better than the people they found themselves locked up with.

Piers rested his head in his hands. 'How in God's name has it come to this? It feels like I'm stuck in some sort of nightmare with no chance of waking up. I've always taken my freedom for granted. That it was my right as long as I stayed on the straight and narrow. Yet here I am eating three meals a day in a cramped cell. There's no canteen like you see in that film, Shawshank Redemption. You're left to perch on your bed chewing burned rice using plastic cutlery and cardboard masquerading as bread.'

Roddy nodded. 'It's grim, I appreciate that, but we're going to put forward the best possible defence that we can for you.'

'The fees your firm charges I expect that as a given.'

Roddy ignored his client's barbed comment. 'Have you had your induction yet?'

A nod. 'Within an hour of arriving I was sent to a training room to watch a power point presentation that's intended to prepare newcomers for what to expect, only there's no real way to dress up being locked up 23 hours a day, is there? We get issued with a welcome pack too, can you believe it? Only instead of a fluffy robe and slippers you get a sheet, a pillow, and a ghastly orange blanket. The gym time they refer to amounts to bodybuilders doing bench presses in the exercise yard. It's soul destroying to have so many choices taken away from you,' he muttered.

Roddy tried to move the conversation along. 'I fast tracked your wife's visiting order.'

'Yes. She came earlier.' He doubted she'd be back though, given what he'd told her.

'Will your friends visit you, your colleagues, maybe?'

Bradley looked at him as though he was mad. 'You're not serious? Who in their right mind would want to step into a place like this if they had a choice? I certainly wouldn't, and I don't blame them for keeping away while it sorts itself out. Just as long as they know that there's been some terrible mistake. That it'll all be cleared up soon. That's all I can hope for.'

'You're forgetting about the CCTV footage, Piers. It's pretty damning. The close up shows you tampering with the tube going into Blake Peters' oxygen tank…'

'All I've ever wanted to do is provide the best medical care that I can. The thought that I'd do something as horrific as I'm being accused…'

'I'm not saying you have. But there have been other cases where medical professionals have used their skills to commit murder and conceal the evidence. That's why the health board couldn't be seen to be lenient.'

'Couldn't be seen to be lenient! I've never been so humiliated in my life. To be removed from the hospital in handcuffs. Whoever leaked my arrest to the press…'

Roddy studied him. 'Could it be possible that you were

suffering from stress at the time?'

'A certain level of stress is required for the job.'

'Self-medicating?'

'You want me to make out I had some form of memory lapse due to a dependency on drugs?'

'It seems the most plausible explanation in my view. We can't argue with video evidence. Look, I'll leave you to mull it over, but don't take too long, we'll need other, impartial medical experts to attest to this if that's the road you intend to take.'

Roddy could see the man's mood deteriorate as he got to his feet. Each step heavier than the last as he made his way out of the visitors' room back to the alien world he'd been relegated to. A world in which he was considered the alien.

*

His cellmate sat on the lower bunk vaping. Piers mumbled a greeting as he climbed onto the top bunk. For want of something to do he pulled the induction leaflet he'd been given from under his pillow and began to flick through it. His cellmate rose to his feet and reached for the toiletry bag issued to each new prisoner. 'Hey, posh boy, OK if I use your shower gel? Only I'm all out of mine,' he asked as he scratched himself.

'Yes, of course,' Piers answered, even though the other inmate's shower gel and soap were on a shelf on the wall. Fear rose up in him. Is this how it was going to be now? He was no longer the one calling the shots. He was on the bottom rung of the ladder; the best he could aim for was to become invisible, not ruffle any feathers so he stayed out of the firing line. He closed his eyes, waited until he was sure his cell mate had left before he opened them again. The feeling inside him was getting worse, not better. He tried to anchor himself with positive thoughts but he felt like he was drowning. He'd woken up in someone else's life. His reputation, his morality, in tatters.

It had been a typical 24 hours on-call day. An anorectal abscess first thing followed by a laparoscopy. The CT1 on call with him meant that nothing could be delegated; each procedure had to be overseen by him for the purposes of patient safety. He was on the labour ward reviewing the patients on the obstetric HDU when his beeper sounded. A clinically unstable patient with an ectopic pregnancy required emergency surgery. A critical case. He ran toward the operating theatre. The anaesthetic room was full by the time he arrived. ICU and theatre staff, a couple of locums first time on shift. Belinda Adamson was clearly in a lot of pain. The small pink cannula that was already inserted wasn't sufficient for emergency surgery. He checked the veins and administered the local anaesthetic, applied a tourniquet then replaced it with a cannula. Everyone knows anaesthetists are control freaks. He liked to plan everything to the very last detail. Why would he have changed the cannula if he'd intended to kill her? What would be the point? He agreed the protocol that should be followed with the rest of the team. The patient's haemoglobin was 60g/L with a raging tachycardia. She needed to get into theatre as soon as possible. He turned to the patient, leaning close so that she could hear: 'You may feel a burning sensation but it'll pass. Now, I want you to count down from 10 for me…'

Everything that could go wrong did after that. But even at the end, when her trembling partner was led white as a sheet into the relatives' room it was agreed what happened was terrible, but one of those freak occurrences beyond anyone's control.

It wouldn't have gone any further, than an internal multi-disciplinary review, if it hadn't been for Blake Peters. That was the case, only two hours later in that same afternoon, that had got everyone into a flap.

Piers lay back on his bunk. Stared at the ceiling. At the overhead pipe that creaked every time he tried to close his eyes. His lawyer said they had it on camera but he already knew that. They'd shown the footage to him before they'd called the police. Even then he could sense the disbelief which matched his own, the futile hope there could be another explanation. He hadn't been drinking and he'd never taken drugs. Yet there he was, caught on tape, every inch a killer.

He swallowed, his mind a series of images of needles and tubes, his hands moving over them like a magician performing a trick. He ran his hands over his face, rubbed the heel of his palms over his eyelids. He pulled the sheet off his bed. Started to wrap it around him.

What was one more death in the grand scheme of things?

CHAPTER FOUR

It was late before they'd gone to bed. Coupland had drifted into a troubled sleep. In his dream he'd been falling, his arms flailing out wide to slow his descent, but his efforts were fruitless, the thud, when it came, inevitable. He'd spent the best part of an hour churning thoughts through his head before reaching for his phone. News of Reedsy's death had found its way onto social media but there was no reference to the allegations that had been made, or that foul play was suspected. He should be grateful, he supposed. Though gratitude at this moment was way beyond his radar.

In the bedroom across the landing Amy pleaded with Tonto to call it a night. Coupland climbed out of bed and threw on his dressing gown before padding through to the nursery. 'Is he playing silly beggars?'

Amy pulled a face. 'When doesn't he? I read somewhere that babies can pick up on things. Maybe he can sense the tension.'

Coupland sent her a look. 'Maybe you're reading the wrong stuff. There's so called experts out there would have you think raising children is a science. There's nothing scientific about it, trust me.'

They'd all been on edge since he returned from Eccles station. He'd tried to hide his frustration, had resisted all attempts to coax him into talking. No good came from baring your soul. Yes, there was tension. But its presence was a constant, had been there since Amy had told them she was pregnant. It was hard enough for a father to realise his daughter wasn't a baby anymore, but Tonto's paternity had put a hairline crack in their relationship that he worried would never heal. It was a complication none of them had asked for, that they were still learning to live with.

Amy stifled a yawn. 'Here, let me take him,' Coupland offered, 'you look dead on your feet.'

'You sure?'

'I'll recite a couple of pages from PACE, that'll have him asleep in no time.'

Amy shot him a look of disapproval that resembled Lynn so much he had to blink several times. 'What's wrong with regular fairy tales, Dad, the ones normal grandparents read to their grandchildren?'

Coupland returned her look. 'What? Fill his head with jealous stepmothers and axe wielding lumberjacks? Neglected kids eaten by cross-dressing wolves?' He shuddered. Some stories just don't have happy endings. Besides, learning the rules of law and order in his infant years might stand him in good stead in later life, though Coupland knew better than to voice *that* opinion. Tonto, as though sensing the handover, stopped his chunnering and stared at Coupland before breaking out into a smile. Coupland lifted him from Amy, blowing a raspberry onto his cheek as he settled him onto his shoulder. It never ceased to surprise him, for something that weighed not much more than a bag of potatoes, how heavy he felt in his arms.

'His nappies are in the changing unit, there's clean clothing in the dresser. I've made up a couple of bottles in case he really won't settle, and his favourite...'

'Ames, I'm a detective. I'll work it out. Now bugger off before someone pulls a body out of the canal and I have to go in.' He rubbed the baby's back the way he'd seen Amy do, stopping once she'd returned to her room.

His favourite times were when they were alone. When Amy and Lynn weren't hovering over him, checking he was holding Tonto properly, or feeding him properly, or bending his arms the wrong way when he tried to dress him. A thought occurred to him. 'I bet you've never been out in the dark yet, have you, kid?' Pulling the crocheted blanket from his cot he tucked it around Tonto before slipping on his beanie hat, making sure his knitted boots were still in place; he slipped past Amy's bedroom door and padded downstairs, out into the garden. Holding him in the crook of one arm he moved towards the flower beds like a judge at the Chelsea flower show. 'A pal o' mine planted these,' he said, 'when your grandma was ill.' His throat tightened then, but he swallowed it away. 'She's added a few plants here and there, keeps it looking nice.' He couldn't put into words how he felt about his family. And now this boy. There was no denying he came from damaged stock, that it was up to Coupland to keep him on the straight and narrow. He'd always suspected that people were born a certain way. Good. Bad. Somewhere in between. The wrong person or the right person had the ability to tip them either way. It all depended on your moral fibre, the ability to feel guilt at the thought of doing wrong. Remorse was over rated; by the time someone felt it the damage had been done. Better to control temptation by the fear of what would happen, wasn't that the premise of law and order? What made Joe Public behave himself and keep anarchy at bay? He'd have to keep a close eye on this scrap; he knew that much, but nothing worth having came easy.

The boy wriggled, drawing Coupland's gaze back over his tiny body. The moon was full and bright like something out of a child's bedtime story. Somewhere in their one-sided conversation Tonto had fallen asleep. Coupland stared at his cherubic face in the moonlight. 'I used to fall asleep every time your mum watched The Lion King,' he whispered, 'but there's a bit I remember, where the baboon holds up the lion cub. I used to like that part,' he added. 'We could watch it sometime.' Tonto slept on, oblivious.

Back indoors Coupland lowered the boy into his cot, smiling as one tiny fist punched the air. He padded downstairs, grabbed a beer from the fridge as he scrolled through his phone. There was a text from DCI Mallender. Looked like he was having trouble sleeping too, given the time it had been sent:

> Heard you're back home. The Super has scheduled a meeting tomorrow morning to discuss the way forward. Someone from human resources will also be present. You are entitled to bring your Fed Rep.

Coupland pulled a face. The HR department consisted of Maggie and a kid on work experience. He'd known Maggie for years; she was married to a beat cop and was on first name terms with everyone at the station. Why the sudden formality? *Everyone leans on their job titles when a bollocking's involved,* he reminded himself before throwing the can in the bin and calling it a night.

CHAPTER FIVE

Reception, Salford Precinct Station

He'd been about to key in the access code on the door marked 'Authorised Personnel Only' when it happened. The shift in the atmosphere that set him on alert. It started with the desk sergeant asking if he wouldn't mind waiting in reception. Coupland knotted his brow as he approached the counter. 'Is there a problem?' he asked, noticing that the civilian working on the computer hadn't bothered to look up or call out a greeting when he arrived like she usually did. Instead she'd busied herself with a data entry task she could normally do blindfolded. Coupland moved to the door and typed the four digits in anyway. His fingers moved over the keypad on auto pilot, but when he turned the handle the door didn't budge.

'The code's been changed,' the sergeant called out, clearing his throat as though something was lodged in it.'

Coupland tutted. 'Give me the new number then…'

The sergeant said nothing. Instead of reeling out the new pass code he sucked in a breath, looked around as though checking they couldn't be overheard. There were a couple of people sitting on the plastic chairs in the waiting area. Relatives with clean clothes and sandwiches to hand into loved ones in the custody suite. Too busy scrolling through phones or taking it in turns to pop out for a fag to pay any attention to the surly detective barred entry from his workplace. 'Sorry Kevin, I'm under instructions not to give it out,' the desk sergeant informed him. 'I was told to buzz DCI Mallender when you arrived.'

Coupland shook his head. 'Better do as you've been told, then,' he said, standing back while the sergeant made his call. Mallender appeared in the doorway a little out of breath as though he'd seen Coupland approach from an upstairs window and had tried to get to reception before him. He held the door open wide as he waited for Coupland to pass through. 'Damn, I'm sorry Kevin,' he muttered when he saw the confusion on Coupland's face. 'The Super's insisting we do everything by the book.'

'Is he now?' Coupland replied, wondering which bloody book everyone had started referring to. 'Reading's never been my strong point,' he muttered.

The meeting was to take place in Superintendent Curtis's office on the second floor. 'Let's get the lift,' Mallender said, jabbing his finger on the call button, cursing when it didn't arrive straight away. 'I'm happy to walk,' Coupland offered, enjoying the senior man's discomfort as they passed officers struck blind as Coupland strode along the corridor. Mallender filled in the silence by asking after Lynn, Amy, Tonto, anything but the reason Coupland had been summoned to the inner sanctum.

Coupland studied the DCI's profile, a look of incredulity on his face. 'If I'd known we were going to be nattering about our families I'd have brought my knitting.'

A crimson flush crept up Mallender's neck. 'I thought I'd save work-related questions for when we go in,' he explained.

'More likely the Super will want someone to note down my answers,' Coupland replied.

He followed Mallender into the Super's office, noting

that the DCI held the door open for him as he passed through. A sea of assorted faces turned in his direction as he approached the long conference table in the centre of the room. 'I thought Maggie from HR was joining us?' he asked.

'No, this is Suzanne Waite from head office,' Superintendent Curtis told him, making the introductions while Coupland took the seat Mallender held out for him. The HR manager's hair was clipped in an 'updo'; strands of it fell about her face giving her an ethereal look. She made a humming noise, as though listening to a soundtrack only she was privy to. Coupland knew better than to be fooled by this, even more so when she failed to return his greeting. His stomach churned in apprehension. Personnel meetings unnerved him, made him feel out of his depth. He supposed that was the point of them, an attempt to demoralise you before the proceedings began. He wondered if he'd been wise not bothering to inform his federation rep of this meeting.

There was an empty seat beside The Super and Mallender moved into it, his eyes remaining on Coupland as if warning him to keep his mouth shut. Suzanne Waite spoke next: 'Perhaps it would be useful to outline the purpose of our meeting today.'

'I daresay it would,' Coupland answered, ignoring the look Mallender threw in his direction.

'We've received the report from Inspectors McAndrew and Smedly following your Professional Standards hearing yesterday—'

'—Blimey, they didn't mess about. Though I imagine the wifi's pretty good in most of the eating establishments off the M62.'

The HR woman smiled but continued as though he hadn't spoken. 'In light of other, more serious circumstances arising over the last 24 hours, we felt it sensible to expedite their findings to help signpost the way ahead vis-a-vis the current situation.'

Coupland furrowed his brow. 'Sorry, you lost me at signpost. You might want to use subtitles given there's a non-graduate in the room or failing that dig out a colouring book and crayons.'

Ms Waite made a humming noise and looked at DCI Mallender as though some sort of translation was required.

'DS Coupland's sense of humour can be a little off key at times,' Mallender said, eyeballing him. 'But beneath that offhand exterior I know he's taking the situation he's found himself in very seriously indeed.'

Superintendent Curtis shuffled the papers in front of him. 'I take it everyone has a copy?' he asked, waiting while Mallender handed a rainforest worth of paper across the table to Coupland. 'I'll leave you to read the full report in your own time, Detective Sergeant, but whilst we are assembled it's worth running through Professional Standards' findings so that we may agree the appropriate remedial action to be taken.' Curtis cleared his throat and began:

'"DS Coupland's account of the events leading up to the capture and arrest of Austin Smith during a raid on premises at Algernon Way concur with that of the complainant, in that he admits to using excessive force during his apprehension, and assaulting him to the extent the complainant suffered a broken nose. Mr Smith's statement claimed that prior to this he'd been about to give himself up. Further investigation of the crime scene following his arrest determined that the window behind where Mr Smith was apprehended could have been a potential escape route. In addition to this a cache of weapons was found beneath it. We feel, on balance, that although Mr Smith suffered an injury during his arrest, his detention was pivotal to the outcome of the raid carried out on the property and to the apprehension of a gang guilty of the trafficking and sexual exploitation of immigrants from Albania. Mr Smith's escape and possible discharge of the hidden firearms could have resulted in severe injury to civilians as well as other officers at the scene. We therefore recommend that Mr Smith's complaint is not upheld."'

All eyes fell onto Coupland who had been doing his best to keep up. As far as bollockings went he'd had worse, he conceded. But the show wasn't over until the fat lady sang. Or in this case, until the humming HR woman reached the bloody chorus.

'Perhaps, DCI Mallender, you'd be happy to read out the hearing's recommendations?'

Superintendent Curtis paused to make it look as though Mallender had a choice in the matter, removing his glasses before he had time to respond. Ever the politician, the Super had done the good cop bit; now it was left to Mallender to tell Coupland his fate. The look Mallender sent in his direction seemed to convey: *Don't shoot the bloody messenger*, causing Coupland's palms to sweat. He wiped them down the front of his suit trousers, flicking off imaginary bits of lint. Mallender picked up the report, continuing where the Super had left off. '"The fact that DS Coupland admitted to using excessive force from the outset is to his credit. It made the direction of our investigation a simple one. However, during our investigation it came to our attention that on several occasions DS Coupland has attended highly stressful situations without availing himself of the post counselling support available to division personnel. This may have contributed in part to the bouts of aggression to which he seems prone. Whilst anger is a natural response to certain life experiences, when excessive, it can be problematical. With this in mind it is recommended that DS Coupland undertake a course of anger management counselling to help "'

'—Whoa there,' Coupland interrupted, sitting forward in his seat. 'For a minute it sounded like they want me to join some happy clappy therapy group. You've got to be kidding me, right?'

The HR woman's humming had gone up a notch, oblivious to the look Curtis, then Mallender sent in her direction.

Coupland tried a different tack: 'Besides, the things I have to say might be subject to Data Protection.' He felt like gamekeeper turned poacher using the obstacle that annoyed him the most when making enquiries as a trump card to get out of Professional Standards' recommendations, but if that's what it took, so be it.

The Super narrowed his eyes so much he looked as though he was suffering a severe allergic reaction. The humming paused as the HR manager regarded him. 'I've done most of the legwork on this, DS Coupland, and have already compiled a list of therapists willing to work with you on a one to one basis. They were briefed in relation to your… current situation, and have demonstrated in one way or another, sound interventions that should be of immense benefit.'

Coupland opened and closed his mouth like a fish out of water. 'Guv?' he said, beseeching Mallender with a stare.

The DCI placed his elbows on the table and made a steeple out of his fingers. 'I appreciate this may not be your preferred course of action, Kevin, but in the circumstances you don't really have a choice.'

'Sorry?'

'The report was written prior to Austin Smith's murder.'

'And?'

'Since then you have been required to help the investigating team at Eccles with their enquiries.'

'So?'

The HR woman paused a tune that was starting to sound surprisingly familiar. 'Let's not be coy, DS Coupland, you were taken in for questioning in relation to the circumstances surrounding his death.'

It was the Super's turn: 'The point is, this was Professional Standards' recommendation prior to the allegations that have been made in the wake of Austin Smith's murder.'

'The anonymous allegations which my lawyer,' Coupland exchanged looks with Mallender, understanding at once why his boss had urged him to get advice, 'is treating as malicious.'

The HR manager was on a roll. 'Even so, we have no option in the circumstances but to suspend you pending a thorough investigation,' she said.

'Which we know is a formality,' added Mallender.

Coupland felt as though he'd been dealt a sucker punch. 'You're kidding me?'

Suzanne Waite locked eyes with him. 'Believe me, this is no laughing matter. I must remind you that it is a condition of our return to work process that you engage fully with the therapy recommended in this report, as you will be unable to return as a serving officer without the therapist's sign off.'

Coupland fell silent; clamping his teeth together so tightly his jaw muscles could be seen working beneath his skin.

The Super put on his concerned face. 'I just want to say, DS Coupland, that you have our full support. I am satisfied with the findings of the hearing and am confident DCI Mallender and your co-workers will facilitate your return to work in any way that they can.'

Forget Hans Christian Anderson and the Brothers Grimm, the best fairy-tales he'd ever heard were spun by top brass.

'By the way, you'll need to hand over your security pass and warrant card,' he added without blinking, 'and leave any items that belong to GMP on the premises.'

'Here's your hat where's your hurry,' Coupland muttered, getting to his feet.

'Oh, and before I forget,' the Super continued. 'We would ask that during your suspension you don't contact any of your colleagues here at the station until the matter has been dealt with fully.'

Coupland's head shot up. 'Surely I can speak to my team, sir? Let them know what's going on?'

'They'll be fully briefed, DS Coupland, you don't need to concern yourself with anything other than engaging with your counsellor and the team investigating Austin Smith's death.'

'Looks like it's all sewn up then,' he said, pulling himself up to his full height.

'Don't forget to take your copy of the report with you, for reference,' Suzanne Waite reminded him, before resurrecting the tune she'd paused earlier.

'What?' said Coupland, 'In case I don't feel like I've been humped enough I can roll it up nice and tight and shove it up my—'

'—I'll walk you out, Kevin,' Mallender said hurriedly, scraping his chair back and gathering up the paperwork in front of him.

Superintendent Curtis had decamped to his desk, was in the process of buzzing his assistant to bring him tea. 'For one,' he emphasised, in case the others took it as an invitation to stay.

Coupland leaned in to the HR woman as she picked up a leather briefcase that had been lying by her feet. 'People say my humour leaves a lot to be desired but yours knocks mine right out of the park.'

She screwed up her face. 'Sorry?'

'Don't be, I found it quite funny as a matter of fact. I mean, I can hardly blame you, endless meetings with clapped out cops like me, it's enough to warp anyone's outlook.'

She looked at him confused. 'I don't follow.'

'The tune you were humming, I couldn't work it out at first. Then I remembered where I'd heard it before. I took my missus to see Pirates of Penzance one Christmas, her choice not mine.' He looked at her and grinned. 'That's where I'd heard it. You know, that song, *A Policeman's Lot is Not a Happy One.*' He looked from her to Mallender then nodded. 'I mean, as song choices go, you couldn't have picked anything better, I'll give you that. Sums my day up just nicely. Priceless...' he muttered, as he doffed an imaginary cap towards her before turning to leave.

It was probably mind over matter, Coupland thought as he passed through reception. No one other than the powers that be knew that he'd been suspended, so the averted eyes and pained expressions were probably down to everyone knowing he'd been dragged into Eccles station the day before.

'That reporter's been here, asking after you again,' the desk sergeant called out as Coupland and Mallender drew level. 'The one that caught you smoking on the fire escape,' he added.

Coupland stared at him pointedly. 'Only because some balloon head sent her over there to look for me,' he answered.

'Don't shoot the messenger,' muttered the officer, dropping his gaze. 'Anyway, she was asking to speak to you, wanted your opinion on Austin Smith's untimely demise.'

'I bet she did,' Coupland said, turning to look at Mallender. 'One for you, I think now, eh, boss?'

Mallender tutted and held out his hand for the scribbled note the officer held up like the winning ticket in a raffle.

'Being suspended has its perks,' Coupland said, enjoying the surprise on the sergeant's face.

Coupland was less jovial in the car park, shaking his head when Mallender attempted to defend the Super's decision. 'They've already decided I'm guilty,' he seethed, reaching for his cigarette pack and lighting up in record time, inhaling as far as his lungs would allow.

'No, they haven't. But they are covering their backsides. It's what happens.'

'But what sort of message does it send out?'

'I didn't think you cared what people thought.'

Coupland looked at him pointedly. 'That's where you're wrong, see. Of course it bloody matters. Folk don't have to like me but they need to know I can be trusted. How's it going to work if every time I turn my back someone's sniping that I'm bent.'

'That's why the Super wants you out of the way. Let the dust settle and attention will turn onto someone else.'

'Whose attention? That two-bit reporter and her cronies? Let's face it, all Curtis is bothered about is how anything makes him look and right now having a tainted DS on his team is the last thing he wants. He's thrown me to the bloody wolves.'

'You're talking bollocks.' It was Mallender's turn to shake his head. The DCI was an articulate man, wasn't prone to swearing in the way the rest of the murder squad did. On a good day their vocabulary made Tarantino sound chaste, only no day was a good one. Coupland reckoned it was the job that did it, brought you up close and personal to things the public never saw. The bruised and battered faces. The smears and sorrow. With photos of damaged victims staring down at them in the incident room, who'd baulk at 'bastard' and 'fuck?' Even Krispy was starting to turn the air blue though Coupland hoped to Christ he knew how to rein it in at home. The boss had always been a different kettle of fish. More refined. He used his tone of voice to convey how he felt, let pauses emphasise their meaning. A rebuke from Mallender was low pitched and lengthy but just as damaging as any tirade from Coupland. And yet he'd just told Coupland he was talking bollocks. Maybe the tension was getting to him too.

'One of these days you'll learn not to take things so personally, Kevin. That not everything that goes on in the universe revolves around you.' He sounded done in.

'Boss?' Coupland studied him as he tried to work out whether he'd overstepped the mark, finally worn the DCI's patience too thin.

'Have faith in the system you've spent your life upholding. Not everyone is incompetent. Some of us take our jobs seriously. We actually give a toss, you know.'

Coupland knotted his eyebrows together. He had a way of appearing ungrateful, Lynn told him as much; he made a note to self to show his appreciation more, even if he didn't bloody well feel it.

'Am I allowed to ask how Alex got on bringing in Tunney?'

Mallender raised an eyebrow. 'Not really, but I can tell you he was picked up from his home last night and charged with conspiracy to murder. He was up before the court first thing before being remanded to Strangeways.'

'You're kidding me? It'll be like home from bloody home.'

'We'll be transferring him, Kevin. We couldn't get anything South of Manchester at short notice but it'll be any day now.'

'Was he questioned in relation to Reedsy's murder?'

'What do you think?' Mallender said, trying not to look put out. 'Of course he was. And he maintains it had nothing to do with him.'

Coupland blew out a sigh. He was aware he was on full view of anyone happening to look out of the CID room window and he sure as hell didn't want to provide a side show. 'Fine!' he said, throwing his arms up in mock surrender. 'I'll bugger off home and sit on my hands, leave you lot to make Tunney see sense and admit he set me up.'

Mallender nodded, satisfied. 'We'll give the press a statement to keep them off our backs for the time being, and I'm relying on you to keep your head down. The only talking I want you to do over the next few days is from a reclined position on a shrink's chair while you tell them your life story. You hear me?'

'Loud and clear, boss,' Coupland said, feeling a weight press down behind his eyes. He reached in his pocket for his keys and bleeped his car open. 'And…thanks,' he said, baring his teeth in what he hoped looked like a smile.

*

DS Alex Moreton stood by the window in the CID room looking down at the two figures talking by Coupland's car. 'I didn't know Kevin was back,' she said, wondering why he hadn't texted her to let her know what happened after he'd been carted off to Eccles station. He'd probably want to tell them all in person, she reasoned, embellishing bits where he could to get his point across; after all they'd be none the wiser.

'DS Coupland's been suspended, Sarge!' Krispy panted as he hurried into the room with a box of doughnuts for their break, red faced for being the centre of attention after repeating what he'd just been told downstairs.

'What makes you say that?'

'The desk sergeant just told me. Said he heard it from the DS himself.'

'I'm going down there,' Alex said, jerking her thumb in the direction of the car park below in time to see Coupland's car reverse out of the parking bay. 'Shit!' she groaned, wondering what the hell was going on.

'Can I have a word?' DCI Mallender stood in the CID room's doorway as though he'd been teleported there from the car park. Alex raised her eyebrows as she followed him into his office.

Mallender didn't bother waiting for her to sit down. 'I don't know what you've heard but Kevin has been suspended,' he told her as he closed the door behind them. Before she had time to respond he ploughed on. 'Not because of Austin Smith's complaint – Professional Standards made a different recommendation regarding that, but because of the allegation that's been made in relation to his subsequent murder.'

'It was an anonymous call, we're not really taking it seriously?' The corners of her mouth turned down in disgust.

Mallender nodded. 'We don't have any choice.'

'For how long?' The DCI shook his head. 'How long's a sodding piece of string? There are procedures to follow…' He avoided her eye as he spoke, in case she saw that he was purely going through the motions. The truth was internal investigations could go on for months. The cost of getting in additional cover would break the team's budget.

'Yes, but this is a formality, though,' she began. 'Kevin is coming back, isn't he? I mean, him helping the inspector at Eccles with his enquiries is just a box ticking

51

exercise, isn't it? No one in their right minds thinks he had anything to do with Reedsy's murder.'

Mallender looked away.

'Seriously, boss? You can't think—'

'—Of course I don't! Not for one minute. But it's more than a formality. We are accountable to the public. We have to demonstrate due diligence.'

Alex studied him. 'And finding the person responsible wouldn't go amiss either.'

Mallender pointed a finger at her. 'Leave it. They won't thank us for stepping on their toes. Let's see what the team at Eccles come up with.'

'Yeah, but boss—'

'—Give them a chance,' Mallender insisted.

'Meanwhile Kevin's expected to sit tight and kick his heels? He'll love that…'

Mallender coughed. 'Not entirely. Professional Standards has stipulated that he goes on an anger management course – it's a condition of his return.'

Alex widened her eyes. 'Should you be telling me this?'

'No. But now's not the time for me to be coy, Alex, you know him better than anyone here, are you telling me he has a handle on his temper?'

It was Alex's turn to look away. 'He's the most fair-minded person I know.'

'That's not what I asked you.'

Alex tilted her head. 'It's probably wise not to get on the wrong side of him,' she conceded. 'But it's not like he's unstable. He doesn't kick off if you look at him funny, only if you've committed a serious crime and are hell bent on lying about it.'

Mallender sighed. Days like today made him question

his job, but having supported the Super's decision he couldn't baulk at it now. He didn't question Coupland's integrity, just wished his fiery sergeant would learn when to keep his powder dry. 'It's a done deal, Alex, the sooner he engages with a counsellor the sooner he can return to work once Eccles give the all clear.'

'What about cover? We're inundated with admin. I've got pre-trial work to do on the fire at Cedar Falls; we've still got Kieran Tunney's involvement in the hit and run to put to bed. You know what it's like when you're liaising with the CPS, the paperwork takes on a life of its own.'

'Ah, well that's the next thing I wanted to talk to you about.'

'We're to do more with less, sir, am I right?'

Mallender held his palms outwards towards her. 'Hear me out. The Super asked me to pass on that he was impressed with how you stepped into Kevin's shoes during the investigation into the arson attack.'

Alex acknowledged his words with a nod. 'It was a difficult time. I did what I could; we all did, especially when we discovered Kevin's mother was one of the victims.'

Mallender nodded his understanding. 'Exactly, and for that reason I'd like you to continue to lead the team. They respect you and as it is Kevin's suspension is going to knock them for six. The Super wants a steady hand on the tiller.'

Alex wasn't used to one-to-ones with the DCI – that was Coupland's remit. She wasn't to know that he used the Super's quotes as a way of poking fun at the system, a passive aggressive resistance to the rank and file that he was a part of. 'I happen to agree with him,' he added on seeing her confusion. 'You'll be the safe pair of hands needed while the storm surrounding Coupland abates. Ashcroft can step into your shoes and DC Timmins is more than capable of taking on additional responsibility.'

'He's an inexperienced DC, sir, everything he's been allocated so far has been under clear supervision.'

Mallender shrugged to show it wasn't up for discussion. Despite newspaper headlines and political posturing there'd been no extra funding for officers at local level, and you couldn't get blood out of a stone.

'There's something else,' he ploughed on; as though he hadn't just tipped a shed load of work on her desk already. 'The Super has stipulated that there should be no communication between Kevin and the team until his suspension is over. Keeps things simpler, that way.'

For you, maybe, Alex found herself thinking. After all, she'd be the one Coupland would ring if he wanted an update on Kieran Tunney's status.

Mallender scooped a file from his desk and held it out to her. 'Something's come in overnight that I want you to take a look at. There's been a suicide on the remand wing at Strangeways.'

'The same day as Reedsy's murder? What are the staff doing there, sleeping on the job?'

Mallender shrugged his shoulders, grim faced. 'It doesn't look suspicious but the coroner's office is already involved and they need us to establish a cause of death as a matter of priority.'

'How come?' 'It's the consultant charged with killing two patients at Salford Royal. I was the SIO on that case and DC Andy Lewis was the arresting officer. The case was watertight, there's CCTV footage catching him red handed tampering with medical equipment used by one of the victims.'

Alex took the file and glimpsed at the contents, trying to put her thoughts in order. What was one more case, she supposed. She was spinning that many plates she could always audition for Britain's Got Talent if her career went pear-shaped.

'Was he a suicide risk?'

'The Governor says not. The officers on his wing said he was subdued when he was brought in, but there's nothing unusual about that. He was probably in shock.'

Alex narrowed her eyes. Adjusting to prison life was a shock to anyone's system but few who ended up there could claim they hadn't seen it coming.

'Despite the damning CCTV footage he was adamant he wasn't responsible for their deaths. If he isn't, then the killer may still be at large, leaving some serious dark and sticky stuff on the hospital's fan. There's going to be a lot of media interest when this gets out. The papers had a field day when he was arrested. There's an opportunity for serious scaremongering if we've got it wrong. The prison governor's already in a tail spin after Reedsy's murder. This has put her and her team under the spotlight.'

'I'm not surprised.'

'As I said, no hint of foul play according to initial reports but we need to be thorough.'

'I'll get straight onto it. What about the team, Sir, do you want to tell them about Kevin or shall I?'

'They're your team for the time being, Alex, you do it.'

CHAPTER SIX

Alex knew time was of the essence in terms of the suicide investigation but she had to update the team – her team, as DCI Mallender had reminded her – on what was going on with Coupland. The CID room was still full when she returned, as though Salford's criminal fraternity had declared a day of rest and all the detectives milling around had to do was catch up with emails and filing. She knew word would have spread about Coupland's suspension and that the boss had summoned her to his office. 'Any excuse for a skive, eh, Turnbull?' she said, clocking him filling two mugs with hot water with the contraband kettle Coupland insisted on keeping in the office even though it went against HR policy. 'Make one for me while you're at it,' she called out, then surveying the rest of the room she said: 'Stop pretending curiosity isn't killing you and gather round for five minutes.'

The detectives listened, moaning and butting in with their own two-penn'orth opinions whenever she paused for breath.

It was Krispy who summed it up best: 'So, let me get this right, Sarge, DS Coupland has been suspended while the powers that be eliminate him as a suspect in a conspiracy to murder Reedsy, even though none of them believe he has anything to do with it. Is that the gist of it or am I missing something?' Apart from the fact that he was a good two stones lighter and didn't possess the gravelly voice of a smoker, Krispy was turning into Coupland's proper little mini-me.

'No,' she replied, supressing a smile. 'Sounds pretty bang-on to me.'

'Is there anything we can do, Sarge?' asked Ashcroft. He'd transferred from the Met two years ago and credited Coupland with his smooth transition into the team.

Alex was already shaking her head, much the same as Mallender had done. 'The best thing we can do is let Eccles get on with their investigation. Last thing they need is any of us getting under their feet trying to do their job for them. Oh, and one last thing...' She looked around the assembled detectives and took a breath. 'The Super has stipulated that during Kevin's suspension we're to keep our distance.'

'Reassuring to know the higher ups have our backs,' Robinson observed.

'I'm merely passing the message on,' Alex said, hands in the air. 'How you respond to it is up to you.'

'Well it's a two fingered salute from me,' said Turnbull.

'And a middle finger show of appreciation from me,' added Robinson.

'I know who I'd rather have in my corner,' said a DC sitting on a desk at the back of the room.

'I'll be sure to pass your comments onto Kevin,' smiled Alex. 'Should I happen to bump into him, accidently like...'

Several heads nodded their approval.

'In the meantime I'll be heading up the team. Now listen up, we're a person down so don't expect to get home in time for cosy dinners with your better halves any time soon.' She turned to Ashcroft. 'I need you to give me a hand preparing the arson case file against Liam Roberts for the CPS. I've a suicide at Strangeways to deal with relating to an ongoing investigation and I don't want us to miss any deadlines.'

Ashcroft nodded. Two detectives made the mistake of avoiding her eye.

'Turnbull, Robinson, you're going to have to take over Sean Bell's CPS case preparation…'

Robinson's shoulders visibly dropped. 'How long's the Sarge going to be out of action?' he asked.

Alex shrugged. 'Your guess is as good as mine. The boss reckons this is just a box ticking exercise, although HR has made it a stipulation of his return that he completes the training recommended by Professional Standards.'

'What kind of training?' the DC from the back of the room asked.

Alex paused; she didn't want to breach confidentiality but at the same time knew this was the stuff that rumours were made of. Secrets traded in the canteen turned into something far more sinister because the people kept in the dark had a tendency to let their imaginations run wild. She let out a sigh as she weighed up what to do.

'It'll stay in this room, Sarge,' said Turnbull.

'Christ, that'll be a first,' she replied, deciding to go for it. 'Professional Standards want him to undergo a course on anger management.'

She was impressed with them really. Their ability to keep their faces straight for a full five seconds. Remarkable in fact, given the subject matter and his reputation.

Ashcroft reached into his jacket and pulled out his wallet. Handed Turnbull a ten-pound note. As did

Robinson and several other DCs. 'Jammy bugger,' one of them muttered as he handed the cash over.

'Seriously?' Alex asked. 'You'd been betting on the outcome?'

'I reckoned he was down for a demotion,' Robinson said, 'but at least none of us bet on him getting the chop.'

'I'm sure he'd be delighted to hear that.'

'It was only a bit of fun Sarge,' said Krispy, crestfallen. 'I was worried they'd transfer him to traffic or school liaison.'

'And this lot convinced you making a few bob on the outcome might soften the blow?' Krispy dropped his gaze. 'He's not out of the woods yet,' she reminded them. 'Until he complies with this training the best thing any of you can do is keep your heads down and get on with the job.'

*

DC Andy Lewis was based in a smaller but much tidier office along the hall from the murder squad, based in a team that dealt with serious assaults and manslaughter. Known as Cueball due to his shiny pink scalp as a result of alopecia he'd suffered since his police training days, he'd done most of the grunt work on James McMahon's hit and run and had no doubt put in the hours putting a case together against Piers Bradley. Two investigations that due to external issues required the intervention of other officers to bring it over the line. Alex knew how frustrating that was. Even though he was below her in rank she wanted to reassure him that she wasn't stepping on his toes, at least as far as the investigation into Piers Bradley went. She'd liaised with him once before on a missing person case and knew he could be touchy.

He looked up as she entered the room, his forehead glistening under the ceiling's strip lighting. 'DCI Mallender called me in first thing, Sarge, he said that you'd be assigned to follow up on the doctor's suicide.'

Alex nodded. 'I'm on my way over to the prison now. I just wondered if there was any relevant background intel you had that would be useful.'

'Well I didn't go in gung ho if that's what the boss is worried about,' he said. 'The evidence pretty much spoke for itself.'

'As I said, I'm not here to check your handling of the investigation, I've been asked to make sure there's been no foul play.'

Cueball nodded. 'Good. He was caught on CCTV so there's no question of his guilt. Now he's lying in the mortuary and I'm going to have to tell the families of his victims that any hope they had of getting answers has disappeared up the Swanee.'

'Any idea why he did it?'

He shook his head. 'He had an unblemished career according to everyone who worked with him. Meticulous. Not so much as a parking fine in his personal life. Happily married too. Stands to reason he was going to go off the rails. Too much walking on water for my liking.'

'Really? Some folk put the effort in where it matters. Whatever's gone on recently, sounds like he was a respected member of his profession.'

'Something the likes of DS Coupland can't be accused of.'

Alex regarded him head on. 'Seriously? You've not fallen for any of that flannel have you?'

'There are rumours flying round he's been consorting with gangsters.'

'Only in the line of his work, same as you.'

Cueball sighed. 'I suppose you're right. Sorry!' he said, chewing his lip. 'So much of what we do comes back to bite us these days. I've just found out about his suspension and don't want to be the next in the firing line if I fuck something up.'

'If it's any consolation I don't think they dare lose any more manpower,' Alex quipped, only half joking. She held up Piers Bradley's case file. 'This was always an open and shut case which is why it landed on my desk.' But still, there were a couple of things she needed to know. 'What was your first impression when you met him?'

Cueball shrugged. 'He was like someone who'd been caught with their fingers in the till. But then he started protesting his innocence which in my view damned him even more.'

'What do you mean?'

'It was like watching one of those crap TV dramas where the actors read out their lines but they don't mean a word of it.'

'Going through the motions?'

'That's how I saw it.'

'I suppose he wasn't used to being on the back foot.'

'Could these deaths have been down to human error?'

'He claimed the first death was a mistake and the hospital board took him at his word. He injected an excessive dose of local anaesthetic into Belinda Adamson in what should have been a routine procedure to alleviate pain. But in the second incident the nitrous oxide and oxygen tubes were swapped – and it was captured on

CCTV. Take a look at the footage. He pretty much went from hero to zero in the space of a day. It's weird when you think about it. All that protesting yet he'd not even tried to cover his tracks. The CPS was suggesting Gross Negligence Manslaughter for Belinda but I reckon we'd have got him for murder if I had longer to build a case. The footage of him tampering with Blake's equipment was a gift.'

Back at her desk Alex decided to do some on-line digging. There certainly wasn't a shortage of information about Piers Bradley. He'd come into the public eye recently because he'd been awarded an MBE in the previous New Year's Honours so there was a lot of media interest in him. 'There's a site called Doctoralia,' she said aloud, looking at Coupland's desk before remembering he wasn't there. Ashcroft was replying to an email from the CPS that she'd forwarded to him; he looked up, grateful for the distraction. 'Patients can rate their experience of dealing with their consultant. He's got fifty-two five star reviews.'

'Any one-star? They're the ones you should be interested in.'

Alex grunted in agreement but shook her head. 'Not that I can see.' His biography was impressive: Consultant and senior lecturer at Charing Cross Hospital before transferring to Manchester in 2010. He qualified in Medicine in Aberdeen, completing his anaesthesia training in Edinburgh. Registered with the Royal College of Anaesthetists, he specialized in local anaesthetic and steroid injections for joint and spinal pain. 'He'd published numerous medical and scientific papers in high-level journals as well,' Alex said aloud.

'Highly respected, then.'

'Indeed. Seems he was about to carry out a research project in Canada.'

'How the mighty fall…'

Ashcroft had a point.

'OK, so that's what his world looked like before...' Alex said, tapping the words 'consultant' and 'arrested' into Google and clicking on the first result that came up:

Dr Death arrested as second patient dies.

A young man died after his oxygen pipeline was connected to the nitrous oxide supply by a senior consultant. Dr Piers Bradley is an anaesthetist with the Greater Manchester Foundation Trust, based at Salford Royal Hospital. Police were called after the man became unresponsive during what was considered to be a routine procedure. Greater Manchester Police said the force was alerted by concerned staff at the hospital. Police Crime Scene Investigators continue to carry out their work at the hospital and at Dr Bradley's home address in Worsley, where he lives with his wife. A local resident said, 'The police have been outside the house all day. I've no idea what is going on.' A neighbour, who didn't wish to be named, said, 'At least one officer has been parked up outside the house since Friday. A friend came and picked his wife up, she didn't look too happy, but we don't know anything more.'

Trust Medical Director, Dr Lynn Brookes-Osborne, said: 'I can confirm a member of staff has been arrested but as this is an on-going situation I am unable to say any more. Patient safety at the hospital is of the utmost importance to us and I wish to reassure our patients and relatives of loved ones coming into the hospital, that they will receive the best possible care from our staff.'

The photo beneath the headline was a head and shoulders shot of Piers Bradley blown up to fit the page. Wearing a shirt and tie and Foundation Trust lanyard, he grinned at the camera, emphasising a double chin that was just starting to show. With close-cropped hair and rimless glasses he looked younger than his 45 years, certainly too young to be a consultant, Alex thought, or was she just getting old? Another photograph showed him being led from the hospital in handcuffs, his face a picture of incredulity.

Police Superintendent Curtis, based at Salford Precinct Station, said: 'We are investigating an incident following reports of two unexplained deaths at Salford Royal Hospital. The first incident involved a patient who became critically ill during a routine procedure. We are unable to discuss specifics relating to the second incident for the time being. A further statement will be made in due course.'

A Greater Manchester Police statement said later: 'Dr Piers Bradley, aged 45, from Worsley, has been charged with manslaughter, and will be remanded pending his trial.'

Alex looked thoughtful.

'Penny for them?' Ashcroft asked, catching her eye. 'Oh, nothing you'd want to part with your hard-earned cash for. Anyway, I'm surprised you asked, given your current losing streak.'

She picked up her car keys and slipped her bag over her shoulder, but before heading outside she popped her head into the room Cueball occupied. 'I take it all the usual financial checks were carried out on Dr Bradley?'

The DC muttered something under his breath before looking up from the paperwork on his desk to reply. 'His finances are squeaky clean, Sarge. A mortgage that makes my eyes water just thinking about it but no missed payments, no debts or HP. Credit card balances settled at the end of every month. Neither he nor his wife have gambling habits, drug habits or partake in dodgy pastimes unless you count cooking holidays in Tuscany or regular trips to their farm house in France.'

'Nice life. Until you kill a couple of patients and lose it all.'

*

HMP Manchester

The prison governor stood to shake Alex's hand, indicating she took a seat on the other side of the cluttered desk. 'Sarita Anand,' she said, introducing herself and Rob Ellis, the doctor seated beside her after Alex had reiterated the purpose of her visit. Early forties, petite with thick black hair which she raked with her hand every five minutes or so, it was clear she was concerned by Alex's presence. 'Let me just say,' she began, before Alex had had time to remove her notebook and pen from her bag. 'From the outset Piers Bradley posed no obvious suicide risk.'

'Yet here we are,' replied Alex. 'So what changed?'

'Risk factors change every day,' answered Sarita. She spoke out of the corner of her mouth as though concealing her words; Alex found she had to lean forward to hear her clearly. 'Short of assessing inmates every day it's impossible to completely head these things off. Besides, it was his first day; his lawyer had managed to get him a visit from his wife. Some have it a lot worse.'

Alex posed her next question to the prison doctor. 'What would you say are the main reasons inmates commit suicide in jail?'

Dr Rob Ellis was in his late thirties with a body mass index that suggested he didn't practice what he preached.

But then, Alex reasoned, the majority of his work here would be dealing with internal assaults and handing out methadone; probably not the reason he took the Hippocratic Oath. Ellis acknowledged her question with a nod. 'The causes of prison suicide are self-evident – social isolation, harsh discipline, lack of privacy, add to that the constant threat of violence, fear, guilt, hopelessness, and depression – they all take a heavy toll on the human spirit.'

'But he'd only just arrived, could he have been a victim of intimidation from another inmate?'

The doctor thought about this. 'To be honest I can't see it. He was on 'A' wing. The only inmates they come into contact with on that wing are other new arrivals, at least for the first 48 hours. We probably would have left him there longer, given his background and lifestyle, as there'd have been a hell of a lot of acclimatising to do.'

'You were satisfied that it was a suicide though?'

'Sadly yes, I've seen enough of them in my time here.'

'He must have been like a fish out of water in many respects, not to mention scared out of his wits,' Alex prompted.

The governor cocked her head to one side. 'You know, you can't always make assumptions about social class. Harold Shipman settled in well here while he was on remand. The other inmates used to queue outside his cell daily to consult with him about their ailments. They said he had a great bedside manner.' The doctor chuckled. 'Before my time here,' he said. 'But they trusted him, even though he killed over 200 of his patients.'

Alex opened her notebook and wrote a couple of things down. Made a point of underlining several words though in truth she'd not heard anything to concern her. It was a tactic Coupland used. Silence unnerved people. Made them feel obliged to fill it.

The governor didn't let her down. 'I imagine it was the impact his new situation would have on his friends and family that tipped him over the edge,' observed Sarita. 'Maybe his wife coming to see him on his first day was too soon. Everything would still have been raw. Perhaps she said something that was a bit too close to home.'

'Maybe he couldn't stand seeing her disappointment,' the doctor concurred.

Sarita jumped as though she remembered something, pulled a clear plastic envelope from her desk drawer. A plastic poly pocket with what looked like a hand written letter inside it. 'He left her a note,' she said, handing it to Alex.

'I'll make sure she gets it,' Alex said, nodding as she got to her feet.

'I'm sorry I couldn't have helped you more. I'll have someone show you back to reception.'

Alex was already shaking her head. 'Oh, I'm not done yet. I'll need to speak to the officer who found him, so if you can point me in the direction of 'A' wing I'll be much obliged.'

The task of escorting Alex to 'A' wing fell to a welfare officer summoned from the visitors' hall and told to report to the Governor's office to chaperone her visitor ASAP.

'Did she give you her "Door's always open" speech?' he asked.

'Not quite, but I've got one like that back at the station so I know how it goes.'

The walk would take them the length of the prison and Alex had to be signed in and out through several security doors to reach their destination. Built in the typical Victorian star shape the prison consisted of five main wings each with four landings. 'A' wing was the induction wing housing unsentenced inmates awaiting trial and sentenced prisoners on their first night.

'Have you been here before?' The prison officer asked.

Alex shook her head. 'No, but there's a fair few in here would recognise my face, I shouldn't wonder.' One in particular, given she arrived on his doorstep uninvited with two dozen of GMP's finest less than twenty four hours since.

The officer opened his arms wide and gave her a sardonic smile. 'In that case welcome to the only hotel in Manchester that's always 100 per cent full.'

'Do you normally work in this part of the prison?'

He paused. 'No, I'm covering for someone off sick. I'm based on the segregation unit on 'E' wing.'

'The wing where Austin Smith was murdered?'

His smile fell away leaving a grim line. 'We've been advised by the union not to speak to the police without a representative present.'

'I wasn't going to ask you anything about it,' she lied. 'It's being dealt with by colleagues from another station anyway.' She paused. 'Were you on shift though, when it happened?'

A nod.

They'd reached 'A' wing where they were met by a further welfare officer who stood so straight it looked as though he had an ironing board up the back of his shirt. 'The guvnor radioed that you wanted to speak to me,' he said, nodding to the officer who'd escorted her as if to say he'd take it from here.

'Quite a tag team you've got,' Alex commented.

'Your safety is our priority,' Officer Ironing Board said, making Alex wonder if he was aware of the irony, given the circumstances of her visit.

'I'm here to see Piers Bradley's cell,' she said. 'I've been asked to prepare a report for the coroner.'

'You know his personal effects have been removed?'

Alex glanced at him sharply. 'Who said you could do that?'

The officer shrugged. 'It's standard procedure. We moved his pad mate to another cell too. The inmates on cleaning duty will give the place the once-over ready for the new occupants.'

'But you knew I was coming?'

'Yeah, but it's standard—'

'—Yes, you've already said that bit.' Alex heaved out a sigh. 'Might as well take a look, given that I'm here.'

They were on the first floor; the doors to each cell on this landing were all shut apart from one. 'Has any unauthorised person had access?' Alex asked as they came to a halt beside the open door.

The officer indicated the closed doors around the landing. 'The men aren't due out for association time for another couple of hours. They get their breakfast cereals with their evening meal so once they're locked up that's it for the day.'

Alex looked down onto the ground floor where inmates gathered around a snooker table, others lined up to use a wall mounted phone. 'What about them?' she asked.

'They're from the second-floor landing, their association time's nearly over, they'll get escorted back to their cells before the inmates on the third floor are escorted down.'

A feeling came over Alex, the type of feeling that warned her she was being watched. She looked up at the fourth-floor landing. A group of men leaned against the landing rail observing the snooker game below. All, that was, bar the man at the centre of the group, whose eyes bore into her skull.

'Why aren't they locked up?' she asked, turning to the officer and indicating the group with a tilt of her head.

The officer didn't bother looking up. 'Although they have to have a mandatory induction because they've just been incarcerated, they are not first timers, in fact they're such frequent flyers I don't know why we don't give them a priority boarding pass and let them check themselves in. We tend to let them stretch their legs more, since they know the ropes.'

Alex looked back up at the fourth-floor landing, at Kieran Tunney already centre stage in his banged-up empire, and returned his stare.

'There's nothing left to see, really,' the officer said, encouraging her to get a move on. She followed him inside the cell. The room was small. If she stood in its centre she could almost touch both walls either side. Stripped of any personal items, all that remained was a narrow set of bunk beds, a sink and a toilet that wouldn't look out of place in an Eastern bloc gulag. A barred window let in dreary winter sunlight casting the cell in a permanent gloom. There was mould around the window frames and stains on both mattresses. The air stank of body odour and something more cloying.

The officer clocked Alex turn her back on the skid marked toilet and offered a smile. 'You get used to it,' he said.

'Only we shouldn't, should we?' she muttered, wondering how cooping men up in their own shit rehabilitated them. 'Where did you find his body?' she asked, trying to focus on the job in hand.

The officer pointed to where she was standing. 'He'd tied his bed sheet to the overhead pipe.' He pointed to the heating pipes that ran across the breadth of the room from one cell to another. 'He must have done it while he was on his bunk. He tied the rest of it around his neck then rolled off.'

Alex knew it didn't need to be a great height if the intent was there. Just a willingness to get the job done. Or desperation, depending how you looked at it. She turned to the officer. 'You seen many of these?'

He nodded. 'Too many to mention.' He shoved meaty fists into his trouser pockets and let out a sigh. 'Five minutes. That's all he needed. How are we supposed to stop it happening when they are locked up in their cells out of sight for so long?' It wasn't really a question, more a show of frustration. 'There just aren't e-fuckin'-nough of us to go round.'

'I understand he'd had a suicide assessment at induction and there had been no obvious risk.' The officer nodded. 'Then there's not much else you could have done,' she said. 'I've seen enough,' she added, turning to go.

As they approached the first set of security doors to leave the landing they were on Kieran Tunney was making his way downstairs from the landing above. 'Hello Miss,' he said, as they drew level.

'Kieran,' she answered, glancing sharply at her companion. 'I thought no one else had access to this landing,' she hissed, not bothering to conceal her displeasure.

'Not unaccompanied,' stated the officer, 'and right now Mr Tunney is being accompanied by us.' She noted the use of 'Mr,' wondering if he addressed all the inmates this way or whether this was another dispensation for the 'chosen few.'

'Just on my way out for my constitutional,' said Tunney. 'Too much time indoors is bad for the complexion. I hope you don't mind me saying, miss, but I reckon it'd do you the power of good too.'

'Glad to see you've settled in so well, Kieran.'

'The pleasure's all mine,' he drawled. 'If I'd known you were coming I'd have asked the chef to prepare something.'

'Not to worry.' She made as if to go on her way but Tunney stayed put.

'When I saw you stepping out of that poor fella's cell I wanted to take the opportunity to say how terrible it is, when something like this happens. I hope you don't mind.'

Alex sighed inwardly. There were a few things she'd like to say to him but she knew damn well there'd be no point other than providing a floor show for his cronies. He'd been less convivial with his arm up his back when he'd been led into the back of the police van the previous evening, but she knew he was playing her, trying to get a reaction. 'Is there anything else, Kieran? Only as you can see I'm rather busy.'

'I'm sure you are, what with being a man down and all.'

'Yeah, well you'd know all about that,' she answered, indicating to Officer Ironing Board that she wanted to crack on.

'It had nothing to do with me, you know,' said Tunney. 'What happened to that trafficking paedo.'

'Yes, you told me that at the station. Shouted it if I recall.' She looked up at his cronies and smirked. 'It seems such a coincidence that you offered to take care of Austin Smith for my colleague – all he had to do was say the word, as I understand it, and next minute he's dead.'

'The big fella moves in mysterious ways. I hold my hand up, Miss, if Mr Coupland had said yeah I would have carried out my promise but he didn't. I look after the folk who look after me, everyone knows that, but the good turns I do are always appreciated. What's the point in giving someone something they don't want?'

'So who killed Reedsy, if it wasn't someone on your payroll?'

'You know, there's a touch of déjà vu about this conversation, which makes me think I shouldn't say any more without my lawyer being present. Besides, you know more than anyone I wouldn't divulge that information even if I knew. I removed someone's kneecaps for being a grass once, I can hardly sing like a canary now, can I?'

'So you'd be prepared to let Coupland's career go down the toilet after he saved your life?'

'What can I say? It's a jungle out there.'

'Not a patch on what it's like in here,' she muttered, turning to the officer impatiently. 'Let's call it a day; some of the wildlife in here is distinctly unpleasant.'

*

Alex's mobile rang as she settled back in the driver's seat of her car and started the engine. Ben's school flashed up on the screen causing her to grab it from the passenger seat. She jabbed the 'reply' button with her finger, swallowing down the fear that something awful had happened. 'Hello?'

'Miss Burke here… Ben's teacher,' the voice on the other end explained as though Alex didn't consign everyone to memory that came into contact with her boys. *'Nothing to worry about, Ms Moreton, I just wondered if we could ask a favour…'* Miss Burke had one of those sing song voices that'd be irritating in most jobs and downright inappropriate in Alex's line of work but perfect for a primary school teacher. She was plump and smiley and everything about her was jolly, jolly, jolly. *'We've had so much support from the parents,'* she twittered. *'And I wondered if it was something you'd be willing to do, too?'*

Alex realised she hadn't been paying attention and that a response of some sort was required. 'Sorry?'

Well used to dealing with short attention spans, Miss Burke chuckled. *'I was wondering if you could come into class to talk to the children about your job? Most of the other parents have participated and the children are very keen to hear what Ben's mummy does when she goes to work.'*

Alex tried to remember what the other parents did for a living. There was a flight attendant; she remembered that much because his gran did the school run when his mum was working long haul. Alex pictured her turning up to deliver her talk carrying conch shells and sick bags armed with funny tales to keep children her son's age amused. There was a vet, a dental nurse, a baker and a mechanic.

How could she talk about her work to a bunch of eight-year-olds? Parts of her job were unpalatable. The rest was downright awful. 'I'm not sure…' she began.

'Oh that's a shame, I think Ben was hoping to show his mummy off, he's very proud of you, you know.'

Alex sighed. 'Well, I suppose I could spare half an hour,' she said.

'That's great,' Miss Smiley said. *'It's important children have an understanding of what's going on in the world around them, don't you think?'*

'I suppose…' Alex replied, eyeing Piers Bradley's suicide note on the passenger seat beside her. When the call ended she picked up the plastic wallet containing the doctor's final words. The slim plastic wallet weighed heavily in her hands. She noticed his writing was neat for a doctor:

What I said to you today was the truth, my love, yet I wish with all my heart that it wasn't.

It felt wrong to read something so private, to be party to a stranger's last thoughts. Even so, she picked up her phone and tapped on the camera icon, took a copy of the note in case she needed to refer to it later.

CHAPTER SEVEN

The house was accessed through a private road which opened out onto an extensive landscaped driveway large enough for several vehicles. Alex manoeuvred her car through the heavy iron gates, parking in front of a detached double garage, beside a four wheel drive that made her Fiesta look tiny. She'd telephoned ahead to check Ruth Bradley had returned to the family home, although she was surprised to see her waiting at the door given her initial reluctance to meet.

'I'm not Ruth, my name's Kirsty Astley, her sister,' the casually dressed woman explained when Alex held up her warrant card to introduce herself. 'She's in the sitting room, I'll take you through.'

'How is she?'

'Like a woman who doesn't know what day of the week it is. One minute she was fussing over what wallpaper to choose for their country house in France, the next minute she's queuing up to visit her husband in jail like some gangster's moll.'

Alex got the impression there wasn't a great deal of love lost between Kirsty and her sister, and even less for her now departed brother-in-law. 'You know he's dead, right?' she asked.

'Of course, but if he'd only done the decent thing *before* he got himself locked up she mightn't feel so ashamed.' Kirsty led her through double doors into a large sitting room decorated in cream damask with pale leather sofas and antique looking side tables. The large bay windows overlooked the village green where a couple of men with telephoto lenses loitered. 'The press have been a real pain in the backside,' Kirsty muttered, 'but she won't let me close the blinds.'

'I don't see why I should hide away, I've done nothing wrong and neither had Piers!'

Alex stepped towards the woman who had spoken, perched on the end of a sofa as though ready to make a run for it.

'Keep telling yourself that, Ruth, and one day you might believe it,' Kirsty scolded, prompting Alex to step between them as she held out her hand to the seated woman.

'Mrs Bradley, we spoke on the phone,' she said, introducing herself before offering her condolences.

Ruth Bradley was skinny – some might say too thin. She looked good in the clothes she wore – a slim fit cowl neck sweater over tailored trousers, but the skin around her face and neck sagged. Her clothes were expensive, her jewellery understated but heirlooms none the less. Alex found herself wondering if she'd ever worked, whether she was the last vestige of women that kept house for their men. In Alex's house it was Carl who did the bulk of the childcare and domestic chores; his string of internet-based businesses had never really taken off. There were times, usually when she'd skipped lunch to sit through a post mortem, that she wondered what it'd be like to be at home all day, to be in the shoes of someone like this. Then she reminded herself of the reason for her visit and forced her mouth into a smile. 'I'm so sorry to be meeting you in these circumstances,' she said, meaning every word of it.

A shrug. 'It's not your fault.'

Alex took a breath, decided there was no way to dress up the reason she was there. 'Due of the nature of your husband's death I am required by the coroner to gather information that will help them determine the cause.'

'I thought the cause was pretty obvious.'

'We need to be sure there was no foul play.'

Ruth's head snapped up. 'You think he was murdered?' She turned to her sister. 'Did you hear that, Kirsty?'

Her sibling was already nodding. 'Only Piers could go to prison and end up getting murdered…'

Alex held out the palms of her hands to both women. 'Please…my investigation into this has only just started, though I haven't seen anything yet to make me doubt the prison doctor's initial report.'

'So it's still a suicide, then,' Ruth said, crestfallen.

'Can I ask when you last saw your husband?' Alex asked.

'Yesterday afternoon… in prison.'

'How did he seem?'

'He was distraught! Perplexed as to what he was doing in such a place. I mean, the whole case against him is preposterous.'

'I need to make it clear I'm not involved in the original investigation. My role is to look into the circumstances surrounding his death.'

'So why do you need to speak to me?'

'I want to get a better understanding of his state of mind. I've read his career history. It would be fair to say his recent actions were totally out of character.'

'Of course they were! He wouldn't harm anyone, let alone someone in his care. That's what I keep telling everyone but no one seems to listen. He was dedicated to his career. A perfectionist. He never made mistakes.'

'The facts speak for themselves, and these weren't mistakes! When will you get that into your head?'

Ruth spun round at her sister's comments. 'You would say that, wouldn't you? You never liked him.'

'Here we go again…'

'How about I make us all a cuppa?' Alex offered, mimicking Ben's teacher's sing song voice in an attempt to smooth things over between the sisters. 'Perhaps you could show me where everything is?' she asked Kirsty pointedly.

*

The kitchen was a large, modern affair: stainless steel units that wouldn't look out of place in an operating theatre. Alex looked for a kettle only to be pointed in the direction of a chrome tap on the kitchen island.

'Permanently hot,' Kirsty said, rolling her eyes as she lifted three mugs out of a handle-less cupboard. She reached into another cupboard and brought out a wooden box containing a selection of teas. 'Earl Grey, Peppermint…'

'Normal' Alex replied, more bothered about restoring peace than quenching her thirst.

Kirsty found something that fitted the bill; placing the tea bag into one of the mugs she filled it with the perma-hot water before passing it to Alex. She added water to the other two mugs then placed them on a tray with a plate containing slices of lemon.

'Do you have milk?' Alex asked her.

Kirsty nodded in the direction of the enormous fridge behind her, waiting while she located some and poured it into her mug.

'I take it you didn't think much of your sister's husband?' Alex enquired.

'He was an arrogant wanker,' Kirsty answered, causing Alex to glance up at her in surprise. 'Our Ruth married into all this, we don't come from money,' she explained. 'She was flattered when they got together, and she's spent their entire marriage trying to live up to his elevated status. Then he goes and gets arrested and everyone can finally see that he was the unworthy one in the relationship.'

'What are your thoughts on his suicide?'

'I'm shocked, obviously, but after recent events I suppose anything was possible.' Kirsty returned the tray to the counter top. 'He was a tad too sanctimonious for my liking. He always wanted to be in control. His way was the only way, you know the sort. Perhaps he was fed up of the pedestal he'd been put on and what he did to his patients was a cry for help.'

Back in the sitting room Ruth had calmed down, though her eyes were bloodshot and her chin wobbled as she spoke. 'I can't believe this is happening. I keep thinking he's going to walk in through the front door complaining about some junior doctor or other. He said they got more stupid every year. I'm sure he didn't mean it,' she added, seeing the look that flitted across her sister's face.

Alex felt sorry for her. She imagined friends were thin on the ground once her esteemed husband had been placed on remand.

Ruth turned to Alex. 'You told me on the phone that

he'd written me a letter. Please, may I have it?'

Alex reached into her bag and pulled out the plastic wallet. 'Here,' she said, placing it into Ruth's outstretched hand, studying her face as she read the last message from her husband. She gave Ruth a moment to take in what she'd read, before pressing on. 'I need to ask you what he meant, when he said he told you the truth yesterday.'

'It was nothing.'

'Obviously it wasn't. It may even have some bearing into my investigation into his death, or the case against him.'

Ruth sighed, turning her head toward the window. Alex followed her gaze. One of the photographers loitering on the green was unscrewing the lid from a flask. Everyone was entitled to a tea break, she supposed. Ruth blinked, snapped her attention back to Alex. 'That's what I'm worried about. When I saw him yesterday he said he'd had time to think. He told me that when he closed his eyes there were images in his head that wouldn't go away. He could see his hands close up; saw himself injecting the woman with a fatal overdose, swapping over that young man's oxygen tube. He said it was like watching a video being played over and over, so much so that he'd started to believe he must have done these terrible things after all.'

She stared at Alex wide eyed. 'What hope did he have if he'd started to believe he was guilty?'

PART TWO

CHAPTER EIGHT

"*City bosses welcome the profile and £30million boost this conference brings to Manchester. Local police say they will balance the right of delegates to attend the conference and the right of protesters to free speech and lawful protest, backed by 1,000 officers on duty over the weekend.*"

Asim Khan sat in the back of his chauffeur driven car watching the news on his phone as his driver slowed at the 'Vehicle Mitigation Point', two concrete slabs that prohibited vehicles over a certain size from entering the conference centre's 'safe zone', and showed his clearance pass to the security personnel.

'Where were your lot this morning?' Asim muttered at his phone, rubbing at the dried egg stains on his new suit. The reporter on screen had followed him up the conference centre steps that morning desperate to get his views on plastic, air travel, vaping, anything in fact, that she could use as a 'filler' while she waited for the senior members of the cabinet to emerge. He'd become accustomed to the shallowness of it all, yet still, the lengths they went to… a political journalist had practically tailed him into the gents at last year's conference, would only leave when he'd threatened to call security. Then again, it hadn't been as grim as the conference two years before that, when delegates and journalists alike were heckled and spat at.

It wasn't how he'd imagined it when he'd studied

politics at university. He'd been an idealist, he realised that now. Determined not to become one of the pompous elite, he'd worked his way up, doing a range of jobs to pay his way before taking a job assisting the local MP whose shoes he stepped into when the politician was sacked following a scandal. He was the party's youngest MP and Muslim to boot. The press couldn't get enough of him even then.

He'd spent yesterday shaking strangers' hands and listening to their complaints, while trying to ignore the foot-high stack of casework from his constituency.

Today he'd been pelted at with eggs.

The rock 'n roll life of a back bench MP.

His driver pressed a switch to lower the partition between the driver and the passenger of the car. 'Where to, sir?' he asked.

Asim massaged his temples. 'Back to the hotel,' he answered. 'It's been a long day.' He switched from the news channel to check through his emails, one hand automatically loosening his tie. Meeting requests, reports he had to read through and comment on before the end of the day, tiresome receptions he had to host or attend. He couldn't remember when he'd last had a holiday.

He'd found it hard to engage with the party sponsor who'd collared him before the conference began and he'd fidgeted all the way through the keynote speech. When a reporter had asked for where he stood on Palm Oil he'd clammed up, requiring his researcher to field the remaining questions from the floor. His foot tapped against the car's foot well.

'We're here, sir.'

He looked up to see his driver peering at him in his rear

view mirror. 'Of course,' he said, picking his briefcase up from the seat beside him as he opened the car door.

'Same time tomorrow morning, sir?'

'Yes,' he let out a sigh. 'Same time tomorrow.'

He exchanged a nod with the doorman as he made his way towards the lift, waving at the receptionist who hurried over to him with several envelopes. 'These arrived for you today, Mr Khan,' she said, handing the envelopes to him.

'How's your mother?' he asked, nodding his thanks as he took them from her. 'Recovering well,' she smiled. 'Starting to complain about everything again so she must be on the mend.'

'Glad to hear it,' he replied before stepping into the lift. When the lift doors closed he slumped against the mirrored wall, took several deep breaths.

Housekeeping had worked their magic on his room, leaving his towels as he'd requested. He could hardly have them changed daily whilst attending a conference addressing protecting the environment. The minibar had been restocked though, making him smile appreciatively at the hotel's discretion. Taking off his jacket and tie, he put them over the chair by the window, before placing his briefcase and mail on the writing desk. He didn't bother opening it; instead he scrolled though his phone one last time before placing it on the bedside table. He moved to the CD player and hit 'Play', before taking off his shoes and socks and padding barefoot to the minibar to pour himself a drink. Exhausted, he returned to the bed, lay back against the pillows and closed his eyes.

He must have been asleep for a while because when he opened them everything was cloaked in darkness.

The only light came from the street and the buildings opposite, casting an eerie glow into the room. Something felt wrong. Very wrong. He felt clammy and disoriented. The air coming from the open bedroom window made him shiver. He became aware of something beside him on the bed. He turned his head; saw in the soft lighting that it was a woman.

'What the hell…?' He sat bolt upright and reached for the bedside lamp. He switched it on as he turned to her. 'You need to get up,' he said, blinking. 'There's been some sort of mistake.'

But the woman didn't move. She lay on her front in a way that made him wonder how on earth she could breathe as her head was face down on the pillow, her arms splayed out either side of her. He reached over to shake her while at the same time taking in what she was wearing. Dominatrix shoes and a PVC skirt. Hair that was obviously nylon. But it was her stockings that sent his heart thudding. For only one was where it was supposed to be. The other, he realised as he swallowed down bile, was tied around her neck.

CHAPTER NINE

The front door was already open when Alex arrived, reminding her that with a baby on the premises only the foolhardy would ring the doorbell. 'Ding dong,' she said, eyeing Coupland as he headed upstairs with his grandson under one arm like a rugby player heading for the try line. 'I take it you've read him his rights?'

'Every one of them. We're hoping he opts for remaining silent but only time will tell on that front.'

'Come through,' Lynn called from the kitchen. 'Amy sweet talked us into watching His Nibs while she went out with some pals. That was before Kev got your text about coming over.'

'Doesn't bother me, I can work my way through a tikka masala no matter what the decibel level. Anyway, how is he?' Alex asked, placing the takeaway bag on the kitchen table then set about unloading the contents.

'Grumpy, hard to settle.'

'And the baby?'

Lynn pulled a wry smile as she opened the cutlery drawer and lifted out a corkscrew.

'Someone's been using my name in vain,' Coupland said as he joined them round the table, making himself useful by bringing the plates out of the oven, his mouth forming a 'O' shape when they turned out to be hotter than expected. Lynn asked if Alex was driving, brought out three large wine glasses when she said she'd booked an Uber.

'I suppose I should be honoured,' Coupland drawled, spooning the contents of the carton nearest to him onto his plate. 'I daresay you've all been told to keep your distance.'

Alex nodded. 'Yeah, well you can imagine how that went down. They'd have come over with me tonight if I hadn't reminded them you keep baby hours now.'

Coupland told her about his meeting with the Super and the humming HR woman. Of the stipulation regarding the anger management therapy.

'The boss kind of mentioned that to me,' she said, pulling a sheepish face.

'So much for confidentiality,' Lynn sniffed.

'I'm surprised it's not on the bloody intranet,' Coupland said, shrugging.

'I think he was sounding me out,' Alex said. 'To see if I thought it was as preposterous as you obviously implied when it was put to you.'

'I may have questioned its relevance,' he admitted, his mouth forming a sly grin, 'But I know when I've been backed into a corner.'

Lynn regarded him wide-eyed. 'Really? I wouldn't have guessed, given you've done absolutely nothing about it.'

'I needed to get my head around the idea,' he admitted. 'But yeah, since I've got no say in the matter I suppose there's bugger all to think about.'

Alex told him about her visit to HMP Manchester following Piers Bradley's suicide.

'I heard about it on the evening news. Never saw that coming. But then none of us thought him capable of killing his patients.' Lynn scooped more rice onto her plate, followed by several more scoops of curry sauce before topping up her wine glass. 'This is the part where I leave you guys to it,' she said amicably, aware the conversation was heading towards a conflict of interest not to mention breach of confidentiality if she stayed. 'There's a murder mystery on TV with my name on it. Don't often get the chance to watch them without a certain person providing a running commentary all the way through.' She got to her feet and padded through to the living room, reminding Coupland to top up Alex's glass.

Coupland did as he was told, an ear cocked towards the baby monitor. Satisfied, he topped his own glass up by a thimbleful.

With Lynn out of earshot Alex told Coupland she'd crossed paths with Kieran Tunney whilst at the prison. 'I'm surprised he doesn't have a suite to himself, though I'd bet money there'll be one waiting for him when he's transferred to the main wing after he's convicted,' she added, deciding not to mention the book that had been running on the result of Coupland's disciplinary hearing. 'The boss says he'll be moved down south when there's a space.'

'Men like Tunney have contacts everywhere. He'll be looked after wherever he rocks up.' Coupland studied his colleague, reckoned he was about to learn the real reason for her visit, rather than the show of solidarity which she originally claimed.

'The thing is, Kevin, now I've had time to think about it, even though Tunney's a shady bugger I think he was telling the truth about not being involved in Reedsy's murder.'

Coupland was grateful to hear someone say out loud

what had been preying on his mind. 'That's my view too. I said as much to Roddy Lewisham but he wasn't so sure.'

'You know the first rule of detection. The simplest reason is most likely the one.'

'Exactly. Maybe Tunney's offer to kill Reedsy was just ill-timed. Think of the company these guys keep. It isn't exactly stretching the imagination to think that there's more than one person wishes them dead.'

'Only it's more than a wish though, isn't it? It's someone willing to see it through.'

'Plenty like that knocking around. We need to think who else had something to gain from Reedsy's murder.'

'He was happy enough to spill his guts after his arrest, it could be one of the others involved in the trafficking gang decided to take him out.'

'Or show Midas how easy it would be to get to *him*.' Midas was the head of the gang that had trafficked Albanians into Salford. Now he was behind bars other gangs would be vying to take over the gap in the market, and take out opposition where needed. As well as home grown 'family firms', Greater Manchester was a melting pot of organised crime syndicates including Yardies, Asians, Eastern Europeans, Turks, each operating within their own networks, collaborating with others when under threat.

'I need to find out who set me up, and to do that I need to find Reedsy's killer.'

'You don't need to do anything apart from let others do their job.'

Spoken like someone spending way too much time in the boss's company, reckoned Coupland. 'Yeah well, we'll see about that. Anyway, why were you sent to check out that doc's suicide? Is foul play suspected?' He swallowed down his disappointment that he was hearing this second-hand, that overnight he'd been relegated to listening to the radio to find out what was happening in his city. 'I take it he just couldn't hack his fall from grace?'

Alex shrugged. 'Possibly, but I can't help but feel there's more to it. I went to see his wife and she's adamant he's been set up.'

'Who's been handling it?'

'Cueball.'

'He's a good guy, needs a steer now and again but nothing you can't handle.' He picked up half a naan bread that was going begging, used it to mop up the sauce that remained in each of the empty foil cartons. 'If I don't watch out you'll be running things like clockwork to the point no one'll want me back.'

Alex blushed. 'Hardly, the boss looks at me when I speak to him as though he's waiting for a punch line. The team's hacked off Reedsy's murder was handed to Eccles, and Krispy's walking round like someone stole his comfort blanket.'

'Early days, they'll all be eating out of your hand soon enough and I'll be nothing more than an anecdote at the annual piss up.'

'Come on, Kevin, it won't come to that.'

'Then why did Mallender tell me to get a lawyer?'

'Maybe he was just giving you some friendly advice. Remember these things aren't always determined by right and wrong but whichever way the political wind is blowing. He doesn't want you used as a scapegoat.'

'Anyway, tell me more about this Dr Death, and what's making you so uneasy.'

Alex shrugged. 'When his wife went to see him in jail he told her he was starting to believe he was guilty.'

'Seems a bit odd, to say it like that.'

Alex narrowed her eyes as he tried to remember his words verbatim before giving up and pulling out her phone. She showed Coupland the copy she'd taken of the suicide note Bradley had left for his wife.

'"What I said to you the other day was the truth…"' Coupland read aloud. 'And you asked her what he meant?'

A nod. 'He told her he remembered doing the things he's been charged with. Namely giving Belinda Adamson an overdose of pain relief and removing Blake Peters' oxygen tube.'

Coupland raised his glass. 'So, it looks like you've got your confession, albeit posthumously. Job done, I'd say.'

Alex was halfway down a second bottle of wine when a whimpering noise came through the baby monitor, slowly building in crescendo until it became a full-blown cry.

'His Master's Voice,' said Coupland, slurping at the coffee he'd just made before getting to his feet.

'And my cue to leave, it's a school night after all,' said Alex. 'I reckon my two will have run rings round Carl. Either that or he'll have given in to Ben's demands and they'll be playing Grand Theft Auto on the X-box munching on pizza. Speaking of which, his teacher rang to ask if I'd do a class talk about the job. What do you reckon?'

Lynn, on her way back into the kitchen for a wine refill, caught the tail end of their conversation. She threw Coupland a look. 'Kev gave a talk when Amy was at school. The head was inundated with complaints afterwards; some of the kids had nightmares, apparently.'

Coupland blew out a sigh. 'No one wants to know what we really do, just that we're there. If you want my advice, take along a squad car so they can take turns sitting in the driver's seat and putting on the blue light.'

Alex pulled a face. 'Isn't the point of careers talks so the kids have a real idea of what the job entails?'

Coupland shrugged. 'Feel free to turn up in your smart suit and talk about blood spatter but take it from me, they don't want to hear it…'

He'd reached the top of the stairs by the time he heard the front door open and Lynn call out goodnight to Alex. He paused in the doorway to the baby's room, watching Tonto ball his hands into fists, punching the air like a drunk at closing time. As though sensing he had company Tonto rolled onto his side and gripped the cot bars, glaring at Coupland as he loomed in the doorway. Coupland rubbed his eyes, hoped to Christ it wasn't a premonition. 'That's better,' he said, as the boy's cries started to subside. He folded his arms, resisting the temptation to get too close. Amy had downloaded some parenting app that advocated leaving babies during the night so they learned to settle themselves. He and Lynn had been given their instructions: soothe, but don't pick up. Easy enough when she was out for the night and couldn't see Tonto's shoulders shudder in temper, the angry tears rolling down his cheeks. 'I know the feeling kid…' he sighed, crouching on the floor so they could eyeball each other. 'How about I keep you company?' he said, pulling a face as he made himself more comfy on the carpet, inching back a little so he could lean against the bedroom wall. It wasn't the first time he'd sat outside a custody cell making sure the occupant didn't run amok. He slipped his hand through the cot's bars, waited while one of Tonto's fists found its way around his finger. 'Good grip,' he said with approval.

Within minutes Tonto's breathing had settled into the regular hum of a sleeping infant, his fingers clinging onto his grandad like a junkie hanging onto his fix. 'Don't worry about me, kid, I'm going nowhere,' Coupland said through half closed eyes.

CHAPTER TEN

He could have predicted the headline. Dictated it word for word if he'd been given half the chance:

Shamed cop suspended following prison death.

DS Kevin Coupland of Greater Manchester Police has been suspended following the murder of convicted trafficker Austin Smith earlier this week. Smith had made a complaint about the detective following injuries he'd sustained during his arrest last year. Coupland admitted assaulting Smith to our reporter Angelica Heyworth and went before a Professional Standards hearing on the day of Smith's murder. The outcome of the hearing has not been made public and it is understood DS Coupland was later taken to Eccles Police Station to help police with their enquiries.

In a statement, a GMP spokesperson said: 'We can confirm that a decision has been taken to suspend DS Coupland following serious allegations relating to an incident at HMP Manchester. That is all we are prepared to say at this time.'

The paper contacted Greater Manchester Police Federation for a comment relating to DS Coupland's suspension. A Sergeant Colin Ross declined to speak to our reporter. DS Coupland was unavailable for comment.

As hatchet jobs went it was thorough, he supposed. The words 'Hung Out' and 'Dry' came to mind but he shrugged them away. After all it wasn't as though anything mentioned in the article was untrue. It made him wonder, seeing the article in black and white like that, if his career could ever come back from this. Despite Roddy

Lewisham's scepticism, he couldn't see what Tunney would gain from having Reedsy killed for the sake of it. Coupland got the impression it mattered to Tunney that he kept him on side, which meant, as he and Alex had concluded the previous evening, that the murder had to be down to someone else. Coupland saw no point twiddling his thumbs while he waited for Eccles station to catch up. It was high time he looked under a few stones, see what crawled out. He picked up his mobile, scrolled through his contacts list until he found the number he wanted.

*

The café was old style. Formica tables and wonky chairs. Windows full of condensation. The coffee was cheap and came out of a jar but Coupland wasn't there for the ambience. Nor was he there for the view, given its location in a retail park in the back of beyond, industrial units as far as the eye could see.

Nexus House, a large modern office block in Tameside, Greater Manchester, was home to several police specialist units including Serious and Organised Crime, Economic, and Cold Case Units. It was also home to the force's Operation Challenger, which worked to dismantle organised crime gangs.

Coupland had arranged to meet Adrian Leigh, a pal from police college days who'd transferred there several years back. He ordered two coffees, declined the cellophane wrapped cake beside the till and sat back and waited.

He'd forgotten how intimidating Leigh looked until he stood in the café's entrance, eyes travelling over every diner until he found who he was looking for. Built like an old-style bouncer, he had a mass of curly hair which was starting to turn grey, and the brooding eyes of a cage fighter. His looks had got him involved in several long-term surveillance operations; it was easy to be accepted into the rank and file of career criminals when you looked like you could handle yourself.

Leigh's face grew serious as he approached the table. 'Listen, I heard about your suspension. I'm not on the investigating team but if there's anything I can do...?'

Coupland acknowledged the offer with a bow of his head. 'Feel free to start a petition or wave banners outside HQ but I don't think it'll do much good.'

'Any reason why this gangster's set you up?'

'Not convinced he has, yet. There's plenty others would want the chance to have a pop at me, him too for that matter, you know how it goes. What better than for some rival to pin *conspiracy to murder* on the two of us, create a smokescreen, then swoop in and take over his patch?'

'It won't stick.'

'If you throw enough mud at something it leaves a stain that looks like shit. Anyway, maybe there is something you can do. I need to know who the possible contenders are.'

'What do you mean?'

'Who is currently on your watch list?'

Leigh stared at him wide eyed. 'Seriously? You shout me crap coffee then expect me to spill my guts regarding covert intelligence operations?'

'Now who's having a laugh. "Covert Intelligence Operations?" You tap gangsters' phones; you're hardly James bloody Bond.'

'I've got officers who haven't slept in their own bed

for months. Round the clock surveillance takes it out of you, you know.'

Coupland sighed. On the few occasions he'd tailed someone there'd always been an officer to swap with when his shift was over. When assigned to watch a suspect, the special ops teams weren't allowed to let them out of their sight. He hadn't intended to ruffle Leigh's feathers, though God knows when he'd become so precious about his work. Then again, lack of sleep made most people arsey over time. Coupland threw his hands in the air. 'Look, I was out of line, my missus keeps telling me I've got no filter when it comes to getting people's back up. I'm in a hole that's partly of my own making but unless my name's cleared I'm out on my backside.'

'Whatever information I gave you would be inadmissible in court.'

'I don't want it for court. I want it to help me decide which trees to shake.'

The look Leigh gave him wasn't hopeful. 'I don't think I can help you. All our resources have been diverted into identifying trafficking networks. Drug dealers and arms traders are getting a bit of a holiday.' He laughed but it was strained. Policing was about priorities, and following the discovery of three dozen Chinese migrants who had perished inside a lorry in Essex, the Home Office had instigated a national response to dismantle trafficking gangs.

'So I'm back to square one then.'

'You sure Tunney isn't behind this?'

'As much as I can be.'

'But chances are he could find out, if he wanted to.'

Coupland's mouth turned down at the edges. He

couldn't deny that was a possibility.

'You told me on the phone that he reckons he owes you for saving his life.'

Coupland nodded.

'Then you know what you need to ask him to do. If he's a man of his word, he'll do it.'

CHAPTER ELEVEN

Coupland heard the radio in the background as DCI Mallender answered his call. 'I know I'm supposed to keep my distance boss, but—'

'—*Can it wait, Kevin? I'm on my way out to the Lowry Hotel.*'

'Alright for some, the Super got you holding his plate for him while he shmoozes? God forbid he should be asked to multi task.'

'*Hardly. A sex worker's body has been found in Asim Khan's suite.*'

'Asim Khan, the MP?'

'*The very same.*'

'And where's he?'

'*Still at the hotel. Adamant he didn't touch her.*'

'Who's your wing man?'

'*I'm meeting Ashcroft there.*'

Coupland suppressed a pang.

'*What is it, Kevin? I can spare you five minutes.*'

'I spoke to a pal o' mine at Nexus House.'

'*You're suspended. You shouldn't be contacting any GMP personnel.*'

'I bumped into him boss, funny how that happens sometimes. You don't see someone for years then you travel ten miles out of your way for a coffee, near Serious and Organised's HQ in fact, and bam, you're swapping stories like the old days.'

A sigh. '*How are the counselling sessions going?*'

'Champion.'

'You haven't started them yet, have you?'

'Maybe not…'

A loud exhale of breath. *'Go on then, what did this pal who should know better have to say for himself when you stalked him at his local coffee shop?'*

'Not a lot really. Other than the local gangs are getting a surveillance holiday since they've been told to focus on traffickers. Said that meant he didn't know who might have it in for Tunney enough to muddy the waters between him and the local constabulary.'

'Not a worthwhile trip then.'

'I wouldn't say that. Our talk about surveillance got me thinking, boss. It's not about what you know, but who you know. Putting the word out in the right place can glean more information than traipsing round after someone in week-old pants.'

'I'm listening.'

'Something you're very good at, I reckon.' Coupland paused, weighing up whether he should risk saying what he was about to, or leave it the hell alone. 'Remember the drive-by shooting we worked on?' he said, deciding to push on. 'You turned up to the location where the witness had been abducted at the same time as me, yet I'd just happened on that info by chance moments earlier. Not that I'm complaining, mind, given the killer was pointing a gun at me.' Coupland could only imagine the look on Mallender's face.

'A lucky hunch, Kevin, you know how irresistible that feeling in the gut is.'

Coupland paused to consider this. 'Well, if you've got any more irresistible urges in your gut please feel free to act on them, because my gut is telling me that Tunney is telling the truth.'

'I'll see what I can do,' Mallender said. *'But I need to get on. This is potentially a very sensitive case. We need to tread carefully.'*

'As carefully as if it was a sex worker accused of killing a politician, I hope,' Coupland replied.

'For pity's sake Kevin can you stop lecturing me and start working on your To Do list instead? Go and see a counsellor!'

'You wouldn't be missing me by any chance, boss?'

'In the same way I'd miss a haemorrhoid, Kevin. Only that's a much smaller pain in the backside.'

Coupland looked up to see Lynn studying him as he ended his call. He hadn't realised she'd been standing in the doorway.

'You're on that phone more now than you ever were,' she observed, her lips a thin line.

Coupland threw his hands wide. 'I can't just switch off. You wouldn't ignore someone who went into labour on the bus just because you weren't on duty, would you?'

Her mouth turned down at the edges as she shook her head. 'No, but if I'd been suspended, I would make a point of complying with the conditions of my reinstatement.' She picked up her laptop that had been left on the counter top. 'You know what you need to do,' she added, placing it on the kitchen table before pointing to a chair. 'Now sit down and get on with it.'

Coupland slumped into the chair with a groan. He lifted the laptop's lid and logged in, clicking on the link sent through to him via email from HR. He could feel Lynn's eyes boring into the back of his skull. 'Pull up a seat if you don't trust me,' he grumbled.

Lynn didn't need asking a second time. She pulled out

the seat beside him and slouched into it, staring at the screen as he clicked on the sidebar.

'Christ, who knew there were so many trick cyclists?' he muttered, scrolling down Suzanne Waite's shortlist of therapists, skim reading names and specialisms, whistling when he reached the end. 'There's a fortune to be made in people's misery. Who knew, eh?'

'Not always misery, Kev. Think of it as self-improvement.'

'You can't improve on perfection, love.'

His grin was almost convincing but Lynn wasn't taken in. 'Shame your bosses don't agree.'

Coupland clicked onto one of the sites and began reading the list of issues the therapist claimed they could cure. Weight Management. Alcohol Abuse. Gambling. He read the list out loud. 'This guy guarantees results in 30 days.'

'Impressive.'

'Yeah, but how can he be so sure?' In Coupland's experience people weren't one thing or the other. The folk he came into contact with were like layers of an onion. A killer wasn't just a killer. They were often liars too, and deluded. Throw in a tendency to think their actions were justified and you had a dangerous combination. 'What if you're a fat drunk that likes a bet on the horses?' Coupland asked, his free hand rubbing at unshaven stubble.

Lynn shrugged. 'Maybe it's a case of selecting the issue you want to be rid of the most.'

'What if their issues complement each other in some way? The gambler might be twice as heavy if they won all the time and ate out to celebrate. And if they drank

105

themselves into a stupor they'd spend less time in the bookies.'

'You would say that,' Lynn replied, furrowing her brow. 'I'm not sure where you're going with this, Kev.'

'Maybe I wouldn't be so angry if I smoked more?'

The fact Lynn looked as though she was considering this made him hopeful. 'Ah, now I get it. Feel free to try out that little theory, only make sure you hand me your door key once you've moved out…'

'I'm only thinking aloud!'

'Think away, but you've had your card marked. There's nothing optional about any of this, Kev,' she said, indicating the laptop and the opened directory of psychotherapists. 'You need to suck it up and get on with it or go and find another job.'

Coupland cocked his brow. 'You might want to work on that bedside manner.'

'There's nothing wrong with my bedside manner. Seriously, Kev, pull your finger out. Select the next bloody therapist you come to if you have to. It doesn't need to be any more scientific than that.' She got up to put the kettle on, lifting two mugs from the draining board and placing them on the worktop before spooning in coffee.

Coupland sighed. Lynn had a point, he supposed. The practitioners had been vetted by HR so all he needed to do was choose one. Closer to home would be handy, he reckoned. The number of five-star reviews might be helpful, too. He worked his way down, randomly clicking on a link, waited for the web page to load. He selected the button marked 'Behavioural therapy', read the questions at the top of the page:

Do you lose your temper easily or find it difficult to let go of frustrations?

Have you reacted out of anger in a way that you later regretted?

Does your rage seem so strong at times that it scares people, including yourself?

'I've found one,' he said, clicking the contact button.

*

DCI Mallender sat in his car outside the Lowry Hotel mentally running through his checklist of actions. The crime scene had been secured within an hour of Rose King's body being discovered. The pathologist had completed his initial examination and CSIs were harvesting forensic evidence from the executive suite Asim Khan had been staying in. The hotel would be closed to new guests for 24 hours. The current guests were in the dining room having their details taken by uniformed officers; their names would be cross-checked against the guest register. He'd left DC Ashcroft to interview the reception and hotel lobby staff, and check through CCTV.

The glass fronted five-star hotel sat on the banks of the River Irwell. It attracted a champagne cocktail crowd including Mallender's father when he entertained visiting associates. Mallender preferred to steer clear of smart places, had chosen to live a life that didn't draw attention to itself as a result of his father's chequered past. He'd hidden his background surprisingly well. No one that knew him would guess he was John Gibson's son, an 'entrepreneur' who'd built up a business empire based on protection rackets and extortion. Mallender's twin sister had been murdered as a child; Gibson served a stretch inside for killing the man blamed for her death.

On release from prison he'd decided to go legitimate, moving into property development, where he could put his connections to local councillors to good use. Despite this, Mallender continued to keep his distance, saving the sparse communication he had with his parents for high days and holidays.

Coupland's call this morning had rattled him. It was clear he had no intention of letting the investigation into Austin Smith's murder take its course. Typical Coupland, if you backed him into a corner he came out fighting. He'd gleaned precious little from his contact at Nexus House, though it was clear he wasn't going to stop there. What Coupland had alluded to during their phone conversation had been right. Mallender had saved Coupland's life once. In a house on Worsley Road he'd shot a hitman hellbent on executing a key witness in a drive-by shooting, along with the stubborn cop who'd refused to get out of his way. They'd never spoken of it afterwards. Coupland had let the rest of the team think he'd told Mallender of his whereabouts that day, and had never sought to get to the bottom of the real reason he'd known where to look. What if he started to dig now and discovered the identity of Mallender's father? Even though the old man's intel had saved Coupland's life, Mallender's career would be over. Was that a good enough reason to let Coupland be thrown to the dogs? Mallender already knew the answer. He pulled out his phone. His father hadn't been 'Dad' on his speed dial since he'd joined the force. He scrolled down until he found the name stored on his contact list as 'Gibson' and hit 'call'.

'It's been a while son. To what do we owe this pleasure?' Despite the rebuke his father sounded pleased to hear from him,

and more than a little curious.

'You've not seen the news then?'

'You mean the item about one of your lot going rogue? I'm surprised that's even making headlines these days.'

'He's a good man.'

'Aren't they all? That's how it starts, Son. A good reputation, a happy marriage, a pillar of the community. Then something comes along and threatens it all and before you know it they need a favour doing…'

'Like getting an inmate's throat slashed? That's a tad extreme.'

'An inmate with an axe to grind, I heard.'

'It isn't like that.'

'What is it like then?'

'He's been set up by someone. Kieran Tunney was looking most likely at first, but it doesn't make sense. Maybe they're both being set up for all I know… what is it?' Mallender asked, when Gibson said nothing.

'I knew it was probably work that made you phone but even so, don't you think you could dress it up as a social call, for your mother's sake?'

'How is she?'

'She's fine. As good as she's been in a long while, in fact. Not that you'd know.'

Mallender swallowed down his guilt. 'You know how it is, Dad, I can't come over too often, the press gets hold of our connection and my career is as good as over.' Not for the first time he wished he could split his family in two. His mother had never wronged anyone in her life. But she loved a man who had and there was a price to pay for that. Mallender pressed on, regardless. 'I need a favour. About that inmate who had his throat slashed…'

109

*

Salford Royal Hospital

Lynn Brookes-Osborne was the medical director of Greater Manchester NHS Foundation Trust. She was several inches shorter than Alex but what she lacked in height she made up for in attitude. With cropped auburn hair styled around an angular face, her build suggested she liked to keep fit. Alex found herself admiring the trouser suit she wore, though on a sergeant's pay it was probably unattainable.

'I appreciate you finding the time to speak to me at such short notice,' Alex said, after introducing herself. 'As I explained on the phone I'm investigating the circumstances surrounding Piers Bradley's death and I hoped you'd be able to fill in some of the blanks before I conclude my report to the coroner.'

The medical director nodded. 'Of course. I'll help in any way I can. I must say we're all still reeling from his arrest, never mind this latest, terrible news. The medical community is in shock.'

'So Piers was well regarded then?'

'Yes. By staff and patients alike. As medical director I had the upmost faith in him.' Lynn pointed to a chair the other side of her desk and waited while Alex sat down before returning to her own chair. The office was large enough for a grandiose desk, two leather sofas either side of a glass table, and a floor-to-ceiling bookcase filled with medical reference books. 'Please ignore the mess,' Lynn said, indicating the cycle helmet and high viz clothing piled up on one seat, a rucksack and a discarded towel on the other. 'I forgot my locker key this morning so have had to dump my stuff in here.'

'I'm impressed,' Alex said, trying to remember when she'd last gone to the gym.

'Don't be, if working in this place doesn't motivate you into staying active, nothing will.'

She had a point, Alex supposed.

'Can I offer you tea or coffee? It's no trouble.'

It never was any trouble when someone else would have to make it, Alex thought, shaking her head and claiming she'd not long had one when in truth her mouth was so dry she could spit feathers.

'Given the CCTV footage there's never been any question of Dr Bradley's guilt, but I wondered if anything that happened to his patients could have happened as a result of an error?' She'd asked this question several times to members of the medical staff a lot less senior than Brookes-Osborne and they'd all come back with the same reply. Still, it didn't hurt to ask the question one more time.

The medical director sighed as she shook her head. 'Not in a straightforward context, no. Anaesthesia is delivered in a controlled and deliberate environment. It has to be carefully measured, administered, and monitored. It's a powerful cocktail of several drugs which are meant to paralyse, block pain, and render a patient unconscious. Any miscalculation of these drugs could have disastrous results. That's why stringent checks are made… and why gas men don't suffer fools gladly.'

Alex nodded. 'There was me thinking my job was stressful…'

'Trust me, by the time you get to occupy this chair you've seen just about every medical cock-up there is and can tell the difference between accidental or deliberate. Look… what happened to Belinda Adamson was rare but it can happen. A moment's lapse in concentration, misreading notes on patients' height and weight, any number of things. But the CCTV footage in respect of Blake Peters made my job easy. It clearly showed Piers tampering with his oxygen tube, causing the patient to suffer hypoxia. Even if he'd survived, he'd have been severely debilitated. This was no accident.'

Alex considered this. 'It's strange isn't it? When I think of medical blunders I think of surgeons slipping with a scalpel. I've never considered the implication of pain relief or breathing apparatus.'

'This is because anaesthetists are kind of in the background of healthcare. You only tend to get to meet them moments before surgery begins.' There was a glint in Lynn's eye before she spoke next. 'They use the same drugs used to legally execute prisoners in some states of America, just much higher doses.'

Alex returned the woman's smile. 'I trust you don't mention that to anyone you're about to operate on.'

'Sadly my time is taken up with admin these days. I don't get to scare nearly as many patients as I used to.'

Alex got to her feet. 'Just one more thing. The CCTV that captured Dr Bradley's actions. Why was it there?'

Lynn frowned. 'We use them to make sure staff are following hygiene protocol in a bid to reduce hospital-acquired infections.'

'Like MRSA, you mean?'

A nod. 'And as a by-product, I hope to see an improvement in patient safety and quality of care.'

'And reduce the incidents of blunders and malpractice

while you're at it…' Alex finished for her.

Another nod. 'The directive came from above so we do what we're told. But as a result of that we caught a killer who might have otherwise carried on undetected, so for me it has proved itself a worthy eye in the sky. After all, the camera never lies.'

What the medical director said was right. Even so, Alex couldn't ignore the feeling of unease that had settled in her stomach.

Feeling peckish, Alex headed towards the ground floor hospital cafeteria where she helped herself to a green tea and a bowl of pumpkin soup.

'I'll have what she's having, said no-one, ever,' the person behind her bellowed as she took her tray to the cashier.

'You can say what you like since you're paying,' Alex replied, waiting while Coupland fished in his pocket for his debit card which he swiped across the contactless payment device. His own choice had been a touch more substantial, a pasta bake with extra cheese and a double shot latte. They found a table in the corner of the room, away from the other diners.

Alex told him the purpose of her visit to the hospital.

'Seems like Big Brother has finally made it onto the wards,' Coupland observed, though it was no surprise, he supposed.

'Surveillance is a hot topic, and not just for staff safety. Medical supplies going missing, equipment going walkabout, the problem's nationwide,' Alex told him.

Coupland considered this. 'If this doc was banged to rights due to the CCTV footage then you've got nothing to investigate. Slam dunk.'

113

Alex pulled a face. 'It seems that way, yeah…'

'But you're not convinced.'

She shook her head, recalling her conversation with Ruth Bradley and her sister. 'He may have been considered arrogant by some but he was a consummate professional, passionate about his patients. If there wasn't CCTV footage actually catching him in the act I don't think anyone would have thought him capable.'

'You're happy the recording's not been tampered with?'

'I'm no tech expert but we're talking about a full-on facial capture in one shot. He never made out it wasn't him in the footage, just that he didn't commit the crime… until his admission to his wife whilst on remand.'

'Surely that makes it even more of a slam dunk.'

'You're probably right. Even so, I think I'll take a look at the tape one more time. Then I really do need to submit my report, otherwise I'll be getting the coroner's office filing a complaint.'

He watched as she took a half-hearted slurp of her soup. Made a point of smacking his lips after guzzling two loaded spoonfuls of creamy pasta. 'Do you want me to take a look at the CCTV? Not like I've got a lot on my plate at the moment.'

'That'd go down well with the powers that be.'

'I'll hardly be making a song and dance about it. I'll give it the once over and let you know what I think. Two heads are better than one, remember.'

She quickly shook her head. 'No need. I'm probably looking for issues where there aren't any. Anyway, why did you want to meet me here?'

Coupland shrugged. 'Seemed as good a place as any.

I can legitimately tell whoever asks that I've just dropped Lynn off for her shift.'

'Fair enough.'

'I rang the boss first thing but he's on his way to a shout at the Lowry.'

'I heard about that. Some MP has killed a sex worker. I reckon that means for the next couple of days the press will be all over the honourable member and you'll be off the hook.'

Coupland took a slurp of his coffee. 'Every cloud...'

'So... why did you call?'

'Just wanted to let off steam, I suppose. I was so sure my contact at Nexus house would be able to point me in the right direction regarding the toe rag who's set me up but it feels like I'm pissing in the wind.'

'Maybe now's the time to get your head down and crack on with this counselling malarkey.'

Coupland sat upright in his chair and lifted his chin. 'I'm already on it. Booked my first session for this afternoon, as a matter of fact.'

Alex failed to conceal a smirk. 'I'd love to be a fly on *that* wall...'

Coupland refused to rise to the bait. 'Do you reckon I'll get a certificate at the end of it?'

Alex shrugged while slurping more soup.

'My first ever certificate. Maybe the Super will do something to mark the occasion.'

Alex tilted her head. 'Yeah, he'll give you your warrant card back. Seriously though Kevin, you will make an effort, won't you? Fully engage with it all, when you're there I mean.'

Coupland huffed out a sigh. 'What do you take me

for? Like I said to Lynn, I'll do whatever is needed to get top brass off my back, and if that means sitting in the Lotus position while someone beats me round the lugholes with an incense stick then so be it.'

*

CID Room, Salford Precinct Station
Krispy looked up from his desk as Alex entered the CID room. 'DCI Mallender's been looking for you, Sarge.'
'Did he say what he wanted?'
Krispy shook his head. 'I told him you were at the hospital. He said you were to go and see him the moment you got back.'
Alex dropped her bag and car keys onto her desk and headed back the way she'd come in.

The DCI's door was open. Despite tapping on his keyboard, he looked up when she hovered in the doorway, something the Super never bothered to do until the task he was working on was complete. 'Come in,' Mallender said, ushering her in with one hand while clicking 'send' on the email he'd been compiling. 'Ready to put the Dr Bradley report to bed yet?'

Alex frowned, sitting in the empty chair in front of his desk when he pointed to it. 'Sorry, sir, but no. There's a couple of loose ends I need to tie up but my report should be ready by the end of the day.'

'Don't apologise for being thorough, Alex. Anything I can help with?'

'Well, you could start by reinstating Kevin.'

'I'm doing all that I can at my end but he's got to make an effort too. When he called me this morning he hadn't even organised an appointment with a therapist.'

'He's seeing someone this afternoon…' Alex winced at her slip up, feeling her cheeks flush under Mallender's gaze.

'Well, that's something,' Mallender conceded, letting it go.

'Is there really nothing more we can do?' Alex asked.

'We couldn't even if we had the resources. The investigation was handed to Eccles for the sake of impartiality. Our hands are tied.'

Alex dropped her gaze. The system stank at times but it wasn't the DCI's fault. There was nothing to be gained rubbing him up the wrong way because she didn't like what he was telling her. She remembered he'd been on a shout earlier. 'I hear we've got an MP in custody.'

Mallender nodded. 'He phoned hotel reception in the early hours yelling for an ambulance but when the duty manager went to his room it was obvious the woman was dead. He was arrested on the spot by the first officers on the scene but he's made no comment other than to ask for his lawyer.'

'How did she die?'

'It appears to be strangulation. One of the stockings she was wearing had been removed and used as a ligature around her neck.'

'Any ID?'

Mallender handed her a file. 'Her name's Rose King. You'll see from what she's wearing it's hard to mistake her profession.'

Alex opened the manila folder and studied the series of crime scene photos inside. 'She's dressed like a low rent Pretty Woman.'

Mallender frowned.

'The film that made prostitution seem attractive. Julia Roberts was in it. It's the kind of get up you'd wear to a Tarts and Vicars party circa 1980.'

'So what's your point?'

Alex shrugged. 'At least we won't have trouble picking her out on CCTV.'

Mallender nodded in agreement. 'Can you get DC Timmins to run a background check on the hotel staff? I've also asked him to cross check the hotel's guest register with the names of people uniforms have spoken to first thing, make sure we haven't missed anyone out.'

Alex closed the file and slipped it under her arm. 'Will do, boss.'

'Alex…'

'Yes?'

'Have you discussed your reservations about the Bradley case with Andy? There may be something he can put your mind at rest with. Besides, he's done most of the leg work. Communication and all that.'

Alex felt a moment's irritation. She'd been meaning to update Cueball but hadn't had a chance to yet. She hated being on the back foot. 'I'll do that right away, sir,' she said, head bowed.

Cueball was less amenable than the last time they'd spoken. 'I've had Dr Bradley's widow on the phone asking when you'd be done with your questions.'

'What did you tell her?'

'I said it was out of my hands, that I'd have to speak with you…'

'Yeah, sorry about that, I should have kept you in the loop and I didn't.'

'So, you've found something then? Don't tell me he was murdered as well?'

'No, nothing like that. Were you made aware he'd left a suicide note?'

Cueball pulled a face like he'd smelled something sour. 'No… to be honest it feels like I've been pushed out of the way since you've taken over.'

'I haven't taken over, Andy; I'm just overseeing the conditions of his arrest and his state of mind prior to his suicide. I should have shared relevant information with you and I didn't, so I apologise about that but for Christ's sake don't turn petulant every time something doesn't go your way. You want to know something, speak up.'

'Sarge…' Cueball muttered, a red flush appearing from his shirt collar.

'Look. I could do with your help over something. I want you to watch the hospital CCTV with me…'

'I've already seen it…'

'Yeah, but humour me, OK?'

Cueball nodded reluctantly, following Alex through to the larger of the two CID rooms, waiting while she dragged a chair from another desk and placed it beside her own for him to sit on. She logged onto her PC and found the file she was looking for, then hit play.

She fast forwarded through the footage until Dr Bradley came on screen, making his way towards Blake Peters' bed:

It was evening. The lights on the ward had been dimmed. At first he stands motionless at the end of Blake's bed, observing the young man who appears to be in pain. What Bradley says to him, and the security he conveys, visibly relaxes him. After a moment or two Blake nods and closes his eyes. Instead of walking away Bradley moves to Blake's bedside, removing the tube going into the oxygen cylinder and connecting it to the cylinder beside it. He does so efficiently and with no emotion, little wonder he doesn't draw attention from the staff who pass by in a constant stream. In the seconds that follow, Blake's eyes begin twitching spasmodically before snapping open. His chest rises and falls rapidly and his stomach begins to jerk. Bradley studies his deterioration, his gaze lingering on the machine monitoring the young man's pulse rate. Satisfied, he walks away. In the seconds that follow Blake's mouth falls open, and a trickle of saliva runs out.

'Callous twat,' muttered Cueball. 'Did you see how he doesn't even look around to check he's not being watched?'

Alex pulled a face. 'But why would anyone pay him any attention, let alone question what he was doing? Even if they did he'd have been able to fob them off or shame them into submission for even challenging him.'

'That's what happens when we put people on a pedestal. They start acting like they are above everyone else.'

Alex didn't disagree. 'OK,' she said finally. 'I'll let the coroner's office know I'm satisfied there's no evidence of foul play in relation to his suicide. I think his conscience finally caught up with him.'

'And you're happy with my investigation?'

Alex nodded. 'Of course,' she said slowly. 'After all he was literally caught in the act. We'll never know if he was truly of sound mind. His actions suggest not but there's no evidence to support that either.' He'd certainly not shown any agitation, or anger for that matter. It was hard to pinpoint any emotion, now she thought about it.

Cueball was on his feet, keen to return to his own desk. 'I'll let Mrs Bradley know you'll be contacting the coroner then. That'll get her off my back at least.'

Alex nodded distractedly. She picked up her phone, keyed in the telephone number for the coroner's assistant and told them what she had told Cueball. When the call ended she slouched back in her chair, drumming her fingers on her desk. Despite her relaxed posture she felt tightly wound, unable to shift the nagging doubt that she'd missed something. Sighing, she sat forward in her chair and stared at the screen.

She opened up her email account and had hit the 'create new' button. Before she had time to think about it she'd entered Coupland's contact details into the recipient's address and typed Hospital File as the heading. In the body of the message she wrote: 'Assuming you're still kicking your heels I've attached the clip I was talking about. Can you take a look at it and let me know what you see?' She hit send.

CHAPTER TWELVE

Incident Room briefing, Salford Precinct Station

'Most of you will now know that Asim Khan, MP, has been detained in custody, arrested for the murder of sex worker Rose King.' DCI Mallender pointed to the photograph on the incident board of a woman in her twenties lying face down on the hotel bed, fully clothed apart from one stocking tied around her neck. 'A bag which we believe to be hers was found in the room. Inside it was a debit card and two hundred pounds in cash, plus three packs of condoms.'

The photograph beside it was a blown-up publicity shot of Asim Khan, taken in the run up to the general election the previous year. 'Mr Khan claims he has no recollection of events in the lead up to Rose's murder, nor of the act itself. His lawyer's downstairs on his phone requesting a super injunction.'

'He's not on legal aid then,' said a DC on the front row.

'Nice work if you can get it,' another observed. 'Amazing what you can afford when the tax payer's stumping up. Bet he was going to put her services through the books as well.'

Mallender nodded at Krispy who'd raised his hand.

'I've printed this photo off Rose's Facebook profile, taken last year on a mate's hen do,' he said, holding it up. It was a typical social media 'pouting' pic favoured by women under 25 and older ones who should know better, in Alex's opinion. Taken in front of a full-length mirror before a night out, by the look of it. A dress so close fitting it appeared sprayed on, boots too high to walk in and hair extensions. She looked older than her 29 years. Dark shadows beneath her eyes and teeth that needed fixing. A combination of drugs, poor diet, lack of self-care. She didn't look as though she normally wore stockings and suspenders on a night out but then last night wasn't entertainment. That was her living, even though it turned out to be the death of her.

Krispy pulled an uncustomary glum face. 'I'm having a problem running background checks, sir. The system's been down most of the day for maintenance.'

'And they say technology is king,' said a DC behind him.

'That's the third time this week,' Alex said, eyeballing the DCI. The division as a whole had been having problems with IPOS, the newly installed Integrated Police Operating System. Users were commonly struggling to log in or found they were logged in as someone else.

'It breaks down so often it's like Groundhog Day,' said Krispy. 'And it takes twice as long to enter any information.' Krispy had been designated the station's 'Super User'. He had attended all the training courses and was as au fait as any of the technical wizards who'd sold the gizmo to GMP, but he was on loan to Pendlebury station for the rest of the afternoon to troubleshoot their system, so his actions were now on the back burner. There was a massive backlog of reported crime that couldn't be cleared fast enough because the network kept breaking down.

Mallender made a mental note to have another sparring

match with the Super about it. He nodded at Krispy. 'Get on to it as soon as you can.'

He looked around the detectives assembled in front of him. 'Hands up anyone who's been able to make progress today.'

DC Ashcroft raised his hand. 'The hotel receptionist remembers seeing Rose, sir. She'd been about to alert the duty manager – there'd been complaints recently by some of the guests about being approached by sex workers in the bar, so the management had asked staff to be extra vigilant – however the doorman persuaded her to keep quiet, claimed she was a 'regular' and wouldn't get in anyone's way.'

'In other words he'd pimped her out for the evening.'

Ashcroft nodded. 'Pretty much. When I spoke to him at first he tried denying having anything to do with her but in the next breath he was saying how he prided himself on providing special guests with anything they wanted and Asim Khan had asked for a pretty woman so he'd obliged.'

'Charming! So we've got a doorman with an open door policy for sex workers as long as they cut him a slice. And presumably the guests in question give him a back hander for services rendered.'

Another nod. 'Got it in one. The doorman claims Khan contacted him by text with the request for a prostitute but it's not Khan's number that comes up when I checked his call history. I've tried tracing it but it's a pre-paid phone, not registered to anyone.'

'Maybe he kept a secret phone for his booty calls?' asked Mallender. 'If so, you need to find it.'

'When's the PM, sir?' Alex asked.

'Not till tomorrow, though it's unlikely to tell us anything we don't already know. Professor Benson has given a time of death as between midnight and 2am.'

'OK, with any luck forensics will give us the evidence we need so we can go ahead and charge him. In the meantime a taste of our hospitality won't do any harm.'

'Be a far cry from his expense account accommodation, that's for sure.'

'My heart bleeds.' Mallender got to his feet. 'I've got to deliver the death message to Rose King's parents. Ashcroft, I want you to interview Asim Khan. Alex, I need you to allocate today's actions and update the duty log. We need a DNA sample taken and I want Khan seen by the duty doc, there's a scratch on his neck I'd like looking at.'

Alex nodded.

Before leaving the station Mallender made his way upstairs to the Super's office. So much of his job involved towing the party line, but on some issues he would not be swayed.

'I didn't know we had a meeting scheduled,' Superintendent Curtis said when Mallender appeared in his doorway after a sharp knock.

'We don't, sir, I'm on my way to notify the family of the woman found dead in Asim Khan's hotel room, but there's something pressing which I don't think can wait.'

'Really?'

'I have serious concerns about this new computer system. It's causing chaos downstairs. I don't know how long I can keep fobbing my team off.'

Curtis was already raising his hand. 'I don't want to hear it, Stuart, it's not like there's anything we can do.'

'Can we not stagger the roll-out, sir? We could continue to use the old system and trial the new one for a couple of months, so we can iron out all the technical problems before we have to rely on it full time.'

Curtis shook his head. 'You know as well as I do that's not an option. Remember this directive has come from the very top. The Mayor himself wanted it rolled out at the same time throughout the division and that's what he's got.'

'But it's not fit for purpose.'

'You're going to tell him that are you?'

Mallender considered this. 'If I have to,' he said, 'but I thought that was your job.'

'Excuse me?'

'Please – hear me out,' Mallender pleaded, stepping onto the hallowed ground uninvited. 'There's been a serious impact on reporting – right now I have no idea what crimes are happening in my area because I can't search for them.' Under the old system as soon as an address was entered, the database carried out a series of searches based on Person, Object, Location, Event. Under the new system, markers were only attached to the person rather than the place, which meant that officers attending an incident were no longer in possession of key facts. 'My team are unable to search for basic information, track crimes, radio in or get information through to the courts and other organisations. It's a disaster in the making.'

Curtis slumped back in his chair. 'Look, on this we're agreed. I've no idea what's a priority on a day to day basis or threatening to the district. I'm running this station blindfolded.'

For the first time that Mallender could remember the

Super looked out of his comfort zone. He realised he was in just as much a no-win situation. IPOS had been thrust on him in the same way it had been thrust on every officer in GMP. With scant training and precious little lead-in time they were learning as they went along. If the organised gangs got wind of it they'd have a field day.

'Look,' Curtis sighed. 'The best I can do is say that where overtime is required to make up time lost on a case due to IPOS stalling then I'll sign it off – I mean it,' he said, making a chopping motion with his hand to emphasise the point. 'Only where officers have been drafted in to input data and fill in gaps in the system. Who knows, maybe I can get some of it back if this turns out to be a much bigger problem than division level…'

Mallender kept his features expressionless but in truth he was satisfied with the Super's response. 'Very well, sir,' he said. 'And in the meantime let's hope we don't have a major emergency land in our laps.'

Curtis regarded him. 'You know, for a moment there, DCI Mallender, I could have sworn that bolshy detective was back in the building.'

*

Brookdale House Therapy Centre was based in a multi-function health and lifestyle complex situated in a mini business park off Chapel Street. The interior consisted of a large atrium with reception desks for the dental and chiropodist practices based on the ground floor. The counselling rooms were on the first floor, accessed by a narrow spiral staircase on one side of the building or lift with clear glass panels on the other, both problematical for folk suffering from vertigo, Coupland reckoned, wondering if it was a cruel marketing ploy by the therapists running their clinics from there.

The waiting area was quiet. There was a TV on but down low. Several actresses known for stints on The Bill and lesser known soaps chatted on screen about the menopause. Coupland glanced at his watch and sighed. The chairs had been arranged in rows, presumably so patients couldn't eyeball each other while waiting for their name to be called. He took a seat at the back of the room, pulled his mobile from his pocket and scrolled through his personal inbox: introductory offers from Russian dating sites and an advert for penis enlargement. Sighing, he pocketed his phone, his attention wandering to the other sad saps waiting their turn as he tried to speculate what had brought them here. No prizes for guessing what the skeletal woman seated on the front row was in for, he thought, his gaze travelling a few chairs along to a woman in her thirties sitting with a boy aged about 5. Her son, Coupland assumed, given they shared similar features, though he was less confident of who was the patient. Both seemed at ease in their surroundings, suggesting their visits were regular. The lad huddled into her as they looked at photos on her mobile.

'Are you here for the meeting?'

Coupland turned to see a grey haired man in a tweed jacket and chinos addressing him. He'd approached from a corridor to the left of the waiting room carrying a cardboard tray of takeaway coffees. Coupland looked around him to see if the man could have been talking to anyone else, but the woman with an eating disorder and the mother and son didn't seem to have heard him. He shook his head. 'No. I'm…I'm here to see someone…

I'm here for a consultation,' he said in the lowest voice he could muster.

'Ah,' the man said. 'Sorry,' before heading towards a room just off the waiting area that had a laminated sign stuck on the front saying 'Meeting in progress.'

Coupland looked down at the work suit he'd worn. He hadn't been sure how to dress for his appointment, thought his daily get-up was the best bet, show them they were dealing with someone with a purpose. He allowed himself a smile. It wasn't all bad, he supposed; at least to the people around him he looked normal, non-threatening, like someone who could have been here in a professional capacity rather than learning how to downgrade their temper.

Another door opened and a woman with a North East accent stepped out and smiled at the mother and son. 'You're looking well,' she observed, holding the door of her consultation room open so they could step inside.

'We're getting there,' the mother said, 'he's started talking about his dad again, since the funeral…'

Coupland found himself wondering if Liam Roberts had received the help he'd needed at the time, he wouldn't have turned into an arsonist, whether it was that simple.

The door to the neighbouring consulting room opened and a man stepped out, waving at the skeletal woman who got up from her chair and moved towards him to exchange a hug.

'How did it go?' she asked.

'I'll tell you in the car,' he answered, slipping his arm around her waist as they headed towards the exit.

Well, I called that wrong, Coupland chided himself. He should have known better, given the nature of his job.

People didn't walk around wearing labels around their necks saying 'killer' or 'rapist', 'drunk driver' or 'thief.' If they did it would make his job a damn sight easier.

'Kevin?' The person standing in front of him smiled and made a sweeping motion with their arm indicating that he step into the room vacated by the skeletal woman's partner moments earlier. Coupland nodded and got to his feet, guessing patient surnames weren't used much in places like this. The consultation room consisted of a low round table with a chair either side. There was a jug of water and one empty glass on the table top, and a box of tissues placed at its centre. A side table had a small vase containing fresh flowers, beside it a bean bag which Coupland eyed suspiciously. 'Sit wherever you feel comfortable,' the therapist smiled, opting for a wooden framed seat with tapestry style cushions. Coupland obliged by plonking himself on the closest chair, a moulded plastic effort even more uncomfy than it looked. He splayed his legs wide in a bid to take up as much space as possible.

'Look,' he began, his gaze dropping to the badge on the therapist's lapel which said 'Sam Freeman'. 'We're both busy people, Sam, and I don't want to take you away from folk who really need your help. So if we can skip a few of the pleasantries and cut to the chase…'

Sam studied him. 'What? When we were getting on so well…?'

Coupland couldn't be sure whether the therapist was having a laugh at his expense but decided that was counter intuitive for someone in the business of counselling.

'The purpose of this appointment is for me to understand what's troubling you, so that I can recommend the treatment I feel is best able to help you,' Sam explained.

A look of alarm flashed across Coupland's face. 'But this still counts as a session, right? It'll show on my attendance record that I turned up and spent an hour with you?'

'I suppose so... though I'm not sure you're grasping what today's assessment is all about.'

'Trust me, I'm a quick learner. You're hedging your bets and if I get on your wick you'll palm me off onto a pal...' he said, reclining into the plastic before thinking better of it and inching forward so he could arch his back.

Sam continued as though Coupland hadn't spoken, opening a spiral bound notepad and removing the top from a ball point pen. Coupland rested his elbows on his knees, arranging his features so they looked *interested*. His eyes scanned the room as though looking for an escape route. The blind was drawn halfway down the single window, keeping out the glare of the winter sun. Two certificates in thin black frames had been tacked to the wall. A photo beneath them of a sullen teenage boy. He felt Sam's gaze fall on him.

'Goes with the turf I'm afraid, the inability to mind my own business.' He was rewarded with a benign smile. Stock in trade in this line of work, Coupland supposed, just as his was glaring.

'Not at his most engaging, I admit. He's been having a few problems at college this year. You know that saying, *You're only as happy as your unhappiest child?* Turns out it's true.'

Coupland thought of Amy. How he'd tried but failed to protect her from the world he inhabited. Sometimes your best wasn't good enough.

'I've read the referral notes sent from your employer's human resources team,' Sam told him. 'I see that your attendance here is a condition of your return to work.'

Coupland swallowed down his frustration. 'You've got to love HR haven't you?' he sighed. 'I mean, you can see I work for the police, can't you? It's not like I work in a regular firm with customers I *have* to be nice to. Yet these suits throw their weight around doling out punishments like I'm the class bully.'

The look Sam sent in his direction was not entirely pleasant, making him wonder if he'd overstepped the mark. 'So you see being sent here as a punishment?'

Coupland furrowed his brow. 'Put it this way, it wasn't on my bucket list.'

'But you *do* find yourself angry in the workplace?'

Coupland shrugged. 'I work in a murder squad and murder makes me angry.'

'So that's all right then,' Sam said, placing the pad and pen on the table between them. 'Case closed. Your outbursts are directly in proportion to your job. There are no issues around the way you relate to people and no one has ever seen fit to make a complaint.'

Coupland dropped his gaze. 'I wouldn't put it like that, exactly.'

'So, how would you put it?' A shrug. Coupland felt about ten years old.

'Do you like your job, Kevin?' The therapist's voice was calm and matter of fact. A voice that never rose in anger or cursed.

'It has its moments.'

'And other times?'

Coupland puffed out his cheeks. 'Being a cop means

you get to see what's going on behind closed doors. The battered wives, the media execs who think snorting coke makes them less of a junkie, and footballers up to their gonads in debt. You learn everyone has a story. Whether they let that story dictate the rest of their life is up to them. What's not to like?'

'You're very philosophical for one so cynical.'

'Not really. The job alters the way you see people, that's all. The way you look at life in general, I suppose. I'm sure it isn't healthy.' He brushed his hand against his jacket pocket, felt the reassuring crackle of his Lisinopril blister pack. He'd started carrying a spare strip of blood pressure meds around with him the way ancient tribesmen carried a talisman.

'Have you ever considered relaxation techniques?'

Coupland widened his eyes. 'If you're planning on burning candles I'm out of here,' he said. 'There's only so much I'm prepared to do in the line of duty.'

'I was thinking more along the lines of hypnotherapy.'

'You're missing the point, doc, I haven't considered any form of therapy. Never thought I needed it.'

He still didn't. As far as he was concerned this was a box-ticking exercise. A hoop to jump through, like going on diversity courses and conducting performance reviews. Everyone knew they didn't modify behaviour. There would still be twats in the workplace, regardless of the number of PowerPoint presentations they were made to sit through. Coupland tried his best to play nice. 'I'm not sure I fully understand what it is, to be truthful. You mean hypnosis, right? My knowledge extends as far as the fellas you see on TV, the ones who make folk cluck like chickens and take off their clothes, I'm guessing there's more to it than that.'

A laugh, although a little stilted. 'You need to get that idea out of your head completely. Tomfoolery, smoke and mirrors, call it what you will, no one in our profession subscribes to that form of cabaret, or exposing people to scrutiny whilst deeply relaxed as a form of entertainment.'

Coupland nodded, satisfied. 'So, tell me what it is then.'

Sam's smile widened, making it look a lot less forced than it had a couple of minutes before.

'Hypnosis is an altered state of consciousness. To use neurophysiological terms—'

'—Terms a complete idiot would understand, if you don't mind.'

Sam nodded. 'Of course. The brain functions in a particular way under hypnosis. Sections that we don't use are suddenly activated. A person in a hypnotic state is completely relaxed, to the point where they may look almost asleep, but if you conducted an EEG on them you would see that their brain is awake and alert.'

'You could say that about one of my DCs,' Coupland said, conjuring up an image of Turnbull.

Freeman paused, good naturedly.

'Sorry, I'm keeping up with you, I promise.'

'Good. I mention it because, how shall I put it? I'm sensing a little resistance. It may help make you receptive to therapy in general.'

Coupland sat up straighter in his chair. It went against his psyche to relinquish control, especially to a complete stranger. It would certainly require a great deal of trust and what cop claimed that as a personality trait? 'If it's all the same to you I think I'll give it a swerve. Not sure I like the idea of someone poking about in my head while I'm away with the fairies.'

'Worried about what I'll find?' Sam smiled.

Coupland thought about the mental images he'd stored over the years. The dead and their loved ones waiting for justice. Shattered lives seeking a closure they'd never get. 'More worried about how you'd cope with it,' he said truthfully.

The therapist nodded, as though his response had been expected. 'I think, on balance, you may be suited to our cognitive behavioural therapist, Andy Robson. He moved to our practice six months ago, and has built up a good rapport with his patients. Shall I check his appointment list to see if he can fit you in?'

'Is he medium height with grey hair?' Coupland asked, touching his temples to indicate the grey strands on the man who'd approached him in the waiting room. 'Dresses like he's one of the country set?'

Freeman smiled fleetingly before nodding.

'He'll do fine,' Coupland said, thinking that if this Andy Robson thought him well enough to be here in a professional capacity he was halfway on the road to being signed off already.

'There's a cancellation for an appointment first thing, shall I pencil you in?'

'Pencil away,' Coupland said, rising from his seat. 'I'll be here.'

*

Lynn was in the living room, enjoying a rare moment of peace. Amy had gone round to a friend's, lugging Tonto and his changing bag with her. 'Think he's teething,' Lynn said, massaging her temples. 'You forget how much racket they make.'

'At least there's nothing wrong with his lungs,' Coupland said, perching on the arm of the sofa.

'There is that,' she smiled, tucking her feet under her and sipping at a herbal tea. 'So, how did it go?'

Coupland turned his mouth down at the edges, flattened his palm mid-air and moved it from side to side. 'What do you think of hypnotherapy? It's used during childbirth isn't it?'

Lynn pulled a face. 'Not by the time they get to us, it isn't. But I know some mums have used it with varying degrees of success.' Her tone implied she wasn't one hundred per cent behind what she was saying, piquing his interest.

'Does it make the pain go away?'

'Depends on your definition of pain and your normal tolerance level. I know it's possible to carry out surgery under hypnosis, but you really need to manage the patient's expectations. Instead of pain they may feel the sensation of tugging or pulling which may be equally distressing or confusing.'

Coupland nodded. 'Sounds familiar, victims' families think that seeking justice will take away their pain but often it's replaced by something just as unpleasant. Graphic images released during trial, secrets, last words. I can't help wonder sometimes whether ignorance is bliss.'

Lynn threw him a cynical look. 'Really? Said the man who can't stand being kept in the dark.'

Coupland laughed, though the sound came out strained. 'Sometimes I wonder what life would be like if I didn't know any of the stuff I know now. If I'd experienced different things, you know, growing up, at work even.'

Lynn folded her arms. 'Well, you'd be a lot more smiley for a start. One of those people that says hello to strangers. Pleasant, even, if push came to shove. But I don't think you'd ever have been carefree, Kevin. That's a step too far. I reckon our DNA is more powerful than you think.'

Coupland considered this. 'So, I'm not screwed up because my mam left my dad, but because she hooked up with him in the first place?'

Lynn's mouth turned down in the opposite of a smile but there was laughter in the look that she gave him. 'That's what I love about you, Sweet cheeks. That *Heads you win, Tails I lose* philosophy that you live your life by.'

'At least I excel at *something*,' he said, wondering how understanding his flaws better could make him a better cop. Sometimes the job required you to do unpalatable things. Yell. Threaten. Push. Drag. If a balloon head wouldn't move you ran straight through him. Maybe counselling would help him think more. Consider his actions in the cold light of day. The reper-bloody-cussions.

He heard a ping that signified incoming email. He pulled his phone from his pocket and tapped in his pin code, waited for his home screen to appear before selecting the email icon. He read Alex's message: 'Assuming you're still kicking your heels I've attached the clip I was talking about. Can you take a look at it and let me know what you see?'

He headed into the kitchen as he clicked onto the link she'd embedded into her message, waited while the file opened. It was the clip of the doctor she'd told him about.

The consultant anaesthetist captured on screen killing one of his patients. Coupland opened the patio door in the kitchen so he could have a smoke while watching. He lit his cigarette and took a long drag on it before hitting 'Play'. He studied the screen, saw the consultant placate his patient with all the charm of a parliamentary candidate at election time. A reassuring hand on the patient's arm, head tilted in concentration as he listened to the poor beggar speak. Next minute he's switching his oxygen tube as calmly as you like. It was as clear a case of 'caught red handed' as you could get in policing. He continued to watch until the clip ended, though he wasn't sure what else there was to 'see' as Alex had suggested. He watched the clip through again, focussing on the doctor as he went about his business. The consultant wore a calm, serious expression on his face. His eyes empty and distant, but then killers often looked that way.

Satisfied, Coupland closed the file and returned to his email account, hitting the reply button. 'The guy's guilty as charged,' he wrote, pressing send. They may never know the reason why Piers Bradley acted so out of character. The truth was they rarely had the resources to delve too much into the 'why' these days; it was enough to know the 'who' as long as there was evidence to back it up. In this case the reason was of little consequence when the consultant's hands can be seen switching lifesaving medical equipment for all the world to see.

'Anything important?' Lynn asked when he returned to the living room.

Coupland shook his head. 'For someone who spends his time dealing with people who do unexpected things maybe it's about time I did the same.'

Lynn narrowed her eyes.

'Don't look so worried, I was thinking we could go out for a bite to eat, that's all. Somewhere nice, I mean, and I promise not to moan about the price.'

'You've got yourself a deal,' Lynn laughed, getting to her feet.

CHAPTER THIRTEEN

Brookdale House Therapy Centre

Andy Robson was one of those people who immersed themselves so much in their work they'd lost all touch with reality, Coupland thought as his counsellor introduced himself. He wore a polo neck jumper over mustard coloured jeans, and ankle boots which Coupland struggled with on a man. The tweed jacket he'd worn during their previous encounter was draped over the back of his chair. Coupland had worn civvies this time: grey joggers Lynn hated, teamed with a zip-up fleece-lined hoody over a t-shirt.

A wall mounted clock opposite the window would mark their progress over the hour. The large hand was just moving away from twelve when Andy picked up his notebook and pen. 'So, how are we going to do this?' Coupland asked. 'I tell you my life story and you tell me where I've been going wrong?'

Andy cocked his head. 'Do you find yourself making snap judgements about most people?'

'Goes with the turf,' Coupland said. 'I have to make decisions about folk all the time. What are they hiding from me, and whether the lie they're concealing is relevant to my investigation.'

'Do you feel that most people lie to you?'

Coupland didn't need to think about the answer to *that*. 'Course they do... I don't mean the big stuff. I expect killers to lie. I'd be out of a job if they handed themselves in after doing the deed. Those are the lies I understand, based on fear of what they'd lose if the truth came to light. Then you get the other sort. The lies folk tell in an attempt to create better versions of themselves. The books they've claimed to read, the films they haven't seen but make out they have, nodding their heads as though they know what their boss or neighbour or new partner is going on about.'

'Does this matter to you?'

Coupland thought about this. 'It flags up a warning light, I suppose. Most of the time it doesn't come to anything but sometimes... sometimes it gets me wondering about what other aspect of their life they're trying to re-invent, and why.'

Andy had folded his arms across his chest, his right hand supporting his left arm as he stroked an impeccably smooth chin. 'My job is very different, Kevin. Within these four walls everything you say to me is safe. In here you can be yourself, warts and all. There are no agendas here. And for that reason my patients are painfully honest with me.'

'The idea of therapy scares the shit out of me.' Coupland widened his eyes. He wasn't sure where the hell *that* came from.

Andy looked pleased with this revelation. 'I can see we're making progress already.' His questioning technique wasn't that dissimilar to Coupland's. He didn't bang his fist on the top of the table or give Coupland the hard stare when he stalled but he did start off with easy questions like length of service, and how long he'd been married, answers that didn't require thought or filter. 'Kevin?'

Coupland realised Andy was waiting for an answer. He smiled apologetically, made a mental note to focus more.

'What was your father like?'

'Was? He's not dead.'

'Sorry.'

Coupland smiled at his apology. 'Not as sorry as I am.'

'No. I mean for not clarifying that earlier. That was remiss of me.'

'My job's all about asking the right questions, too,' Coupland sympathised. 'It can send you down a whole host of blind alleys if you get it wrong.' Like his own job he supposed, if Andy called it wrong the consequences could be dire. 'Anyway, he was a bastard… My dad, I mean,' Coupland added when Andy looked confused.

'Was he outgoing, introverted?'

'Does it matter?' Coupland thought about it. 'Quiet I suppose. Not shy as such. He didn't seek company though.' A bit like me, he thought with a shudder.

'Being on the outside makes you a good observer.'

'I can't say that I saw that in him,' Coupland replied, though in truth he'd had little opportunity to see his father beyond the role of oppressor. 'Hard as nails,' he found himself muttering. Something else that had been levelled at Coupland over the years.

Andy had a tendency to use long words and cross his legs whenever he asked a question, which Coupland found unsettling at first but half an hour in he'd started getting used to it. There were only ten minutes of their session to go when Coupland realised he hadn't stopped talking. The therapist had a way of nodding every time he paused for breath, as though encouraging him to say more. Coupland finally leaned back in his chair, wishing he'd chosen one of the comfier seats.

'So, when your mother left, your father withdrew his emotional investment in you, as a form of punishment perhaps?'

'I'd maybe have an opinion one way or another if I understood what you said.'

'Your father was hurting. Maybe his withdrawal from you was his way of dealing with his pain.'

'I wish he had withdrawn! Instead his contempt for me seemed to get worse.'

He told Andy about the beatings. The abuse his mother suffered before she left. Even so, he wasn't convinced about the value of sharing. If he wanted sympathy he had Lynn for that. Otherwise wasn't it raking over old coals?

Andy seemed to read his mind. 'You should never underestimate the potential effects our experiences have on the rest of our lives,' he summed up as the clock's large hand edged nearer to twelve once more. 'That pain can lay dormant for many years, then manifest without warning, triggered by something we didn't see coming.'

Coupland raised an eyebrow. 'So I gave Reedsy a pasting because my mam left us.'

'Who is Reedsy?'

Coupland shook his head. 'Doesn't matter.'

Andy consulted his diary. 'I can fit you in same time next week,' he said, already moving his pen to write Coupland's name into the relevant space.

'Tomorrow,' Coupland said. 'I can't go back to work until you sign me off.'

'You need a period of reflection between our sessions, Kevin. We can't hurry the process along.'

'My team is running with one man down. You don't

want folk thinking they can get away with murder, do you?'

Andy eyed him before flicking back several pages in his diary. 'I suppose I could fit you in last thing tomorrow,' he said, scribbling Coupland's name in and snapping the diary shut before Coupland came up with another objection.

*

Afternoon briefing, Incident Room, Salford Precinct Station
DCI Mallender looked on as a happier looking Krispy kicked off proceedings.

'The IT system's been up and running since late last night so I've been able to run background checks on the hotel staff, sir. Barring minor violations they're all clean. The guests interviewed by uniforms at the scene crosscheck with the names on the guest register. One guest who'd been in town for business had to leave early because his wife had gone into labour but I contacted him this morning.'

'And?'

'She's had a little girl, sir.'

Mallender stared at him. 'Had he seen our victim in or around the hotel on the day she was murdered?'

Krispy blushed. 'No, sir.'

Mallender spoke about his visit to Rose King's home to break the news. 'Her parents said they'd been waiting for this kind of call from the moment they learned she'd started turning tricks for a living. She'd got into debt a few years back, made a couple of wrong choices, owed an ex-partner money and couldn't see a way out. She'd only recently moved back home. The post mortem was carried out this morning. Rose suffered from inhibition of the vagus cranial nerve. Her hyoid bone was broken. The stocking had been pulled so tight around her neck that it had torn the skin and caused bleeding. Even with that force it would have taken her two to three minutes to die. Skin found beneath her fingernails matches the DNA taken from Asim Khan yesterday.'

Alex raised a hand, waited while Mallender nodded at her. 'The duty doc found more scratches on Khan's neck, the kind of defence wound a strangulation victim might make.'

'Any sign of intercourse?' asked DC Ashcroft.

'No.'

DCI Mallender's mouth turned down at the edges. 'Maybe he just wanted to talk, or look.' He regarded Ashcroft. 'How did he come across during your interview?'

Ashcroft leaned forward in his chair. 'He's sticking to his original story. That he was shattered when he returned from the conference. All he wanted was a drink and a lie down. He's adamant he didn't ask the doorman to send a girl up to his room, yet someone sent that text.'

'OK, so he's smart enough to use another phone,' said Mallender.

'A search of his hotel room, constituency office and home has failed to find any further device let alone the one correlating to the mobile used to ring the hotel's concierge.'

'Maybe he had the presence of mind to hide it somewhere else.'

'Like where?'

'I don't know, slip it into someone's bag in the lift, anything's possible.'

'It doesn't matter. Forensics came through and his prints are on the cash found in Rose's purse and on the stocking used to strangle her. There's no semen on the bed or around the room so we can rule out him being into erotic asphyxia.'

'Like being a common or garden strangler is so much better,' Alex muttered.

'He's nothing like you'd imagine,' Ashcroft added. 'He's like a rabbit in the headlights. I've seen him on TV being interviewed by that Peston fella. He always seemed a decent guy.'

'For a politician, you mean.'

'Yeah, obviously…'

Alex held up a photograph of Rose King's clothing: thigh high boots and a dress which left little to the imagination, a faux fur jacket which when worn would have barely covered her midriff. 'The sex trade in these kinds of establishments is all about anonymity. Who'd want to advertise what they were planning to get up to, especially in a five-star hotel during conference week with the press crawling round everywhere?'

'Someone who didn't give a toss?'

Ashcroft was already shaking his head. 'He doesn't come across that way. The hotel staff said he was down to earth and polite, he remembered details they'd mentioned in passing about their families and took the time to ask after them.'

'Maybe he was carrying out some sort of fantasy. You can request your favourite "type" from any of the escort agencies trading in Salford and they'll do their best to oblige, albeit with a low rent version unless you're able to pay top dollar. The agency texts the women with instructions on how to dress, how to do their hair…'

'Just another way of making them invisible,' observed Alex. 'So the punters don't see them as women. As wives, sisters, mothers, daughters. To some men they aren't even human.'

'But Asim wasn't one of them. He was respectful, considerate. He doesn't fit the demographic in any way,' persisted Ashcroft.

'Whether he does or he doesn't, we found a receipt for a cash withdrawal in his jacket pocket for £200 taken from a cash machine in Media City,' said Turnbull, who had been the crime scene manager.

Mallender clapped his hands together, satisfied. 'This gets better and better. Charge him. Just one thing, the super injunction he requested has been rejected. Seems several media organisations submitted an argument that the gagging order was unjustified and interfered with the principle of open justice.'

'What, since when do the press have principles?' Turnbull smirked.

'Principles or not it'll be all over the front pages tomorrow,' said Mallender. 'I've warned Superintendent Curtis that his presence may be required on the station steps again.'

Alex made a bee line for Ashcroft once the briefing was over. 'Mind if I sit in when you speak to Khan?'

Ashcroft shrugged as he took a final swig of his coffee. He pushed back his chair as he got to his feet. 'No time like the present,' he said, 'the desk sergeant's buzzed through to say his lawyer's in reception.'

*

Asim Khan was of Pakistani origin, slim built with dark hair turning grey at the temples. His salt and pepper trimmed beard was at odds with thick dark brows. His eyes pierced into Alex's as she entered the interview room. 'Am I being released?' he asked, turning his attention to Ashcroft when she didn't reply.

'Please Asim, leave the talking to me,' his lawyer said, resting his hand on his arm.

'I shouldn't have to watch what I'm saying, I am innocent!' Khan said, shaking off his lawyer's hand and spreading his arms wide. 'That poor woman, such a terrible, terrible thing! How did it happen?'

Ashcroft took the seat opposite Khan, Alex the one beside him. 'Wait while I put the tape on,' Ashcroft said, pressing a button on the digital recorder between them on the table. 'My name is Detective Constable Ashcroft, Mr Khan, I interviewed you yesterday. This is my colleague Detective Sergeant Moreton.'

He waited while Khan's lawyer spoke his name into the recorder.

'Rose King's post mortem was carried out this morning, and it confirms she was strangled between the hours of midnight and 2.00 a.m. the day before yesterday. Fibres on her clothing show she was murdered where she was found, in the bed of room 210 at the Lowry Hotel, which was booked in your name and occupied by you at the time. The forensic lab confirms that skin taken from underneath her fingernails matches the DNA sample you provided yesterday. For this reason, Asim Khan, it is my intention to return you to the custody sergeant who will read out the offence to you and take your fingerprints…'

'None of this makes sense!' Khan objected. 'I swear…'

'Stop talking,' instructed his lawyer, turning to address the detectives. 'I must have five minutes with my client.'

Ashcroft glanced at Alex, who nodded. 'Of course,' he said, switching off the digital recorder before getting to his feet.

*

DCI Mallender was tucking into a shop-bought sandwich and can of sparkling mineral water when Alex put her head round his door and knocked. 'Asim Khan's lawyer's considering a defence of diminished responsibility.'

Mallender's head shot up, meerkat-like. He put his sandwich down reluctantly and eyed Alex. 'So he's confessed then.'

'That's the thing. One minute he was outraged at the suggestion we'd consider him for murder, next minute he's all downcast and humble.'

'Let me guess, somewhere in that mix he was informed his skin was found under the victim's nails.'

Alex smiled. 'Pretty much, yes…'

'Sarge?'

Alex turned to find Ashcroft hurrying towards her in the corridor. 'Sorry for interrupting but thought you'd want to hear this.'

Alex glanced back at DCI Mallender and smiled apologetically. 'No rest for the wicked,' she said, pulling his door to. 'Where's the fire?' she said, facing Ashcroft, who was normally a cool cookie. She'd have said out of all the detectives in the murder squad he was unflappable, yet something was bothering him.

'Asim Khan's brother has rocked up to reception

demanding to see the person dealing with his brother's arrest. I went down to speak to him. He's obviously been in communication with Asim's lawyer as he knew he'd been charged and was hopping about like an Easter Bunny on a trampoline.'

'Go on.'

'He's not buying any of it.'

'What do you mean?'

'The whole fat cat MP and call girl stereotype he claims we've fallen for.'

'What we think of the man's politics is neither here nor there. His lifestyle choices say more about him than the party he represents.'

'That's his point though. He reckons we've all been too quick to jump to conclusions.'

Alex pulled a face. 'The evidence speaks for itself.'

'He reckons someone's trying to set Asim up.'

'By committing murder? That's a bit low even by politicians' standards.'

Ashcroft leaned in close, as though what he had to say was for her ears only. 'He's claiming there's no way in a million years his brother would hire a prostitute for the evening.'

'Oh, and why's that then?'

'Because he's gay.'

*

Irfan Khan was shorter than his brother and carried a few more pounds, but there was no mistaking the family resemblance, particularly the piercing eyes hooded with thick black brows. His hair was worn flatter, combed back, already starting to thin, unlike his bushy beard which he wore longer than his politician brother. He wore tan coloured moleskin trousers and wool jacket over a check shirt. Ashcroft had taken him to the cleanest interview room. The opaque window was bigger and let in more light, although it was still too high to see out of. A cherry scented air freshener made the room smell sickly sweet.

'Are you the one in charge?' Khan's brother demanded, rising from his seat.

Alex smiled and pulled out the chair opposite him, inviting him to sit down once more. 'I am one of the senior officers, yes,' she said, introducing herself while Ashcroft took the seat beside her. 'I appreciate you felt the need to come in, Mr Khan, however, I'm not entirely sure how I can help.'

'I know these are enlightened times, DS Moreton, but not for the Islamic faith. Homosexuality is considered a sin in our community and Asim would be shunned by his family and friends if he "came out". Given his position in society, there are many who would feel he has brought shame on the family and... well... I would fear for his life.'

'He's murdered a sex worker, Mr Khan; the shame will still be there.'

'You are not listening!' he snapped. 'There is no way he would seek female company for the evening, let alone pay for sex with an escort.'

'He changed his plea to guilty an hour ago, why would he do that?'

'Don't you see? He'd rather be thought of as a murderer than a gay man! He had no choice!' Irfan took several breaths which seemed to calm him. 'I know my brother was gay from an early age. I never saw it as odd, just him. But we knew even then that it had to be kept a secret. He was terrified of being forced into an arranged marriage and for that reason kept his lifestyle hidden from view. He's had partners over the years, decent men who wouldn't dream of selling their story to a tabloid. If you want evidence of his sexuality I can give you their names, as long as you ensure discretion.'

Alex glanced at Ashcroft before getting to her feet. 'DC Ashcroft will take the names and contact details of Mr Khan's previous partners and we will follow up this line of enquiry.'

'Is that it?' Irfan demanded.

Alex studied him. 'The victim had Asim's skin under her fingernails. Whether he invited her into his room or not, the fact remains he killed her.'

'Keep it low key for the moment,' she said to Ashcroft before leaving the interview room, meaning make sure the press don't get wind of it. They'd have a field day hunting down Khan's ex-lovers before the police got a chance to, asking them for statements on the basis they'd publish something anyway. They'd have to move fast. It was close to clocking off time but the team would work on until the names supplied by Irfan Khan had been contacted and verified. Though even if they established Khan's sexuality she couldn't see how it would alter the outcome of the investigation. He was guilty of Rose King's murder, end of. She returned to the CID room wondering if there'd been a full moon lately, whether that might explain why people in this city were acting so odd. Her thoughts turned to Coupland and what he would say if she said as much to him. She smiled to herself as she moved to the window and looked out at the ink-black sky. Who was she trying to kid? She knew perfectly well what that lump of a man would say. He'd turn his world-weary gaze on her and tell her to *get a bloody grip*.

CHAPTER FOURTEEN

Brookdale House Therapy Centre

Andy Robson's previous session must have ended early as he was already in the reception area when Coupland arrived. 'Can I make you a coffee?' he asked, holding up a mug as he headed into a door behind reception.

Coupland nodded, giving a thumbs up when Andy asked if he took milk, shaking his head when he asked about sugar. He'd forgotten to bring his sweeteners with him but he'd prefer to go without.

'Go on through,' Andy urged. 'I'll be with you in a minute.'

Coupland took the opportunity of being in the therapist's consulting room unchaperoned by flicking open his diary and scanning down the names to see if there was anyone he recognised. Curse of the job. Andy's iPhone lay beside it; Coupland looked back through the open door along the expanse of the reception area to check no one could see before pressing the 'Home' button. Several notification banners displayed themselves on screen. An Amazon delivery was due at Andy's home that afternoon. A reminder for an appointment with his dental hygienist for the following day. A local news bulletin featuring the headline: 'Sex Fling MP kills Call Girl in Top Hotel' had been saved as a bookmark on his news feed. Coupland heard footsteps heading towards the room and stepped in front of the phone, turning to thank Andy as he handed over his drink. If the doctor was surprised at Coupland's pleasant disposition he didn't show it, though he did suggest that Coupland took a seat so their session could begin. A quick glance at the screen showed that it had returned to its former dormant state, so he did as Andy asked.

'I found yesterday's session very interesting,' the therapist smiled, crossing his legs as he settled into what Coupland now recognised as his 'listening' mode.

Coupland shot him a disbelieving look. 'You need to get out more, then,' he said. 'Or be more choosy about the clients you take on.'

Andy tilted his head. 'Don't put yourself down. You've overcome a brutal childhood yet forged a successful career for yourself.'

'I wouldn't quite put it like that...' Coupland muttered.

'And a happy family life,' Andy added.

Coupland found himself flinching, the way he always did when his family and happiness were uttered in the same breath, as though the Fates were waiting for him to get ahead of himself. Didn't pride come before a fall? 'It's not all been plain sailing,' he said, thinking of the fear they lived under of Lynn's remission ending, of Tonto turning out like his father.

'Even so. You're what I would call a high functioning individual. You've refused to let your experiences drag you down. From what you've shared with me, I would say your coping mechanism has been to compartmentalise your problems.'

Coupland shot him a look. 'Is there any other way?'

Andy nodded his approval. 'Compartmentalising is a

cognitive response. Something you train yourself to do. It's helped you get on with your life up to a point.'

Reedsy, Coupland thought. I'd been a functioning train wreck until I lamped that toerag.

'You talked a lot about your father yesterday. Would you say he was good at his job?'

'A good cop you mean?' Coupland thought about this. 'Till he started drinking. He was addled half the time after that. No use to man nor beast.'

'So, you feel you've done better than him.'

Coupland's mouth turned down at the edges. It wasn't something he'd thought about much, let alone articulated. 'I suppose so,' he said eventually. His father had never achieved the rank of sergeant; something that Coupland knew grated on him.

'It matters to you that you are a better person than he is, I can see that. Is that why it's important to be a good cop too?'

'Never thought about it.'

Andy settled back in his chair. 'I think I might like to have been a detective if I hadn't got into counselling.'

Coupland wished he's had a pound for every time someone told him they would love to do his job. 'There's a lot less to it than you'd imagine,' he said, thinking of the many ways that his hands were tied these days, what with red tape, data protection, and the right to remain bloody silent.

Andy nodded. 'I know, but it must be the ultimate cerebral challenge to second guess what a criminal is going to do next.'

Coupland huffed out a sigh. 'That's the thin end of the wedge. Before that comes hours and hours of interviewing people, asking the same questions over and over until someone slips up. It's hardly rocket science.'

Andy looked disappointed. 'Working out your suspect's motive must make the job easier?'

Coupland laughed. 'You've been watching way too many crime dramas. Evidence, means and opportunity are all we need to prove someone has committed a crime.' Television viewers, like most members of the public, liked their perpetrators to have a motive as it helped them make sense of acts so far removed from their own world that they couldn't comprehend them. But the law didn't require it.

'Anyway, shouldn't we be doing breathing exercises or does discussing the finer points of policing count towards you signing me off?'

'There's a method to my madness, if you'll excuse the pun, Kevin. If a patient finds it hard to open up I often get them to talk about something in their comfort zone. It helps them relax, be more receptive to my suggestions. It makes my job so much easier too.'

Coupland nodded. 'I do much the same thing with suspects. I let them prattle on as though I give a toss about their job or their kid's school or the meeting they have to get to, and all the while I'm studying their "tells", the way they avoid eye contact when they're lying through their teeth, how they cover their mouth with their hands when they're trying to hold something back. There's more to it than that, of course,' Coupland added. 'But then I wouldn't be able to get a measure of you if I revealed all my secrets.'

Andy's laugh was nervous. 'I'm happy with the progress you're making. In my opinion you're an asset to the Force, Kevin. The sooner we get you reinstated the better,' he said, making sure he met and held Coupland's gaze as he said it.

*

DCI Mallender's Office, Salford Precinct Station
DCI Mallender was reading through the CPS case file DCs Turnbull and Robinson had prepared in relation to Sean Bell's hit and run slaying of James McMahon. He hadn't anticipated so many spelling mistakes, and was about to send the whole file back with a reminder he was the SIO, not a bloody proof reader, when his mobile phone rang providing a temporary reprieve. 'Gibson' flashed up on the screen.

'You wanted me to find out who had Austin Smith wiped out and I did. You sure you want to know?' his father asked, getting straight to the point.

'That's the business I'm in, if you hadn't noticed.'

A pause. *'He was murdered on someone called Midas's say so.'*

'He's the head of the trafficking gang Austin Smith worked for.'

'Seems the paedophile network he supplied with migrant kids was getting nervous. This Reedsy fella used to deliver the poor mites right to their door, like the human equivalent of Deliveroo. He knew the faces of all the main players, if not their names, and he certainly knew where they liked to hang out.'

'So, he was a liability then.'

'Got it in one. Midas was told to take him out of the picture and he did.'

Mallender considered this. 'Isn't he worried the same thing will happen to him? Surely he's just as dangerous to this network?'

Gibson spat out a laugh. *'Nah, you're forgetting how it works, son. Men like Midas use lackeys like Reedsy to do their bidding. Not just because they don't want to dirty their hands but as a form of insurance. By getting Reedsy to do all the meet and greets, and fetching and carrying, he removed himself from the firing line should there ever be a question of whistleblowing.'*

What he said made sense, if you were a gangster and lived by their code of ethics. It was a world GMP had learned to navigate, albeit two steps behind the biggest contenders.

'Look, I appreciate this, thanks.'

A pause. 'Remember, these are dangerous men, Stuart. They make Kieran Tunney look like a girl guide leader. Tread carefully.'

'This paedophile network. Did your contact mention any names?'

The sound of air being sucked through teeth. *'What? Names I decided not to pass on to you? Give me some credit.'*

Another pause. Mallender pictured him puffing on his cigar as he gathered his thoughts. A word in the right ear, or a word in the wrong ear for that matter, could glean more information than a formal investigation but you had to trust your sources. *'Look, I heard about a fella once. We're talking a good few years back now. Built like a wrestler but had a remarkable memory. He was renowned for it. Never committed anything to paper. He was called the Dutchman because he'd spent six years in a Dutch jail. Taught himself the language for something to do. The Assets Recovery Agency took £3m off him under the Proceeds of Crime Act, and everyone knows they can't find their arsehole with two hands and a mirror, so you can imagine how lucrative his line of business can be. Back in the day rumour had it he answered the door holding an axe, now he stays in the*

159

finest hotels, rubbing shoulders with the cream of society.'

'You think he's the Mr Fixit for the paedophile ring?'

'Seems I'm not the only one.'

'What do you mean?'

'You lot have had him under surveillance for the last six months.'

*

A startled Superintendent Curtis glared at the interloper who'd entered his office without knocking. 'It's you, DCI Mallender,' he huffed out, rising from his seat. He had his dress uniform on. Drinks and canapes and an afternoon pressing flesh beckoned. 'Is there a reason for this intrusion? I'm expected at the town hall for a reception.'

The detective pal Coupland had contacted either wasn't high enough up the totem pole to know what had been going on or he was playing the long game and wanted a much bigger catch regardless of the casualties. Either way, GMP had been taping The Dutchman's calls and somewhere in the telecoms transcriptions would be his order that Reedsy be terminated.

Handling the Super was difficult at the best of times but Mallender knew all the tricks. What the higher ups wanted was to be absolved of blame. To have someone they could point to if things went belly up.

'I've no time for explanations, sir,' Mallender began, giving Curtis the opportunity to claim later on that he was acting in good faith. 'But I need you to make an urgent call to your equal number at Nexus House. The Mayor'll have to wait.'

*

Coupland was making his way back to his car when his

phone rang. When DCI Mallender's name flashed up on the screen he hit the 'reply' button, positioning the phone into the crook of his neck while he lit a cigarette.

'I have some information for you,' Mallender said, before repeating what his father had told him.

CHAPTER FIFTEEN

HMP Manchester

Kieran Tunney's grin was as wide as that comedian with all the teeth, as he took his seat at the table they'd been allocated. 'Well, well, well, Mr Coupland, nice of you to drop by. It gave me a fuzzy feeling inside when I was told you wanted to see me.'

'I don't see why you're so surprised, Kieran. You offer to wipe Reedsy off the face of the earth for me and Lo and Behold, not only has Jesus ended up with a new sunbeam but I had to hand in my warrant card.'

'I'm guessing you've got it back again.'

'It doesn't quite work like that. I'm about to be reinstated, though I'm tarnished goods now.'

Tunney pulled a sympathetic face. 'I know how that feels.'

Coupland waved his platitudes away. 'That's as a result of the choices you made, Kieran, and the choices you keep on making. That's not how it is for me.'

'So why are you here?'

'You owe me.'

'I offered to pay you back.'

'And I said no. At the time. In the manner you were suggesting. But now I've thought of a way you can wipe your debt clean.'

Tunney settled back in his seat, intrigued. 'Fire away,' he said, making a grand sweeping gesture with his right hand.

'I know who ordered Reedsy's murder. But I want you to join the dots up for me. I want to know who actually did the deed.'

Tunney folded hefty arms across his chest. 'You're having a laugh, aren't you, Mr Coupland? Rule number one: Never grass. It's the law of the jungle.'

Only one of them, Coupland found himself thinking. He pulled on a smile. 'I thought you'd say that.'

'So why did you ask?'

'Because I wanted to see if I could call it right, and I did.'

'So?'

'Like I said. I've come into some information. It's Kosher, not tittle tattle, and I think it may sway your decision.'

'I doubt it, Mr Coupland. Didn't you see the news headlines the other week? "Salford: the city with no witnesses." Apparently getting the public to help you lot is like getting blood out of a stone.'

'It all depends on the context though, Kieran,' Coupland said carefully, 'and I know, above all else, you're a man of honour.'

A smile passed over the gangster's lips.

'Your word is your bond.'

Tunney tipped his head forward magnanimously. 'Can't disagree with that.'

'Have you heard of a fella by the name of The Dutchman?'

Tunney's smile slipped. 'I'm acquainted with the name, yes.'

'Have you ever done business with him?'

'No...' A pause. 'He works with bigger fish than me. Sharks, even, and you know what they say about sharks. It's not the one you see that you need to worry about...'

'...It's the one you can't see,' Coupland finished for him.

'If the truth be told I've heard things about him that are unsavoury... I can't say I share his values.'

Coupland nodded, satisfied. 'If I told you he's instrumental in providing a high-level paedophile network with child migrants, how would that make you feel?'

'It would make my skin crawl, Mr Coupland. Men like that... there aren't words for them, truly.'

'The Dutchman ordered Reedsy's hit because members of his network were worried he would be able to identify them, should a deal be done with the police at some point down the line. The person who killed Reedsy was paid with trafficking money, Kieran, will likely already have been promised he'll step into his shoes on his release. Think about it. Another monster ferrying children around the city to be fucked by so called pillars of society.'

'Enough, Mr Coupland!' Tunney growled, holding up his hand. He looked as though he was going to be sick. 'You don't need to say any more. I'll do it. I'll find the name of Reedsy's killer. Can I ask, though, what will you do with the information?'

Coupland nodded, as though he's been expecting this too. 'There'll be a trial,' he said. 'He'll probably get his sentence extended. But I reckon he'll be useful in helping those way above my pay grade to actually pin something on this Dutchman that'll make him talk and lead them to these sick bastards.' Coupland laughed, but the sound caught in his throat. 'Maybe I'm being naïve and the world doesn't work like that anymore. Maybe some folk really are above the law.'

Tunney nodded. 'I would imagine naivety is a prerequisite to do your job, Mr Coupland, otherwise you'd never get out of bed in the morning.'

Something occurred to Coupland. He stared Tunney in the eye. 'If you do this thing for me, it doesn't make us friends.'

The gangster's nod was slow. 'It makes us even, Mr Coupland. And that will do for now, don't you think?'

*

Brookdale House Therapy Centre
Coupland was distracted during his session with Andy. He answered his questions with little resistance, made no caustic comments when he referred to his childhood, and kept his sarcasm in check when he spoke about the division's top brass.

'We seem to be making real progress today,' the therapist said as he made notes in Coupland's patient file. Coupland merely nodded. 'Thanks for your time,' he said at the end of the session. If Andy had asked him at that point if he remembered what they'd talked about, or anything that had been covered during the previous hour, he'd have been unable to answer. His mind was working overtime. Churning through his conversation with Kieran Tunney the day before. A cold-blooded gangster guilty of murder and intimidation. He wondered what form his help would take. Tunney had claimed once that he and Coupland had much in common:

That crime paid both their wages.

That they put family first.

That respect *mattered*.

Coupland had refused to accept there were any commonalities between him and the hardened crime boss. Each time Tunney suggested they were cut from the same cloth he'd sneered. But now, there was no denying it, on this one thing Coupland was certain they absolutely agreed. Scumbags who moved children from one continent to another to be fucked by 'respectable' men were the scourge of the earth. And if he had to join forces with a gangster, albeit temporarily, to bring a lynchpin to justice?

Bring it on.

He was reversing into the roadside space outside his home when a news bulletin came on the radio:

"Police and specialist prison officers have been called in to deal with a riot that has broken out at HMP Manchester."

Coupland slammed his foot down hard on the brake to stop him from going into the stationary car behind him. 'Well, well, well,' he muttered, turning up the dial on the volume button.

"Mobile phone and drone footage is emerging showing inmates knocking through weak cell walls and rioting inside the Category A prison. Prisoners can be seen dancing and running around the walkways, with some holding batons. It is alleged that a prisoner is being held hostage, but that has been denied by the governor, Sarita Anand, who claims that order is already being restored to the prison, which became notorious after rioting broke out in 1990, injuring hundreds and leaving two dead.

"A spokeswoman for the Prison Service said inmates in the affected wing will be transferred to other jails."

'Once you've bloody caught them,' said Coupland.

"The spokeswoman added a 'full assessment' would be carried out and those involved would face prison adjudication hearings as well as an investigation by the police."

Tunney didn't do anything by half measures, he'd give him that, Coupland conceded. Sometimes a sledgehammer *was* needed to crack a nut.

CHAPTER SIXTEEN

The call, when it came, was first thing. With no reason to get up at the crack of dawn each morning Coupland had allowed himself to sleep in, sometimes staying in his pit long after Lynn left to start her shift, enjoying her grumbling at the sound of the alarm. He must have slept on after she'd gone out this morning as he woke with a start, his hand scrabbling for his phone but missing and sending it to the floor instead.

'Shit,' he barked, reaching for it and stabbing the reply button.

'*I didn't wake you Mr Coupland, I hope?*' asked a familiar voice.

'Been up ages,' Coupland answered, unsure why he felt the need to lie.

'*You've been listening to the news, I imagine?*'

'Enough to know someone in the big house has been pulling an all-nighter, Kieran. Surprised the neighbours don't complain.' He could picture the smile forming on the other end of the line.

'*You'll be pleased to hear order has been resumed. The screws have got us on lockdown…*'

'And yet you still managed to call…'

'*I believe in treating people fair, Mr Coupland. There's a couple of screws in here know I'm not a bad guy. Will look the other way every now and again as long as I'm not taking liberties.*'

'And the riot, Kieran, what was that about?'

A chuckle, long and low. *'Merely a distraction. How else was I going to get to Midas other than via the roof? We're in different wings, after all. While a couple of old lags waved bed sheets in the air, I was having a full and frank discussion with our local human trafficker.'*

'The news report mentioned a hostage situation.'

'Most people are amenable when they're hanging from a window, you should try it.'

Coupland blew out a sigh. 'That's how I ended up in this mess in the first place. I'll give it a swerve if it's all the same to you. So, have you got a name for me?'

'Oh, I've got a name for you alright, and the location of the weapon he used if you're sharp, no pun intended. Due to the damage caused to the wing he's in, the fella you're after has been moved to another prison while the place is cleaned up, but if you move quick enough you'll find the blade he used to kill Reedsy is still under his mattress. You got a pen and paper handy? I'll need to spell it out for you, he's Turkish.'

'Try me.' Coupland listened to the name he gave him, consigning it to memory.

'By the way, it was his brother who made the anonymous call pointing the finger at you. No ulterior motive, just brotherly love. Isn't that sweet?'

'The cockles of my heart are roasting,' Coupland replied. Not far from the truth given his career was toast. And all thanks to someone he'd never even met.

'We quits now, Mr Coupland?'

'We're quits,' Coupland replied, listening to the dialling tone as Tunney ended the call. He swung his legs over the edge of his bed, swaying as a tide of dizziness swept over him. The surge in adrenaline had made his blood sugar dip. A coffee and a cigarette would restore it but first he needed to make two calls. The first was to DCI Mallender, to give him the Turk's name and get him to send a team to the prison to retrieve the weapon that killed Reedsy and collect DNA samples from the killer's room.

The second call was to Andy Robson, demanding an urgent appointment. Once Reedsy's killer was arrested and charged, Coupland had every intention of reporting for duty. And if he needed a bumper session with his therapist to get a certificate that said he was fit for purpose, then one way or another he'd fucking get one.

*

DCI Mallender's Office, Salford Precinct Station
When the call came through from the governor at HMP Manchester that a search of Yusuf Kanak's cell had uncovered the weapon used to kill Austin Smith, DCI Mallender was inundated with detectives offering to collect it. The fact that many were due to clock off shift didn't matter, nor the fact that each of them already had more work than they could handle. Coupland would do the same if one of them was in jeopardy, and everyone knew that. He settled on DCs Turnbull and Robinson, if for no other reason than it meant whilst they carried out this task they couldn't make any more of a pig's ear out of Sean Bell's CPS file.

He'd just finished reading the case file DC Ashcroft had prepared against arsonist Liam Roberts; it was meticulous, ready to submit to the CPS without any alteration. Mallender rewarded him for this by passing Sean Bell's file onto him, which to his credit he took without complaint.

An hour later Turnbull and Robinson appeared in the doorway of Mallender's office with a photograph of the 'shank' used to kill Austin Smith. A small wooden block with a razor blade embedded into it had been stowed beneath Yusuf's mattress. Dried blood could be seen embedded in the wooden ridges and around the blade. 'CSIs have swabbed it for fingerprints and will cross check flakes of blood taken from it with Reedsy's blood sample collected during his post mortem. The weapon's been handed into the evidence management unit and right this minute an angry Turk is stomping round his custody cell demanding his prayer mat.'

'Get it for him,' said Mallender. 'He's going to need it. Pick his brother up as well, if we can't get him for perverting the course of justice we can at least let him know he's on our radar.'

Both detectives nodded. 'Does this mean the Sarge can come back to work?' asked Robinson.

'It means we can start on the paperwork that will allow that to happen. Dot the 'I's and cross the 'T's so that the CPS, HR, The Super and Uncle Tom Cobley for all I care are happy that everything is watertight.'

For that reason, Mallender thought as he looked at his watch, deciding a couple more hours before he clocked off would be needed, there was only so far he could abuse DC Ashcroft's goodwill. He'd do the sodding paperwork himself.

CHAPTER SEVENTEEN

Coupland entered the CID room to a round of applause. It was one week since Yusuf Kanak had been charged with the murder of Austin Smith and three days since Coupland had completed his final session with Andy Robson. He hadn't wanted a fuss, all he really wanted was to forget about the last two weeks and get on with his job. Despite this, Turnbull, Robinson, Ashcroft and Krispy formed a Guard of Honour as he made his way to his desk.

'Steady on, folks,' he groaned. 'I've been allowed back in the building, not awarded the gallantry medal. Let's show a little perspective.'

'Great to have you back Sarge,' Krispy called out.

'No offence, like,' he said quickly when he saw a frown flit across Alex's face.

'None taken,' she replied as she rose from her desk to punch Coupland on the arm. The paperwork on his desk had been replaced with two scented candles and a bottle of lavender massage oil. A spikey stress ball still in its box took pride of place in the centre. Coupland shook his head as he sat down. 'Honestly folks, you shouldn't have. Really,' he said, taking the ball from its packaging and holding it over his head as though about to lob it at someone.

'Can I make you a cuppa, Sarge? Chamomile tea, Fennel and ginger?' Krispy asked, heading towards the kettle.

'Everyone's a wise guy, eh?' Coupland answered, shaking his head. 'I'll have my usual with something sweet and sticky to go with it.' he said, eyeing the box of creamy doughnuts on Krispy's desk.

'We didn't want the occasion to go unmarked,' Alex told him. 'So you get first dibs.'

'Now you're talking,' Coupland acknowledged, prodding several with his index finger before taking his pick.

'Bloody lucky that riot started,' Turnbull observed, making and holding eye contact with Coupland. 'Otherwise those prison officers might never have found the weapon used to kill Reedsy. Talk about a stroke of luck.'

Coupland raised a brow. 'You've been at the Omega 3 supplements again, haven't you Turnbull? Some days there's just no stopping you.' He saw no point in discussing the understanding he'd come to with Tunney. Few would make sense of it. He wasn't sure he would if it were someone else in his shoes.

'Kevin, a quick word before you get carried away. A couple of formalities we need to run through.' DCI Mallender stood in the corridor as if to stress Coupland's presence was needed immediately.

Coupland nodded, licking chocolate icing from his finger and thumb as he got to his feet. He followed Mallender along the corridor into his office, taking the seat in front of his desk while the DCI shut his office door behind them.

'I take it one of the formalities is the Super coming downstairs to personally hand my warrant card back.'

Mallender's smile was good natured as he slid the top drawer of his desk open and pulled out the very same thing. 'The Super's otherwise engaged,' he said, handing it over. 'But he asked me to pass on his relief at your reinstatement.'

'I bet he did,' Coupland muttered, placing his ID back in his lanyard before lifting it over his head.

'You've no idea of the trees that have been shaken to get you the names you needed,' Mallender said, fixing him with a stare.

'Oh, I think I have,' Coupland replied, staring back. 'But you didn't need to muddy your shoes, and I appreciate that.'

'It was the Super who nailed it though. Spoke to his equal number at Nexus House to requisition the telephone transcript that had the Dutchman on record ordering Midas to kill Reedsy.'

Coupland's eyes widened. 'Why would the Super bother, though? I mean, it's me we're talking about. I've been a thorn in his side since he came here and caught me using his parking space. It didn't seem to matter that it was only the once, he'd marked my card good and proper.'

Mallender snorted. 'I wouldn't get too carried away. It was less about you and more about vanity. I knew he wouldn't stand for someone in his peer group deciding what information they would share or choose to keep shtum about. Knowledge is power, and it didn't hurt that he'd played golf with the Deputy Chief Constable the previous week.'

'The sacrifices he makes for this station knows no bounds.'

'You might want to cut him a little slack when

your paths next cross, Kevin, just so he doesn't regret intervening on your behalf any sooner than he has to.'

Coupland leaned back in his chair and pondered this. He tried to remember what Andy Robson's closing words had been at the end of his last session. Something about being less confrontational; already the therapist's words of wisdom were starting to blur into one another. He glanced up to see Mallender pushing what looked like a questionnaire towards him.

'HR need you to complete this form and send it back to them.'

Coupland read the heading on the front page: '*Returning to work after a suspension.*' 'Who thinks these bloody things up?' he asked. 'I mean, someone gets paid good money for this.'

'And you're getting paid to fill it in when I'd rather you spent the time getting up to speed on the cases that have come in during your absence, but we don't always get what we want.'

'I suppose I could write that I'm full of remorse, and that I fully intend to use the strategies the doc gave me.' Coupland offered in an attempt to make amends. 'You know, whenever I feel tempted to go off on one.'

Mallender nodded. 'That should do the trick.'

Something else had been niggling away at Coupland, he reckoned now was as good a time as any to ask the question. 'What's going to happen to the Turk's brother?'

'I spoke to DI Sharpe this morning. No charges are going to be brought against Salim Kanak for making the malicious call. Nexus House are confident that he's already engaging with the trafficking gangs they've been trailing and are readying themselves to swoop. With any luck he'll be swept up in their net.'

Coupland got to his feet and turned to leave; shoving the form he'd been given into his jacket pocket causing Mallender to frown.

'Make sure you add that you've had time to reflect and that if the same circumstances arose you would do things differently,' he called out as Coupland opened the door.

Coupland looked up at the ceiling. The DCI had better not hold his breath while he waited, although he knew better than voicing *that* thought out loud.

*

Alex was subdued when Coupland returned to the CID room. She was matter of fact when she brought him up to speed on the cases that had come in during his absence, taking little credit for the careful handling of Asim Khan, which could have turned awkward in a number of ways. 'His brother's convinced he's been set up though,' she said, handing him the case file with a shrug.

'I'd be more interested in what Khan's lawyer thinks,' said Coupland.

'Khan has instructed him to plead guilty though he's considering going for diminished responsibility.'

Coupland shrugged his shoulders. 'Either way it's a result. So what's bugging you?'

'Nothing.'

'You might want to tell your face that.'

'It's just that…'

'Go on,'

'It's been a juggling act while you've been away. I don't think anyone with kids has put them to bed these past two weeks, let alone said more than a passing hello to their partner.' She caught the look that flitted across his face and pulled a wry smile. 'Ignore me, I'm just knackered, I know it's hardly been a walk in the park for you either.'

'Well I'm back now and if it's any consolation I can see the work that's been put in, though I'm not quite sure why so many desks are overflowing with paperwork, I thought we'd gone paperless.'

Alex told him about the computer network malfunction and the inability to conduct data searches on suspects across the division let alone with other forces.

'You couldn't make it up,' Coupland said after uttering several expletives.

Alex's nod was impatient. 'Never mind that, now you're back you can take your share of the paper mountain, doesn't look as overwhelming when the piles are divided up.'

Coupland took the papers she gave him and carried them over to his desk. He thanked Krispy for the mug of coffee he'd left on it, relieved the threat of herbal tea had been nothing more than that. The coffee was lukewarm so he gulped it down and, when the caffeine hit its mark, he arranged his work into some semblance of order. He tried logging onto the computer system but the error message that flashed across the screen confirmed that the network, for want of a better technical word, was kaput.

He rolled up his sleeves before disappearing into the corridor only to return five minutes later dragging an out-of-commission whiteboard from the basement. 'There's plenty more where these came from,' he said, eyeballing several DCs as he made his way towards Krispy's desk.

'Do you mind sharing what you're doing with the rest of us?' Alex asked, as several detectives followed him out of the room returning with more whiteboards until the office began to resemble a training centre.

'If the database is as temperamental as you've told me then we need to duplicate the information we enter into it until we are sure it can be retrieved reliably. I don't want the team responding to calls only to find half an hour later we've no record of where they've been sent.'

Alex looked crestfallen. 'I should have thought of that.'

'Why would you when you're caught in the middle of it all? It's easy when you're not wrapped up in a case to be objective, let's hope I'm being unnecessarily pessimistic.'

'Pessimistic, you?' she laughed.

'Better safe than sorry,' Turnbull cut in, dragging a whiteboard behind him.

Alex moved closer to Coupland and kept her voice down. 'Spoken by a guy who makes Eeyore look like he's on uppers,' she muttered.

Coupland pulled a chair across to Krispy's desk and asked him to try logging in. When the system granted access he trawled through data that had been entered over the previous two weeks, photographing each screen with his mobile before printing out the images and blu-tacking them to the whiteboards which he'd lined in a row along the back of the room.

'I think we're in breach of just about every data protection regulation there is, Sarge,' Krispy said, careful that the other DCs milling around the room couldn't hear.

'Would you rather respond to a domestic clueless that a colleague had been threatened at the property the night before, or turn up with the appropriate back up?'

'I'd want my backside covered,' Krispy said, jutting

his lower jaw forward as he interrogated the data with a renewed sense of vigour.

Coupland watched with satisfaction as Robinson handed round a box of highlighter pens taken from the stationery cupboard and the detectives set to work highlighting key names and locations flagged up by the computer, cross referencing them to investigations currently underway. 'I want to know where these fuckwits come from who oversee these projects,' he griped, 'signing off new systems when they're not fit for purpose. A recruitment job lot if you ask me, all on a mass exodus after buggering up the NHS...'

Something caught his attention. One of the whiteboards was out of line from the others; it wobbled when he touched it. He looked around for something to wedge underneath it, remembering the HR form he'd stuffed inside his pocket during his meeting with Mallender. He pulled it out, folding it over several times before shoving it under the wonky leg. He stood back, regarding the finished result with something close to pride. 'You're in charge of keeping these boards up to date, Krispy. Every action and outcome logged. You enter it onto IPOS then you write it on here.'

'What if I run out of space, Sarge?'

'Use the bloody walls if you have to. This place could do with redecorating anyway. We run this dual system until those earning the big bucks tell us that lump of metal is operational.'

*

Alex tapped three times on DCI Mallender's partly open door before entering. He'd been reading the contents of a file on his desk, his eyes registering relief at the interruption.

'Now Kevin's back we can take Batman and Robin off admin duties permanently,' he told her. 'The report they prepared for the CPS looked like it'd been typed up by hyperactive three-year-olds. Have they never heard of the space bar?'

Alex smiled in agreement. 'Leave it with me, boss. I'll take it back and re-do it but I'll show them what I've done so they know how it's supposed to look next time around.'

'No need. I gave the file to Ashcroft, and I must say he turned it round in record time, good standard too.'

'Oh really?' Alex tried not to look too put out. 'Actually sir, I wanted to talk to you about Kevin's return…'

'Oh yes?' Mallender pushed himself out of his seat and stretched his spine before moving round to where she stood. He perched a buttock on the top of his desk. 'I thought you might,' he said, eyeing her. 'Starting to feel surplus to requirements now that he's back?'

Alex's cheeks flooded with colour. 'No, it isn't that. Christ knows there's precious little enough time to get on with the regular job as it is, and I'm genuinely relieved that he's been reinstated.'

'But…'

'But… I'd be lying if there wasn't a twinge of something at the thought of handing the reins back.'

'I understand. I've been thinking along those lines myself. You've stepped into Kevin's shoes every time with ease and I wouldn't want you to think your efforts weren't going unrecognised. We can give you more cases to lead on from within the CID team but I feel it's time you consider working towards the inspectors' exams.'

It took all of her effort to keep her face looking nonchalant.

'There's a new course on Leadership that HR have circulated, I think you should take a look.'

Alex felt horrified and elated in equal measure.

'We'd base your assessments on your current workload so it's not as if you'd be taking on extra cases.'

'I should hope not, sir, there's a whole new level of crazy going on at the moment.'

'Is that a yes, then? Courses like this get snapped up quickly.'

Alex didn't need to think about it. Carl was virtually looking after the boys full time, and there was no doubt the extra money her promotion brought would come in handy. 'Count me in,' she replied, waiting until she was back in the corridor before punching the air.

*

'Glad to see something's put a smile on your face,' Coupland observed when Alex returned to her desk.

'I'll tell you why later,' she said, imitating a zip fastening in front of her mouth to indicate it was for his ears only. She regarded Coupland's handiwork with the whiteboards. 'How come you've put Piers Bradley's details up there when the case has been put to bed?'

'Same reason everything else is going on. If you can't be certain information relating to it can be retrieved when you want it we need to safeguard it – the coroner hasn't recorded a verdict on his death yet, they could still ask you to check something.'

Alex pulled a cynical face. 'Not like you to be so diligent.'

Coupland looked put out. 'It's how I always used to work before the tech guys came along and made everything so damn complicated. Remember I'm from the pen and paper generation. Cross checking files meant reading through your body weight in barely legible post-it notes, but it worked.'

'You're loving this, aren't you?' she smiled.

'What? Showing top brass that shiny isn't always better? That maybe there's still a place for hairy arsed cavemen like me?' He grinned. 'Course I am.'

She moved over to his desk and lowered her voice. 'The boss is putting me on a leadership course, reckons I should start working towards the inspectors' exams.'

'No surprise there,' said Coupland. 'Always said you were destined for great things.'

'It won't be a problem, will it?' She sounded anxious, a lot less sure of herself than she had been ten minutes earlier.

'What? You being the boss of me one day?' Coupland thought about it. 'At least I know you've been out there and earned your pips, unlike some I could mention…'

The phone on Alex's desk rang. Three strides and she'd lifted it from its cradle. 'Sergeant Moreton…'

Not a rank she'd be using for much longer, Coupland reckoned, returning his attention to the whiteboards. His gaze ran along the list of names written alphabetically across the top of them until he found Asim Khan. He skimmed down the notes beneath it, pausing at the statement from his brother claiming the politician was gay. His claim had been verified by several partners, interviewed in their homes by DC Ashcroft. 'The press will get their "angle" then,' he said when Alex came off the phone. 'Khan's sexuality will be the big reveal he hoped would never happen.'

Alex nodded. 'Still can't fathom why Rose King was sent to his room. Was it some form of prank? A joke that seriously backfired?'

Coupland turned to Ashcroft who was typing up a report at his computer. 'What state was Khan in when you first spoke to him?' Ashcroft looked up from his screen, the look on his face saying he could have done without the interruption. 'He was in shock, almost incoherent at first, but he seemed to pull himself together.'

'But then somewhere along the way, after first claiming he didn't harm Rose, he admits to killing her.'

'Yes, Sarge. It says so there, doesn't it?' he reminded him, nodding towards his paper data system.

Coupland's thoughts were going off at a tangent. He needed to put them in some semblance of order. It was hard reviewing information he'd had no hand in collecting. 'I'm trying to understand what this isn't telling me,' he said, narrowing his eyes like a clairvoyant conversing with the dead.

'What do you mean?' He scanned down the printed notes until something occurred to him. 'Did anyone check the CCTV footage of the reception area?'

Ashcroft nodded. 'I did. There's no sign of Rose King entering the hotel, Sarge, the doorman has already admitted to smuggling her in using the staff entrance.'

Coupland batted away his answer. 'No, I mean footage of Khan coming into the hotel after he was dropped off by his driver.'

Ashcroft nodded. 'There's nothing to see, other than he looks done in.'

'We know the doorman booked the girl,' Ashcroft added. 'He was cagey at first, obviously didn't want to land himself in it. He has an arrangement with a local escort agency. They provide the girls and he gets a share of the fee.'

'Did you tell him that according to PACE that makes him a pimp?'

'Words to that effect, Sarge. It certainly made him a lot less reticent.'

'What we don't know is who instructed the doorman, am I right?' Coupland thought some more. 'Show me the footage of Khan entering the hotel.'

Ashcroft swallowed down a sigh, tapped several keys on his keyboard before turning his PC screen so that Coupland could get a better look. He studied the CCTV footage frame by frame, Ashcroft hovering by his shoulder in case he found something he'd missed. The camera positioned in the reception area captured Khan nodding at the doorman as he entered the hotel lobby, then taking mail from the receptionist while he waited by the lift. The camera inside the lift captured a very different Khan to the public figure engaging with hotel staff. Once the lift doors closed he slumped against the mirrored wall, rubbing the heel of one hand over an eye before pressing his fingers into his temples.

'Is this the face of a man so horny that when a call girl he didn't book knocks on his room door he lets her in?'

'Wrong gender, remember, Sarge.'

'Fine, company then. Does he look like someone craving company so much he pays for it by the hour?'

Ashcroft shook his head. 'Looks like me when I've pulled a double shift, Sarge. All I want is a beer and a decent kip.'

'And any uninvited callers?'

'They get sent packing, assuming I can be arsed answering the door in the first place.'

'Agreed. So why did he answer?'

'Politeness? Curiosity? It's easy to think the worst of everyone when you're in this job but there was no reason for him to be wary.'

'So he does the one thing that will change the course of his life and in doing so, end Rose King's. He opens the door.'

The last footage of Khan showed him exiting the lift when it reached his floor. He emerged from the lift head down, rubbing at the base of his neck. His fingers were slender, uncalloused, those of a man unused to the toil of physical labour. A slim wrist protruded from a pristine shirt, the cufflink so understated that the gem at its centre had to be real.

Coupland furrowed his brow. Wondered whether the item that drew his attention was significant, or whether there was no meaning attached to it at all. He filed the thought away. 'He's claimed all along he didn't ask the doorman to set him up with this girl, and no phone has been found to link Khan to the one used to contact the doorman in the first place.'

'On top of that we now know he's gay.'

'Agreed.'

'So why did he let her in? And why in hell did he hand over £200?'

*

HMP Forest Bank, Salford

HMP Forest Bank was a new-build privately run prison in Pendlebury. It was considered progressive for a category B prison, its website referring to inmates as residents, as though staying there was optional. Despite the exterior being pristine because it was relatively new, the visitor's area was like any other, fit for purpose and nothing more. A far cry from the gentlemen's clubs and swanky hotel lobbies befitting a Member of Parliament.

The man sat across from Coupland in the room reserved for legal visits looked nothing like the MP portrayed in the life-sized cardboard cut-out in the window of his constituency office. The man in that photo wore a pinstripe suit, arms folded, exuding confidence and integrity. As far away as was possible from the dishevelled husk sitting before Coupland now, charged with strangling a woman he'd hired for sex.

'It's a question I keep asking myself over and over,' Khan replied when Coupland asked him the questions that had been bugging him. Khan's shoulders stooped as he leaned onto the table separating them as though needing every bit of support he could get. 'Truth is I don't really remember anything about that evening, other than I killed someone.'

'Are you in the habit of letting strangers into your hotel room?' Coupland pressed, pulling out his notebook in case Khan's answer merited writing down.

'My client's already accepted the charge against him and is awaiting trial; I can't see what the purpose of further questions will achieve, unless you're looking to incriminate him in something else.' Khan's lawyer was as impeccably dressed as his client used to be, dark hair slicked back with gel suggesting he was younger than he looked, or trying hard to give that impression.

Coupland turned to him and flared his nostrils. 'My, someone woke up bent out of shape this morning. As I've already explained to you, I'm trying to clarify the timeline of events that occurred on the night Rose King was murdered. I wanted to make myself better acquainted, as I've been out of circulation.'

'We all know the reason for that,' the suit muttered, not bothering to hide his smirk.

'Whatever…' said Coupland, turning his attention back to Khan. 'Only I'm back now, and I want you to talk me through what happened in the run up to finding Ms King beside you.'

Khan's shrug was slow. 'There's nothing to tell. I woke up and she was there. I thought I was dreaming, I'd been so tired. All I'd wanted to do when I got back to the hotel was get some sleep. I didn't bother ordering any food, just made do with the snacks in the mini bar and helped myself to a couple of drinks.'

'And there was a knock on the door,' Coupland prompted.

Khan's brow creased. 'There must have been, although I don't remember hearing anything.'

'Go on…'

'Well, like I said. I don't remember anything after that.'

'You don't remember handing her money?'

'Of course not.'

'But you remember waking and seeing her beside you on the bed?'

'Yes.'

'What was your first thought?'

'I thought I was hallucinating. Except I've never taken drugs so I can't really claim to know how it feels.'

Coupland shifted in his chair until he was an inch or two closer. Laid his hands flat on the table. 'OK, once you realised you weren't hallucinating, what happened then?'

'I couldn't see her face at first but I thought she was asleep, so I sat up and tried to wake her. She wouldn't move and when I rolled her onto her side I could see that her eyes were already open. That was when I realised something awful had happened.'

'You make it sound as though you had no control in the matter, yet you have since accepted responsibility for her death. Why is that?'

'My skin was found under her nails. There are still marks on my face from where she scratched me. If I'd read that in one of the tabloids I know what I'd be thinking.'

'Yet you remember nothing.'

'No. But...'

'What?'

'No one will ever know how shocked I am by what I've done. Truly.' He looked at his lawyer then back at Coupland. 'I simply don't have a violent bone in my body. I've always respected women...' Khan's words hung in the air while Coupland wrote something down in his notebook.

'So, you couldn't wake her. What did you do then?'

'I dialled 999, but then I thought I'd better call reception too. I thought they might have a doctor who could come out, just in case there was a chance, you know, that she could be saved.'

'Smart thinking for someone daft enough to let a

strange woman into their room.'

Khan's head shot up. 'That's the thing though. She wasn't strange.'

Coupland tapped an ear with his hand as though he couldn't hear properly. He narrowed his eyes. 'Sorry, I'm confused. Are you saying you knew this woman after all?'

'No. But the more I think about it the more she seems familiar in some way. I suppose it's the reason I let her in.'

'Familiar how?'

Khan looked around wildly. 'I don't know!'

Coupland found himself asking questions that Andy had asked him during the previous week. 'Have you ever suffered from blackouts? Periods of depression or psychosis?'

Khan's lawyer sat up straight in his chair. 'Hang on, you're stomping your size elevens all over my client's defence. I must advise Mr Khan not to answer anything more until I have the opportunity to speak to him in private.'

Coupland shrugged as he pushed himself to his feet. 'All good things must come to an end,' he said. On the face of it the facts he'd gleaned were no different from the information contained in the statement Khan had provided during his initial interview with Ashcroft and the second interview that Alex had sat in on. However, he'd managed to ascertain that the victim had seemed familiar to Khan; although in a way the MP couldn't put his finger on.

Back in his car in the car park reserved for visitors, Coupland opened his notebook and re-read the last entry he'd made. 'I've always respected women,' Khan had stated. Coupland was wary of the sweeping statements people made. The tendency society had to lump folk together by their physical traits. What was it with the R word? Did Khan's claim mean he put women on a pedestal? Or did he feel that treating them no differently to men deserved special recognition somehow, some plaudit to show he was a decent guy? Had he spent his life demonstrating he didn't have a bias? Or had it come about as a result of him being a prize moron somewhere in his past and he didn't want his behaviour to come back and bite him now he was in the public eye? Coupland knew in the grand scheme of things it shouldn't matter. There was enough evidence to keep the CPS happy. Even so, he made a mental note to watch the recording of Khan's initial interview as soon as he returned to the station.

*

CID Room, Salford Precinct Station
The recording showed DC Ashcroft sat across from Asim Khan and his lawyer in one of the interview rooms. The MP was dressed in civvies. A cashmere jumper over expensive jeans. He hadn't shaved, and his hair looked as though he'd raked through it with his hands. He appeared drowsy at times, responding to Ashcroft's questions with sluggish one-word answers. Ashcroft seemed to become aware of this as he began pushing for more details if none were offered. Despite his surroundings and the reason why he was there Khan showed no alarm. Over time he became alert, engaging, a participant in a TV debate rather than a suspect in a murder enquiry.

Alex wandered over to Coupland's desk to see what he was looking at. 'How did your interview with Khan go?'

'Despite claiming that he didn't know his victim, he admitted to me that she looked familiar.'

'Maybe he thought she was a constituent?'

'A constituent who happened to be wearing PVC boots and a cut away dress?'

'Well, if you want to be pedantic, she did live in his constituency. The two don't have to be mutually exclusive,' Alex said, throwing him a look.

Coupland supposed she was right.

'You've seen the interview tapes,' she added. 'You've got as good a picture of him as any of us now.'

Coupland's nod was slow.

'There's no doubt Khan is our killer, Kevin…'

'That's not in dispute,' Coupland conceded, even though his gut told him they weren't looking at anything close to the full picture.

PART THREE

CHAPTER EIGHTEEN

It had been a long day with a pig of an evening ahead of her. Her stomach wouldn't stop rumbling as she sat in the driver's seat. The noise was long and melancholic, and she knew all at once why they were referred to as hunger pangs. She hadn't anticipated the sugar craving would be quite so strong, nor the temptation to give into it. She'd been so good, too. Better still, she was starting to feel the benefit, starting to feel good about herself in a way she hadn't for a long time. She tried to remember when she last felt so in control but the memory brought shame. Mind you, everyone made mistakes, she reminded herself as her stomach groaned for the umpteenth time. She needed to be careful though. Couldn't afford to let her blood sugar drop. She hadn't meant to miss lunch but there'd been a meeting in the staff room which had over run. There was a pack of fruit pastilles in the glove compartment but she refused to give in. She needed to refocus. Get a grip. The last thing she wanted was to swap one dirty habit for another.

She swore as she looked at the clock on the dashboard. She wished this lot would get a move on. Having parents turn up to watch their precious offspring compete slowed everything down. The fuss they made in the changing rooms afterwards: drying their daughters' hair, and making sure their sons hadn't left anything behind in the cubicles. That was why on gala days she left them to it.

No point trying to chivvy little Johnny on with his mum breathing down your neck. Some of the swim team were assembled by the entrance but it was their mothers who held them back, comparing finish times and personal bests, competing with each other about the number of hours their little darlings spent training each week. Not like it mattered. Like any of them were going to give Rebecca Adlington a run for her money any time soon. Sighing, she hit the 'play' button on the CD player, settled back in her seat as she closed her eyes.

*

It wasn't a conscious thought, more a feeling.

The woman knew on some visceral level that something wasn't right with her son's teacher. Her body language had been wrong all day. She'd been fidgety, irritable, unwilling to stop and chat, never mind tell the kids how well they were doing. When she'd popped over to the minibus to let her know the stragglers wouldn't be much longer she'd given her a blank look, sweat beading on her forehead. Something was terribly, terribly wrong, she thought as she made her way back to the group assembled by the main doors. Even so, nothing prepared her for the moment of impact as she instinctively reached for her child.

*

"A terror suspect arrested after a school minibus crashed into the entrance of a sports complex at high speed is not believed to be known to the security services, police have said. Three pupils have been killed and two severely injured when the bus ploughed into the group of pupils as they stood with their parents outside the main front doors of Ellenbrook Leisure Centre. Rooftop camera footage

shows the bus travelling at speed before mounting the pavement where the swim team from Greenoaks Primary School were assembled. A woman in her late 50s was arrested after the incident on suspicion of terrorism offences. No one else was in the van and police have advised no weapons have been recovered from the scene."

An image of Superintendent Curtis, standing on the front steps of the station, came onto the screen. Several microphones and mobile phones were held in front of his face as journalists jostled to get the sound bite they needed. His face was drawn.

"Police and the intelligence services are working to establish whether the suspect of this atrocious crime is part of a wider terror cell and if she had received assistance from others in planning the attack."

He paused. The harsh camera lighting emphasised the creases around his eyes. His jaw muscles moved even though he'd stopped talking. Coupland understood there were times in this job when words didn't cut it. When they failed to convey the emotion felt. The press officer beside Curtis cleared her throat, turned her head slightly in his direction as though urging him on.

'*"It appears to have been a deliberate act,"* he continued, *"but what the motive is we can't answer at the moment."*

'Has the suspect been formally identified, Superintendent Curtis?' asked one of the journalists jockeying for attention.

Curtis glanced at the press officer. *'That's all I'm able to tell you at the moment,'* he said, stepping away from the expectant faces in front of him. *'Thank you.'*

Coupland listened to the Super's briefing on the large screen in the CID room as he waited with other officers who like him had been on a rest day but on hearing about the attack had returned to the station to offer their services. DCI Mallender had been in attendance as he'd been the most senior officer closest to the scene but he'd become surplus to requirements once the Serious and Organised team arrived from Nexus House.

'They'll be stood down too once counter-terrorism get here,' he told Coupland. 'All we're allowed to do is preserve the scene.'

No mean feat when passers-by became roving reporters, zooming their smart phone cameras on victims and responders alike as they recorded a running commentary for their followers. When disaster struck these days everyone wanted a piece of it, spouting out rhetoric as they competed for how many 'likes' they got on social media. Right now the area was on lockdown. CSIs from the forensic imaging unit were surveying the carnage using 3D lasers.

'Any update on the victims?' Coupland asked.

'A woman has also died at the scene. Eyewitnesses say she managed to push her son to safety, just couldn't move fast enough to save herself. Two casualties are trapped under the vehicle and are being treated in situ, the rest have been taken to the Royal.'

Coupland blew out a sigh. 'And the driver?'

'Minor cuts and bruises. She's been taken to hospital under armed guard so she can be checked over before she's transferred to Nexus House for questioning.' Mallender looked wrung out, the horror of what he'd had to deal with etched in his face.

Coupland suspected he was in shock. Not just by what he'd seen, but what people were capable of. 'Is she one of those stand-alone terrorists, do you think? Trying to grab attention for whatever cause she's fighting for?'

Mallender shrugged. 'We don't even know she's a terrorist. You know the protocol; it's treated that way until we're told differently.'

'At which point it's down to us to pick up the pieces.'

'It's what you sign up for every day you put your warrant card round your neck. You serve where you're told to serve. You're not the Lone bloody Ranger.'

Coupland felt his cheeks redden. The boss was lashing out at the frustration of it, but even so. 'If we carry on using that not-fit-for-purpose computer system before the gremlins have been fixed *every* officer out there is the Lone bloody Ranger, boss, and I know damn well none of us signed up for *that*.'

Mallender raised his hands in a show of surrender; he had no intention of arguing the toss on that one. It was the adrenaline that was making them edgy. In the aftermath of a major incident the lines became blurred, not helped by the fact that the press were carrying out their own investigation, releasing information in real time which hadn't as yet been verified. Victims' identities were being made public before loved ones had time to digest the information; photos of the suspect and her family had been shared on-line, fuelling a lynch mob mentality that in certain pockets of the city could be downright explosive.

So far they'd gleaned precious little information: the driver of the minibus was a primary school teacher, Linda Strong, who'd been waiting to return the pupils to school from a swimming competition. She had driven the Ford Transit, which had passed its MOT test two weeks earlier, several times before, both in the UK and abroad, and was described as a competent and experienced driver by the education officer at Salford Council.

'The press will be gathering like vultures at the school,' Coupland observed, still staring at the TV screen.

'Someone from the Education Department is going over there to help the head teacher manage the situation,' Mallender replied. Decisions would need to be made: How and when to tell the other staff and pupils, never mind what to tell them. Whether the school should close for a couple of days.

'We could go over there, Sarge, make sure they're not hindered,' Turnbull suggested. 'You know, stop the bloody reporters shoving cameras in the kids' faces when they come out to meet their parents. Bastards will do anything for a bit of sensationalism.'

'Good point,' said Coupland. Aware that he wasn't officially on duty so it wasn't his call he turned to the DCI for approval. 'Boss?' he asked, moving into his line of vision as like his own, Mallender's gaze attention hadn't wavered from the screen.

'Agreed,' Mallender said, stepping away to answer his phone. 'Muster up some uniforms,' Coupland told Turnbull. 'You won't be short of volunteers, tell 'em to form a human shield if they have to.' Turnbull gave a thumbs up sign as he made his way to the door.

'Sarge.' Ashcroft called Coupland's attention back to the TV screen. Also on a rest day, he'd been at the gym when news of the incident broke out. He turned up at the station wearing tracksuit bottoms and a slim fit top beneath a padded gilet. A get up like that would have made Coupland look sweaty and fat but on Ashcroft it emphasised his athletic build. All he needed was a couple of stripes etched into his scalp and he could be mistaken for a professional footballer.

The TV report showed mobile phone footage of the incident as it unfolded. Taken by an onlooker quick witted enough to hit 'record' as the bus veered towards a group of children, though not quick witted enough to shove them out of harm's way. The footage showed the van going the wrong way round the turning circle in front of the building.

'To be fair he probably thought he was filming some idiot ignoring the one-way system. Probably planned to upload it on Facebook with a close up of the reg number to name and shame the driver.'

Only it was clear very quickly that the driver had no intention of turning round the circle. Instead she gripped onto the steering wheel and stared straight ahead as the minibus lurched forward. At this point the person filming moved his phone to follow the bus's trajectory, his attention homing in on a group of school children standing by the leisure centre's entrance. He could be heard shouting a warning as a woman moving towards the children hurled herself towards a boy, shoving him out of the way as the bus made impact. There'd been no time for screaming.

Coupland turned away. His hands shook as he raked them through his hair, willing himself not to ball them into fists. There was no place for anger, he reminded himself. Anger clouded your judgement.

A DC beside him spoke: 'My sister's kid goes to that school. Can't swim to save his life but that's not the fucking point.'

'Maybe on this occasion it is,' Coupland said to him. 'Maybe you shouldn't be here,' he added, knowing that his words would go unheeded. The tension in the room was palpable. The detectives around him were in a holding pattern, waiting for instructions from those on high. Despite local police being the first on the scene, being the ones to alert control that the act was deliberate, the ones to administer first aid and perform CPR, the ones to evacuate the leisure centre in case more attacks were to come, the ones to lay their jackets over victims and hold children as they cried, until the powers that be made their position known and decided who was running the show, all they *could* do was wait.

DCI Mallender pushed his way back to Coupland's side. His voice was low. 'That was my equal number at Nexus House,' he said, indicating the call he'd taken moments earlier. 'The Super's tied up with press briefings so his calls have been diverted to me.'

'And?'

'It is not thought this person is known to either MI5 or counter-terrorism, Kevin, which means…'

'She's ours,' Coupland finished for him, raising his voice so the others could hear.

CHAPTER NINETEEN

Counter intelligence services handed the case back to Salford Division with such speed the words hot and potato came to Coupland's mind. Uniforms standing guard at the hospital had been instructed to arrest the driver of the minibus and bring her to Salford Precinct station.

Coupland was on his way to the bank of interview rooms ahead of her arrival when his mobile rang. It was DCI Mallender: *'Change of plan Kevin, meet me in the car park.'*

'How come? I thought we were going to interview Linda Strong?'

'We are. Only she's been committed to a psychiatric hospital.'

Coupland couldn't recall when he'd last made the trip across the M62 to Liverpool. A wedding reception next to the Liver Building, if he remembered it rightly, a colleague who'd been transferred during the riots in 2011 had met his future wife as they stood shoulder to shoulder holding plastic shields up against an angry mob.

'And they say romance is dead,' Coupland muttered.

'Sorry?'

'Doesn't matter,' Coupland answered, glancing at the DCI as he checked his smartphone for messages. 'Any news?'

'They're operating on one of the pupils who'd been trapped under the vehicle,' Mallender replied, his voice

203

not holding out much hope.

Coupland drummed his fingers on the steering wheel and stared ahead. 'I don't get it. Why send her to a high security hospital?'

Mallender blew out a breath. 'She was deemed unfit to go into police custody. She's to undergo a second psychiatric assessment before we even get to go near her.'

Coupland's mouth formed a grim line. 'I didn't think they took women there anymore.' There'd been an abuse scandal way back, big enough to result in changes to the admissions process.

'When the situation merits it,' Mallender said, 'And it's safe to say these circumstances are exceptional.'

The high security psychiatric hospital was one of three in the UK that took patients considered a danger to the public. On first impressions, it looked and felt like a prison. Cameras, gates, alarms. Visitors fingerprinted and searched. In addition to that each patient was individually monitored around the clock, cameras tracking every action. If they needed to move from one part of the hospital to another they would be escorted by staff in constant radio contact with the central control room.

Home to some of the North of England's most notorious killers, for the most part the hospital operated beneath the public's radar. The fact the press hadn't got wind of the newest patient was evident by the lack of vehicles in the car park, which suited Coupland just fine. The last thing he wanted was his ugly mug captured on camera for Lynn and Amy to see when they watched the evening news. He'd already checked in with them, told Lynn it was all hands on deck now the big guns weren't coming into town.

Linda Strong was being held in a single storey detached ward, accessed via several sets of air-locked doors. Coupland and Mallender marched down the corridor of the segregated female unit behind a duty psychiatrist responsible for deciding whether she could be questioned. Late thirties with a permanent frown, Lauren Fitzgerald had made her feelings clear when they'd walked into reception stating they were there to interview the hospital's newest arrival. She'd relented after some persuasion from Coupland. 'But only with me present,' she'd cautioned. 'If I say it's time to call it a halt, we call it a halt,' she'd added, her gaze lingering on Coupland as though she'd marked him out as the difficult one.

The corridor was empty apart from two plastic chairs. The floor had recently been cleaned; either that or everyone who walked along it wore fluffy white slippers. Coupland looked behind him and saw the footprints he and Mallender left in their wake.

'This is against my better judgement,' the doctor muttered as she reached in her pocket and brought out a set of keys. 'She needs to undergo a full assessment before I can say with certainty she's fit to be questioned.'

'Easy to say when you're not the one who has to face the parents of the kids she's wiped out or maimed,' Coupland said. He took a deep breath in, exhaling his frustration in a long sigh. Anger didn't get you anywhere, he reminded himself, other than up folks' noses. He moved his lips apart in what he hoped was a smile.

'That's why I agreed to help you,' Dr Fitzgerald hissed. 'Though I'm already beginning to regret it.'

'We're very grateful,' Mallender said. 'It's important all the emergency services pull together at this time.'

The sound of crying coming from the other side of the door, interspersed with low, inconsolable moans, interrupted them. Coupland slid his gaze in the doctor's direction. Caught the hesitation before she swallowed it away. Fitzgerald knocked before turning the key in the lock and pushing open the door. 'Ready?' she asked, turning to both detectives.

'As we'll ever be,' said Coupland.

Linda Strong lay on a single bed, curled into a ball, arms wrapped around her legs. At the sound of someone entering her room she sat up, staring at her visitors with heavily drugged eyes. She was a stout woman, five foot two at most, long greying hair she left loose despite the hairband she wore round her wrist.

'Where's my husband?' she asked, her eyes locking onto Coupland. 'I thought you were my husband.'

Coupland dropped his voice as he introduced himself and DCI Mallender, explaining that they were the only people, for the time being, permitted to speak to her. Her husband was currently in Salford Precinct station helping police with their enquiries, providing a detailed history of his wife that might fill in some of the blanks. Alex Moreton had phoned Mallender to report that Mr Strong was dumbfounded, utterly shocked at what his wife had done. 'We'll let him know you are safe,' Coupland reassured her. 'You'll get to see him soon, I'm sure.'

'Please,' the doctor cut in hastily, 'don't make any promises we can't keep.'

Strong banged the heel of her palms against her head and cried out in anguish, causing the doctor to hit the panic strip. The nurse that arrived pushed a trolley containing a syringe and a phial of diazepam, proceeded to administer it without a word being said.

'How did you know that's what she needed?' Coupland asked.

'It's what they all need,' she told him. She turned her attention back to the patient. 'You're safe,' she soothed. 'You're in this body, you're in this room, nothing can harm you.'

Strong leaned back against the wall before sinking to the floor, her left hand plucking at the band on her wrist list like a sleepy harpist.

What shocked Coupland was not the level of torment in the woman's eyes. Nor was it the speed with which the sedative worked. It was how ordinary she looked. The kind of woman who went to Zumba on a Wednesday night and helped behind the counter at a bring and buy sale, assuming they still existed. The kind of woman you didn't really notice.

Unassuming.

Unremarkable.

Until she ploughed a minibus into a group of school children.

How the hell did she turn into a monster?

'Can you remember anything about what happened?' Coupland asked her. 'Anything at all?' Linda looked at him dead-eyed.

'That's the problem,' she answered, her voice barely more than a whisper. 'I remember all of it.'

CHAPTER TWENTY

Superintendent Curtis remained standing as he looked around the assembled officers. Some had been on duty for 24 hours but were refusing to go home until they heard more about the minibus driver who had been apprehended at the scene.

'At 2.34 p.m. a call was made to control, reporting a vehicle had driven into pedestrians outside Ellenbrook Leisure Centre. A log was created and sent to Nexus House, alerting Armed Response Vehicles to the locus. The initial belief was that this was an act of terrorism but that was dismissed when counter terrorist agencies confirmed Linda Strong was not known to them.

'Strong has been detained at Ashworth Security Hospital and DCI Mallender and DS Coupland have been over there this afternoon to question her.' He nodded at the DCI as if to say 'Over to you.'

Mallender got to his feet and turned to address the assembled group. 'Our first attempt to question Strong has proved frustrating. She became distressed and the medication she was given rendered her incoherent. An assessment will be carried out on her tomorrow to determine her state of mind.'

Coupland was already on his feet, waiting to continue with the briefing on Mallender's nod. The DCI inclined his head.

'Initial blood tests carried out when she was taken to

the Royal are clear – she wasn't over the limit or off her face on drugs. We can only fathom she's had some form of psychotic breakdown.'

'Is that it?' the DC he'd spoken to earlier called out from the back of the room.

'Not sure what more I can tell you that will make it any better,' Coupland responded. 'Nothing we hear will make it palatable. But at least we can reassure the community it was a one-off incident.' Coupland cleared his throat. 'Arrangements have been made for the recovery of the deceased victims from the scene and to take them to the mortuary. Staff from the council's Children's and Adult's Social Care services are in attendance at the school, along with bereavement counsellors. We're doing all that we can.'

He looked around the room. Nothing he could say right now would lift their spirits; all he could do was focus on basics. Make sure nothing was overlooked. 'I want anyone who isn't on shift to bugger off and get some kip. I need you bright eyed and bushy tailed. Our work isn't done yet just because the perpetrator has been detained. There's a mountain of statements still to take.'

Alex moved around the room, giving out actions to the DCs who were meant to be on duty, rejecting offers to stay on from those who should have clocked off hours ago.

'I'm heading over to the locus,' Coupland said, plunging his hand into his jacket pocket for his car keys. 'Want to come along?'

The look she sent in his direction told him there were a million other places she'd rather be but she nodded anyway, making a mental note to go to the gym when she finally clocked off as she'd be ready to knock seven bells out of something by then.

*

'So, how long have we got you before you're whisked away to better things?' Coupland asked the moment Alex had fastened her seat belt and leaned back against the cloth upholstery.

She shivered. She'd changed her car recently, upgraded to a leather interior with front seat warmers. Dreaded to think what Coupland would say the next time she drove them anywhere. 'What do you mean?'

'Before you get your Inspector's pips and I have to start calling you Ma'am?'

Alex let out a laugh. 'It'll be ages yet. I've not even sent in my application… though I'm starting that leadership course any day now.' She saw no point in hiding anything from him; besides, Coupland was like a dog with a bone when it came to getting information out of someone. Just because they weren't in the interview room with fluorescent lighting above them didn't mean this wasn't a grilling.

'Yeah, but we both know it's a formality. You'll pass the exams with flying colours.'

Alex didn't contradict him; false modesty irritated the hell out of her, though it was a different kind of fear that made her baulk at his words. 'What if I *do* get through first time? Everyone hates a swot.'

'So what? You take twice as long as you need just so no one gets upset?' Coupland threw her a look. 'Maybe you're right to be worried. If you're that thin skinned you shouldn't bother.'

'Thanks for the pep talk, Grasshopper!'

Coupland raised his brows. 'Pardon me, I didn't realise you wanted a cheerleader. Wait on while I get my twirling baton out of the boot of my car...' He ignored the scowl that flashed across Alex's face. 'If you want inspiration buy a book. One of those cheesy business ones that they sell in airports. If, on the other hand, real life perspective is what you're looking for, you've come to the right man.'

'You're annoying at times.'

'I know, but I'm right though, aren't I? You want the promotion but don't want to look too keen. Well, throwing your hat in the ring says you are dead keen, and if someone doesn't like that it's their problem.' He looked thoughtful for a moment, 'Just be aware that once you step on that conveyor belt you need to be prepared for the unexpected. You could get a call that moves you overnight to another station, division, or squad, and you – and Carl – need to be ready for that.' Alex didn't respond, instead she mulled his words over. The boys were young enough not to be disrupted by any move they'd need to make, and Carl, well, he was more house husband than entrepreneur these days anyway; he seemed happy taking on the bulk of the domestic chores. She'd need to talk to him though, and sooner rather than later, but on one thing she was certain. She was ready.

Alex hunkered down in her seat, staring out of the passenger window, jumping when Coupland pressed the heel of his thumb on the horn as he swore at a cyclist. Shop fronts drifted past, then flats.

Coupland indicated right, then right again, slamming his foot on the brakes when a learner driver pulled out in front of him. 'Shouldn't be on the bloody road!' he seethed under his breath.

Alex looked at him. 'I thought you were supposed to be all happy clappy now?'

'Happy clappy? I'm so laid back I'm practically horizontal,' he said. His attempt at humour was forced but it did the trick, the mood becoming sombre once more as they approached their destination.

They arrived at the leisure centre in time to see the first body being lifted into the back of one of three private ambulances waiting nearby. They stood in silence, heads lowered, until the process was repeated twice more. When the final ambulance's back doors closed, the convoy began its journey to the city mortuary at a funereal pace, accompanied by a police escort. Only when the final vehicle was no longer in view did the remaining personnel begin the task of clearing the site. Removing swimming bags and satchels strewn across the pavement. Shoes thrown off in the impact. Broken glasses and blood. Whoever had coined the phrase fairer sex was misguided. With the right weapon even a middle aged woman could cause unconscionable harm.

The minibus had been moved during the rescue and removal of the children trapped beneath it. A vehicle transporter had been booked to take it to the police compound for further examination and testing. Coupland moved over to where DC Turnbull logged the contents of the glove compartment before placing them into paper evidence bags. 'Anything of interest?' he asked. Turnbull shook his head. 'A few CDs and a pack of fruit pastilles,' he replied, tossing them into the evidence bag with everything else. Coupland gave the mangled bonnet the once over before making his way back to Alex.

'Glad I didn't see it happen,' she said. Some images were indelible.

'So, what did you make of her then?' Alex asked. 'Any reason why she'd have lost the plot like that?'

Coupland shook his head as he blew out a breath. 'I've no idea. I'm not convinced she has. By the time we left her it was like a veil had come down. Communication was nigh on impossible. I doubt we'll be let near her again any time soon. She was asking to see her husband, but the doc wasn't keen on that happening either.'

'Her husband's in a state of shock. As are their friends and neighbours. No one can make sense of it. They've a happy marriage. No financial problems. She's well respected by her colleagues. Their daughter's getting married next year and she was really looking forward to it.'

'Where did you interview the husband?'

'He came to the station.'

Coupland considered this. 'How about a home visit?'

*

'All this on a teacher's salary?' Coupland asked as he took in the doubled fronted house with ivy growing around a freshly painted porch.

'He's in IT, some sort of consultant.'

'Say no more,' Coupland responded, rolling his eyes. 'As long as he has nothing to do with the system the division's limping along with we'll get along just fine.'

Derek Strong stared at the detectives standing on his doorstep brandishing lanyards. If he recognised Alex from their initial meeting he didn't show it. He looked to Coupland like someone whose innards had been scraped out.

'Can we come in, sir?' Coupland asked when it became obvious from the man's blank expression social niceties were beyond him. Strong nodded and stopped to one side to let them pass.

They followed him into the living room, taking in the chaos brought about when serious crime officers had turned the place over in an attempt to determine whether his wife was a threat to national security.

'Have you got friends or family?' Coupland began, his eyes scanning the contents of the sideboard strewn across the coffee table, the now-empty bookshelf with books scattered around the floor. They'd have been looking for evidence of terrorist allegiance, ETA, IRA, ISIS, Coupland mused. Instead they found Joanna Trollope. 'Someone who can give you a hand putting everything back?'

Derek regarded Coupland as though he were the one who'd lost his handle on reality. Like everything would be OK once the DVDs had been filed away in alphabetical order. He fixed hooded eyes on Alex. 'When can I see Linda?' he demanded.

Alex threw a look at Coupland.

'It may be some time yet,' Coupland answered. 'I went to see her this afternoon,' he added, confident this would make him more agreeable.

'How is she?'

'She's not great.' Coupland answered, deciding truth was the best bet. 'Dazed, confused, the assessment she's to undergo will give us an idea of her level of understanding.'

'So she's had a breakdown?'

'I'm not a medic,' Coupland said, 'I can't answer that

one way or another.'

'So why are you here?'

'I wanted to ask you if you could think of any reason why your wife would do something like this?'

'Your colleague's already asked me that!' Derek snarled, jabbing his finger in Alex's direction. 'Don't you share information?'

Coupland nodded. 'Of course we do, but I find that people forget things when they're in a state of shock. The statements I've read taken from your neighbours give an account of a happy marriage.'

'It is.'

'Your wife is highly regarded by colleagues and pupils alike.'

'She's dedicated to that school.'

Coupland nodded as those these were the answers he was expecting.

'Are you doubting what I've told *her*?' Derek said, glaring at Alex as though she was the cause of his pain.

'No. It's just that in my experience people recall what they expect to see,' Coupland explained. 'We're creatures of habit. We notice things, then after a while we stop noticing and make the rest up to suit the situation.'

Derek gave him a strange look.

'Do you drive to work or take the train?' Coupland asked.

'I go in by train…'

'So imagine someone gets on the same carriage as you every morning, day in, day out. A couple of months later I ask if you've seen them lately and chances are you'll say yes without thinking, even on the days when they may be ill or on holiday.'

Derek slumped into an armchair nearest to him. Let out a sigh so long Coupland expected him to fold into himself, like a deflated lilo or forgotten party balloon.

Coupland looked around the living room. Ignoring the mess, he could see that the furniture was expensive. A bit old style for his liking, but then you got away with big pieces when there was plenty of room to move between them. His attention was drawn to a cluster of framed photos atop the cleared-out sideboard. Derek with the daughter Coupland assumed was getting married next year. 'Does your daughter live here?'

'No, she's in Boothstown with her fiancé. They're on their way over even though I told them not to bother. Once the press get wind of where we live we'll get no peace.'

Coupland wasn't about to contradict him.

Alex asked what his daughter did for a living though Coupland had already stopped listening. His gaze swept every surface. Looking, learning. His mind working overtime. Beside him Alex made a noise like she was trying to clear phlegm. It was only then that he realised the conversation had stopped.

'Has there been anything worrying your wife?' he asked, moving about the room.

'No.'

'Is there a friend she confides in?'

'We don't have secrets.'

The number of times people trotted that old line out to him over the years. Coupland shoved his hand in his pockets. 'A work colleague maybe?'

'There was no one in particular.'

'Weddings can be stressful.'

'It's all in hand. Our daughter gave us plenty of warning, no shotgun wedding here.'

Coupland nodded. He stooped to pick up a photo that had been lying face down on the floor beside the sideboard. Linda was smiling at the camera, relaxed as she leaned back against a balcony, a swimming pool with loungers behind her. She was holding a cocktail glass, grinning like she'd consumed several of them already. Two fingers around the stem of the glass were stained yellow.

'Last year on holiday,' said Derek, reaching to take it from him. Coupland didn't blame him for being precious about the photo. They hadn't known it at the time, but it was the last holiday they'd have together.

'I'll speak to the hospital about you going to visit,' Coupland said when they were ready to leave.

Derek looked at him, surprised. 'Why are you bothering? She's done a wicked thing; I wouldn't blame you or your colleagues for not giving a toss.'

Coupland searched within himself to find the right words. To find any words, that would make this awful situation better. 'When something like this happens there are many victims, not just the obvious ones. We'll do what we can to help you through this.'

He ignored the look Alex shot in his direction as Derek followed them to the front door. He didn't need to be told they didn't have the resources for hand holding, that that was the purpose of Victim Support. A bit of compassion, that's all he was thinking. This man had lost his wife to a detention of some sort; whether in a prison cell or in a hospital ward, it wasn't yet clear. One thing was for certain though, she'd never be released. When he walked his daughter down the aisle next year, his wife wouldn't be waiting for him on a front pew.

*

Coupland dropped Alex back at the station in front of the main steps, telling her there was something he needed to do when she asked why he hadn't turned into the car park. The drive to Brookdale House gave him an opportunity to think. To work out the questions he wanted to ask. Though it pained him to say it, talking about his childhood had made things clearer somehow. Purged wasn't a word he'd ever used but it suited the situation, given the precipice his career had been teetering on.

The waiting room was full of now familiar faces. The skeleton woman who waited for her partner. The young boy and his mother. Each person occupied the same chair they'd been sitting on when Coupland had shown up for his first appointment, as though they'd marked out their spot and were guarding it furiously.

A patient was following Sam Freeman into a consultation room. 'I'm surprised to see you, Kevin; it must be bedlam for you and your colleagues at the moment.'

Coupland nodded, grim-faced. 'That's why I'm here. There's something I wanted to get some perspective on. Is Andy about?'

'He's out this afternoon. Is it something I can help you with?'

Coupland considered this. 'I suppose… though I can see you've got your hands full,' he replied, gesturing around the waiting room.

Sam turned to the woman now seated in what Coupland had come to regard as the triage room. 'Can you give me five minutes?'

The woman glanced at Coupland before returning to the waiting area. Sam ushered Coupland in, closing the door quietly behind him. 'How can I help you?'

'I'm guessing you've been keeping up with the news?'

Sam nodded. 'Shocking…'

'I tried interviewing the suspect this afternoon, only…' He paused to find the right words; he was dealing with a professional, didn't want to come across like an non politically correct Neanderthal, even though in truth that's what he was. 'I don't want to break confidentiality—'

A look flashed across Sam's face. '—Then you mustn't…'

'Christ, you're not making it easy.' He'd built up a rapport with his own therapist. Andy would have understood the importance of Coupland turning up like this, would have weighed up the pros and cons of breaking with protocol if the situation merited it. Besides, he'd confessed to a fascination with police work, would probably have jumped at the chance to help out. Coupland realised he had to tread carefully. 'OK, a hypothetical question then. I've seen many things in my line of work…'

'I can imagine,' Sam said, making Coupland clench his jaw.

No, you haven't got a bloody clue, he wanted to say but decided to keep his own counsel. 'I've seen people blank incidents out, you know, after something traumatic, that's not unusual. Even perpetrators of crime, if they protest their innocence enough, begin to believe it. But this… there's a situation I'm dealing with that's off the scale.

This person is so horrified by what they've done, if they hadn't been found holding the proverbial smoking gun I wouldn't believe them capable of the crime they've just committed.'

'Most people are capable of anything, Kevin, you should know that.' Freeman's tone was harsh, as though he was being unbelievably dim.

'Agreed, but there needs to be a catalyst though, a final straw that breaks the camel's back.'

'And is there a catalyst in this scenario?'

'I can't see one… that's the problem.'

'The brain constantly deceives us. It simply can't recall every detail of our actions or what we see, so instead, the occipital lobe – that's the visual processing centre – adds what it assumes is there. The brain isn't a video recording – it's more like a photo album, and in between those pictures it fills in the blanks. The result is that false memories can be created more easily than any of us want to believe. There will be incidents you are absolutely convinced happened a certain way… but didn't.'

It was pretty much the explanation he'd given to Derek Strong, without the technical words.

'Can it trick us in reverse, though?' he asked. 'Instead of remembering an event that didn't occur is it possible to have no recollection of something that *has* happened?'

'Of course.'

'So a happy, stable person can commit a terrible crime and because it doesn't fit with their "photo album" of good memories and experiences, they may genuinely believe it never took place?'

Freeman nodded. 'Yes. You only need to think of the Nazi war criminals brought to justice decades after the war. Kind old men that doted on their grandchildren, no hint of the atrocities they'd once been capable of.'

Coupland was conscious the clock on the consulting room wall was telling him he'd taken up rather more than five minutes of the therapist's time. But he wasn't done yet. He needed to know something else. 'Is it possible for the brain to heal itself, so that in time the person in question remembers what they've done?'

Freeman's face grew serious. 'It's possible. But to have that kind of memory rekindled would bring unspeakable torment. You wouldn't wish it on your worst enemy.'

I wouldn't be so sure, Coupland thought to himself as he left Freeman's office. There were several killers he'd put away over the years where unspeakable torment sounded just about right.

*

Incident Room, Salford Precinct Station
The incident room was in chaos. Coupland eyed a civilian member of staff as they dragged a large package into the corner of the room and began to unwrap it. 'What's going on?' he demanded, as another civilian appeared with an identical package and set about unwrapping that as well.

Krispy huffed out a breath. 'IPOS has crashed and burned, Sarge. No one in the division can operate it. Some fella's coming up from Milton Keynes to take a look, but he won't get here until tomorrow.'

'Christ, is he travelling here on foot?'

'Prior commitments, apparently.'

'And it's really knackered? We can't just turn it off then restart it like we do with everything else round here?'

Krispy shook his head. 'It's not as simple as that. The system is networked to the rest of the division but at the moment we can't establish a connection.'

Coupland's face remained blank.

'Imagine turning on Sky Sports to watch your team play only to find that annoying circle going round and round in the centre of the screen and naff all else happening.'

Coupland understood immediately, though not for the reason Krispy imagined. Living in a house overrun by women he'd lost all rights to the TV remote control. It was more likely a failure to view their favourite soap on catch-up that would cause the mood in their house to plummet. He hoped to Christ that Tonto's arrival would balance things out a little.

'Emergency buttons won't work while the system's down, Sarge. I thought you'd want me to start logging everywhere the team go.'

Coupland's day was getting better and better. With no way of calling for urgent assistance how could any officer go out on patrol with confidence?

'DCI Mallender has sanctioned the use of personal mobiles as an interim measure, and given me money out of petty cash to pick up more whiteboards from Argos in case we run out.'

Coupland threw his arms out wide. 'Jesus wept; I could build a better network out of paper cups and a cereal box. You did good, kid,' he added, going over to the whiteboards he'd carried from the basement the previous day. Each board was full of Krispy's childlike scrawl, but it was legible, the information clear. A log of incidents the team had dealt with over the last two weeks with updates and outcomes recorded against them. 'Why are some entries circled in red?' he asked.

'The families of Dr Bradley's victims want to know if anyone else will be pursued in respect of their relatives' deaths following his suicide.'

'He was a consultant anaesthetist, the Pablo Escobar of the hospital; I doubt he needed anyone to hold his hand.'

'DS Moreton has gone to the coroner's office. I'll update the board once their decision comes through.'

Coupland moved closer to the board so he could read the comments without squinting. His attention turned to a red circled entry beside Asim Khan's name. 'When did this information come in?' he demanded.

'A couple of hours ago.'

A search of Khan's home had found a prescription for anti-depressants, yet Coupland remembered the MP's blood work had come back clear. 'The prescription was dated a month ago,' Krispy advised. 'He obviously had no intention of taking it to the pharmacy… I was preparing this for our next briefing,' he added quickly, his mouth drooping at the edges in case Coupland was disappointed. Coupland nodded, distracted, his mind already elsewhere.

*

The drive to the accountancy firm where Irfan Khan worked took fifteen minutes. Coupland didn't bother looking for a parking spot on the busy main road, left his Mondeo parked on double yellow lines in front of the office block's entrance and stuck a well-worn piece of cardboard with 'Police Business' scribbled across it on the dashboard.

Asim Khan's brother was put out that Coupland

turned up at his place of work unannounced and made no attempt to hide it, greeting Coupland with all the warmth of a firing squad commandant. 'What is it with you people?' he said after Coupland had introduced himself and Khan had ushered him into his office, away from prying eyes and ears. 'Isn't it bad enough you hound my brother until he confesses to something he didn't do; now you're intent on ruining my reputation by coming to my place of work.'

'It's not like I'm in uniform,' Coupland reasoned, perching on Irfan's desk when the offer of a seat wasn't forthcoming. 'No one would know I was a detective if it wasn't for your reaction.'

Irfan ran a withering look over Coupland's crumpled suit, 'Trust me, they'd have worked it out.' He moved to the window that looked out onto the office floor and closed the blinds. 'The other partners said I could take as much time off as I need, but I don't want this to be an opportunity for them to ease me out. It's a tough world out there, I can't risk starting again at my age.'

'Your brother's coping well with his new surroundings, by the way,' Coupland drawled. 'Given the circumstances.'

Irfan looked crestfallen. 'How dare you insinuate I'm not concerned about Asim! Of course I'm worried about him. When I'm not at work I'm either speaking with his lawyer or updating family members of his plight.'

'Maybe if they'd shown a little consideration in the first place none of this would have happened.'

'What do you mean by that?'

'Hiding the fact that he's gay from his nearest and dearest appears to have taken its toll.'

'I don't follow.'

'Did you know Asim had been prescribed anti-depressants?'

Irfan looked confused. 'No, but I suppose that makes sense, now. He'd become withdrawn some time ago, I kept asking him what was wrong, but he said he was fine. I couldn't understand why he wouldn't confide in me when I was already keeping his biggest secret.'

'Any idea, apart from the obvious, about what could have been worrying him?'

'The job was clearly stressing him out, and I suppose you could be right, keeping part of his life under wraps must have put him under a lot of strain. He told me public events had started to make him feel anxious.'

Coupland clicked his tongue. 'Personally I'd have recommended a change of career.'

'But politics is his vocation! He's good at his job, he genuinely gives a damn. I told him he should see his doctor. That they would arrange for him to see a counsellor and give him tablets as an interim measure.'

'It seems he took your advice about going to his GP, only he didn't bother taking his meds, which gives me a sneaking suspicion he didn't see any therapist either.'

'Ah, well that's where you're wrong. Maybe he didn't mention the medication because he had no intention of taking it, but he did say he'd started going somewhere to learn how to de-stress. I assumed he was going to yoga.'

Coupland kept his face in neutral, his eyes running over the office's drab décor and standard issue furniture. He got up to leave, making a mental note to get DC Robinson to have a word with Asim's GP, but before that he wanted to hear what reason the MP had for not telling the duty doctor who treated him in custody about the meds he'd been prescribed. He looked back at Irfan. 'Are you an equal partner in this firm?' he asked.

Irfan paused before answering. 'No.'

'Thought not,' Coupland said before closing the door behind him.

Outside, a traffic warden circled the Mondeo like a vulture circling offal. He watched as Coupland exited the building and unlocked the car with his key fob.

'Are you blind?' the warden demanded, pointing to the yellow lines that ran the length of the roadside.

'Are you?' Coupland shot back, pointing to his cardboard sign.

'No need to be like that,' the warden said in his best official voice. 'I'm only doing my job.'

'Me too, or at least. I'm trying to.' He made a point of not raising his voice, of keeping his demeanour pleasant. He stepped towards the driver's door but the warden moved to block his path. 'I have the authority to give you a ticket if I want to,' he said, his tone teetering on petulant.

Coupland leaned in close until their noses were touching. 'Be my guest,' he growled. The motorists of Salford beeped their horns as they drove by, pleased to see a traffic warden get his comeuppance. Coupland straightened himself, sweeping his hand dismissively. *There's no place for anger,* he reminded himself, *only reasoned argument.* 'Knock yourself out,' he said to the warden instead. 'Just remember the money to pay the fine has to come from somewhere, that when push comes to shove it'll be staffing that's cut back.'

The warden shrugged, issued him with a ticket anyway.

*

CID Room, Salford Precinct Station

The prison video link kept breaking up, making Coupland wish he'd driven the 15 minutes to Forest Bank prison rather than endure the stilted conversation he was now having with Asim Khan's lawyer, who'd insisted on being present when Coupland informed him of his intention to speak to his client. Coupland reached into his jacket pocket for his note book; from a different pocket he pulled out a pen. Just because they weren't in the same room there was no reason why he couldn't perform the same rituals. Whether he'd hear anything worth writing down was another matter.

'When officers searched your home they found a prescription in your name for antidepressants. I want to know why you weren't taking the medication prescribed you, Mr Khan.'

'How is this relevant, DS Coupland?' asked his lawyer.

'It shows whether Mr Khan did all he could to manage whatever was troubling him. I mean, the doctor wouldn't have prescribed medication if it wasn't necessary, would they?'

A smile flickered on the lawyers' lips, although it could have been static from the transmission. The last thing he'd want was for it to be shown Khan was culpable in his mental decline by not taking his meds. Coupland watched as he leaned towards his client, said something in his ear.

Khan shook his head. 'I have nothing to hide, DS Coupland,' he said, leaning towards the camera to make his point. 'I've been suffering from stress, that's all; the GP gave me the prescription as a precautionary measure.

If I had felt the need to take the medication I would have taken the prescription to a pharmacy but I did not. In some ways it felt good knowing it was there, a form of insurance, if you like.'

Coupland noticed every time Khan spoke his right hand automatically moved to his left, to a spot on his wrist, as though checking for a watch that wasn't there.

'DS Coupland,' Khan said suddenly, causing Coupland to look up. 'How is Miss King's family?'

Coupland regarded him. 'As you would expect. Though I don't think the news has fully sunk in.'

'Please, could you tell them how sorry I am? If there is anything I can do, any assistance I can offer, maybe help towards funeral costs?'

'OK, you need to stop talking,' his lawyer said sharply, bringing the meeting to a close.

Coupland had heard a great many things in his time, but a killer offering to pay for his victim's funeral was a first. He blew out his cheeks, enjoying the lawyer's discomfort. 'I'll be sure to mention your remorse next time I see them,' he said truthfully, 'but I'll swerve telling them about your offer, if it's all the same to you,' he countered, breaking the connection.

CHAPTER TWENTY-ONE

Briefing, CID Room, Salford Precinct Station

DC Andy Lewis sat towards the front of the room beside DCs Ashcroft and Turnbull, on one side, Krispy and DS Moreton on the other. DCI Mallender sat at the end of the row. Cueball's colleagues had opted to stay at the back of the room along with Robinson who had arrived late so was relegated to a draughty seat by the window. He threw a sullen look at the back of Cueball's head, intercepted by Coupland who was waiting to begin. He readied himself for a rebuke, a reminder that they were all part of the same team and that he shouldn't sulk because he wasn't sat with his mates, only to be blindsided by a smile.

Coupland walked over to one of Krispy's whiteboards and pointed to Piers Bradley's photograph. 'The coroner has confirmed she is satisfied with DS Moreton's report into the consultant's suicide, concluding that he died by his own hand. Given that we are in possession of CCTV footage which shows Bradley was responsible for the death of Blake Peters and the witness statements taken following Belinda Adamson's death, we have advised the CPS that we aren't looking to interview anyone else in connection with this matter. The case is now closed.'

Cueball slapped his hand down on the desk top and muttered several oaths. A DC at the back of the room kicked the filing cabinet he'd been leaning against.

The moment the news of Bradley's suicide had been announced they knew the case would be dropped but still, the hours they'd put in. Coupland knew it was a kick in the gut, and he didn't envy them delivering the news to the victims' families.

He looked over at DCI Mallender, 'Anything you want to add, boss?'

Mallender nodded, turning in his seat so he was facing as many of Cueball's team as possible. 'I don't need to remind anyone there are no winners here; none of us could have predicted this outcome. It's pointless apportioning blame, there's nothing more the prison service could have done other than put everyone who steps over their door on regular observations, but it isn't feasible.' He took a breath as he looked around the room, readying himself to deliver the next blow. 'I might as well tell you that I took a call from Ashworth Hospital this morning. Linda Strong's psych assessment has been carried out.' He paused. 'She's not fit for trial.'

The room erupted into angry protests.

'What's the fucking point of us?' a DC demanded.

'The country's going to the bloody dogs,' said another.

Coupland let the volume rise; they needed to let off steam, to threaten what they'd do, how different it would be, if they were in charge. The truth was Coupland sided with them every step of the way. He floundered for something positive to say, some rousing speech that would bring order and focus to the team once more. He sighed, decided in the circumstances it was better to let them run out of steam.

After a minute or two DCI Mallender signalled that it was time to rein it in.

'Pipe down folks,' Coupland called out, 'this isn't a mothers' meeting. We need to crack on.'

The decibel level dropped to a grumpy whisper; a couple of stern looks from him restored silence once more.

Mallender nodded his thanks. 'Is Asim Khan's lawyer still claiming diminished responsibility for his client?' he asked.

Coupland readied himself for his answer to trigger more protests. 'He is…' He held the palm of his hand out to stave off unasked-for comments. 'Although the confused state he was in when Rose King's body was found is very different from the person I saw today. Turns out he'd been prescribed meds which he hasn't been taking, which I'm hoping Robinson can update us on.'

Robinson nodded, opening his notebook and scanning down the page before speaking. 'According to Khan's GP he's been suffering from stress for the past six months. He was also anxious about the party conference, said he needed something to help him relax.'

'So the prescription found at his home was the only time his doctor had prescribed anything like this?'

'Yes.'

Coupland considered this. 'Did you ask about the stress management classes his brother mentioned?'

'Yes, only he wasn't going to yoga. He told his doc he'd found a counselling centre he could attend privately, said he didn't want to wait around.'

'Did you get their contact details?'

Robinson nodded. 'His GP had referred other patients there in the past, when the NHS waiting lists were in danger of breaching directives. I was going to call round there after the briefing Sarge, see if they can't shed more light on Khan's state of mind, though he sounds pretty switched on to me.'

Coupland nodded in agreement. Khan's recovery was remarkable if outward appearances were anything to go by, so his counsellor's opinion would be crucial. 'Where are they based?'

'An outfit just off Chapel Street,' Robinson answered, referring to his notes. 'Brookdale House Therapy Centre.'

Coupland blinked. 'What's the therapist's name?' he asked, even though the answer was already forming in his head. The same therapist who had guided Coupland through his anger management course, who, if he remembered rightly, had bookmarked Asim Khan's arrest onto his smartphone news feed. 'Andy Robson, by any chance?' he asked, noting the surprise on Robinson's face.

'You know him, Sarge?' asked Turnbull, ever slow to catch on.

'Course I bloody well know him, I've been attending appointments with him for the best part of two weeks.'

'No, that's not why I asked,' said Turnbull. 'I mean, it partly is, but not for that reason. One of the items I collected from the minibus Linda Strong drove into the schoolchildren was a CD that had been jammed in the disk player upon impact. It was one of those self-help guides according to the label… Now I'm not saying that it's from the same place that you've been going to, Sarge, or anything like that, but given that Khan went there for support for his anxiety I'm wondering if there's a chance she could have gone there for treatment too. I mean it could all be—'

'—I hear you, Turnbull,' Coupland said, stopping him mid-flow. 'Hands up those who believe in coincidence?'

Not one person raised their hand.

'Thought not, I mean, it's right up there with rocking horse shit and flying pigs isn't it, in terms of likelihood.' Coupland turned to the bank of whiteboards once more, recalling the holiday snap of Linda holding a cocktail glass. The nicotine stain on her fingers. 'OK, there's every chance Linda Strong could have sought professional help to give up smoking. Can you go down to the Evidence Management Unit and get me that CD?' he asked, nodding his thanks to Turnbull who was already on his feet.

'What about Piers Bradley?' Alex asked. 'If we're taking a straw poll on coincidences shouldn't we be checking whether he was receiving treatment there too?'

Coupland thought about this before nodding. 'Can you go and speak to his widow? In fact scratch that,' he said, turning to Cueball. 'Can you do the honours?' he said, hoping that involving him in this new development would take some of the sting out of his own case closing.

*

Coupland rang ahead to check Andy Robson was working before heading over to Brookdale House. He wasn't sure what was pissing him off the most, that Andy had failed to mention he'd been treating Asim Khan, or that he'd quizzed Coupland on issues relating to the case without declaring there was a conflict of interest. Had it been idle curiosity, he wondered, or something more?

Andy was standing in the doorway of Sam Freeman's office when Coupland walked into the reception area. They were discussing some conference they were due to attend later in the year.

'Kevin!' Andy beamed as he turned at the sound of Coupland's footsteps behind him. 'I heard you were coming in to see me, how can I help?'

Coupland looked beyond him into Sam Freeman's office, but his colleague was answering an incoming call.

'I suggest we go to your office,' Coupland said, wondering if Freeman really hadn't mentioned his visit yesterday or whether Andy was playing deliberately dumb. Coupland wasn't buying it. 'Why didn't you tell me Asim Khan is one of your clients?'

Andy looked surprised. 'You didn't ask.'

'Don't play the village idiot, Andy, it doesn't suit you. Feigning interest in police work so you could ask me about my job...'

The therapist's face fell. 'I'm sorry,' he said. 'I couldn't tell you I was working with Mr Khan due to client confidentiality, but you're right, I shouldn't have abused my position by asking about your work during our sessions.'

'I need to inform you I'm here in a professional capacity,' Coupland warned him. 'So think carefully before you answer. Unless you want my opinion of you to sink even lower.'

Andy's cheeks flushed crimson. 'Of course,' he said, finding a spot on Coupland's tie and staring at it.

'Can you tell me why Asim Khan came to see you?'

'As I've already said, I'm bound by client confidentiality—'

'—Which ceases to exist when there is a perceived threat to life or, in this case, in the event of a murder. Do you see where I'm going with this?'

A nod. 'Mr Khan presented with all the hallmarks of stress. His GP had prescribed anti-depressants which he told me he didn't want to take. We spoke about how his position in the community made him feel, about the pressure his sexuality put on his relationship with his family.'

'So you knew he was gay?'

'Yes. Like most people who come here, at first it was hard to coax information out of him but as time went on he started to trust me more.'

'What would you say his opinion was of women? Did he share any violent thoughts with you?'

'Not at all! As for what he thought about women… it wasn't something we discussed. His relationship with men was what caused him the most angst.'

'What about Linda Strong? What was keeping her awake at night?'

Robson's face blanched, telling Coupland that Turnbull's spot had been a lucky one. 'When I heard on the news what she'd done I was as shocked as anyone…'

'Not so shocked that you let the police know that another of your clients had run amok around the city?'

'I didn't think.'

'Seems to me you do very little thinking in your job.'

Andy regarded him, wounded. If he was disappointed Coupland wasn't deploying any of his anger management strategies he'd have to suck it up.

Coupland could feel his temper rising, had no bloody intention of reining it in. 'Don't give me that look like I've pissed on your chips, five people have died at the hands of your clients. I need to take you down to the station for questioning, see how accountable you really are.'

'You can't be serious? How in God's name can I be held responsible for my clients' actions?'

Coupland wasn't entirely sure himself, but reckoned some tough questions down at the station might give him a clue as to what the answer might be.

*

Interview Room, Salford Precinct Station

'Look, I really don't see how I can help you with any of this, Kevin,' Andy said as he followed Coupland through to the bank of interview rooms towards the rear of the station.

Coupland shuddered out a breath. 'I've already told you I'm on the clock as far as you're concerned. It's DS Coupland now.' He opened the door of the nearest interview room and jerked his head towards the table and chairs at its centre. 'In you go,' he urged when Andy paused in the doorway. 'In case you haven't noticed we're not in your consulting room, you don't get to be the one calling the shots anymore, or haven't you worked that out yet?'

'Don't let your anger cloud your judgement, DS Coupland. I'm not guilty of anything.'

Coupland carried on as though Andy hadn't spoken. 'Wait here,' he instructed, 'I'll be back soon.'

Alex was in in the CID room overseeing Krispy's handiwork with the whiteboards. In her hand was the photograph of Piers Bradley which Krispy had unpinned now the case was closed. 'S'funny isn't it?' she said, as Coupland approached. 'The tabloids love their front page photos of "Evil Monsters", and more often than not

Facebook or a friend with an axe to grind can oblige. A miss-timed photo with the perpetrator squinting at the camera, or worse still, glaring, or taken out of focus, to make it look like they've crawled out from the shadows. Yet this one made it onto all the front pages despite him looking like… well… someone you'd trust your life with.'

Coupland glanced at the doctor's photograph; it was the same one that had been plastered on the front page of every newspaper since his arrest, the type of photo found on ward notice boards telling patients who was who: Bradley dressed in shirt and tie, NHS lanyard around his neck. The newspapers had cropped the image to include just his head and shoulders, but in this picture, which was a copy of the original, his arms were folded across his chest, showing a skin coloured rubber band around the wrist of his right hand. Coupland felt the familiar tingle that told him something wasn't right, but he was buggered if he could see it. What was he missing?

He took a copy of the photo with his phone.

'Something wrong?' Alex asked. 'I'm not sure. But given the nature of my relationship with Andy I'd like you in on this interview. Neutrality and all that…'

Alex nodded. 'Already ahead of you on that one, just give me a minute while I get the questions I've compiled.'

Some officers would feel threatened by Alex's efficiency, but Coupland saw no point in resenting someone for doing things by the book, not if it saved him having to. There was no doubt he had a reputation as a cop that got results; if he'd shared Alex's thirst for paperwork he'd be an inspector by now. The Force was old school, it was easier for men to coast into jobs that women or ethnic minorities had to slog for. He took in Alex's tailored trouser suit which looked new and expensive. Looked down at his own ensemble that had seen better days. Nothing a trip to the dry cleaners couldn't sort out. Running a damp sponge over his tie wouldn't go amiss either. That, and remembering not to head butt the clientele.

He leaned against Alex's desk while she retrieved her notebook, checking his phone for messages. A missed call from DC Andy Lewis. He hit the 'call' button and waited. 'Hope it's good news, Cueball,' he said by way of a greeting.

The DC's voice sounded lighter than it had hours earlier in the incident room, a lot more animated. 'Piers Bradley was scared of flying, Sarge. He and his missus holidayed in France every year – they've got a holiday home in Picardy, so they could drive over. Only it turns out he'd been offered a secondment to take up a research post in Canada. There was a lot riding on it career-wise so he should have been made up, except for the small matter of him dreading the flight. He'd gone to Brookdale House to learn strategies that would help him relax.'

'Had he now?' said Coupland. 'Was he given a CD?'

'Mrs Bradley isn't sure, but given Piers committed his crimes at work my bet would be he kept it at the hospital. I bagged everything up from his locker and office and took it to the EMU, I can take a look through it when I get back, Sarge.'

Coupland grunted his thanks before ending the call.

'OK, so we've scored a hat trick on the coincidence front,' said Coupland, when Alex waved her notepad at him, her brows knotting in confusion when instead of heading out to the corridor he returned to his desk. He tapped several keys on his computer while telling her what Cueball had discovered, clicking on the first of three links he'd had Krispy bookmark on his internet browser.

It was easy, when you thought you already knew the turn of events, to look at a piece of CCTV footage and interpret actions that backed up your theory. Coupland studied the clips with fresh eyes, moving his seat to one side so Alex could drag her chair across and sit beside him. Three video clips they'd watched several times over. Piers Bradley removing Blake Peters' oxygen tube. Asim Khan swiping his hands across his face in the hotel lift. Linda Strong driving her minibus into a crowd of schoolchildren.

This time Coupland looked for similarities. All three offenders were slack-faced, had the same blank expression around their eyes. The lights were on but there was definitely no one at home. Neither detective took their eyes away from the screen. When they reached the end, Coupland rewound each clip so they could watch them over a second time.

He pointed to Khan's wrist as he swiped his face with his hand in the lift. 'He's wearing a band like the one Piers Bradley is wearing in the photograph we had on the whiteboard.' He pulled out his phone and showed her the copy he'd taken of it, enlarging the image on screen with his fingers so she could get a close up view. 'When I spoke to Khan by video link he kept reaching for something on his wrist that was no longer there. I couldn't work out why it was bugging me then I remembered the band had caught my attention the first time I watched the clip. We can't tell from the footage taken outside the sports centre whether Linda Strong was wearing one but a call to Ashworth Hospital can clarify that.' He looked over at Krispy who'd been following their conversation from his vantage point beside the whiteboards.

'I can do that, Sarge,' he said, taking Lauren Fitzgerald's contact details down from the board to make his call.

Alex regarded Coupland. 'Well, we've established a connection in that they're all Robson's patients. But what's the relevance of the elastic band, and more importantly, does it matter?'

Coupland considered his answer. Alex's question was reasonable, wasn't that why he was running his theory by her now, using her as a sounding board in case he really was off his head? Besides, it was her initial doubts when she'd been investigating Bradley's suicide that had got him looking closely at the case in the first place. 'I was given a load of literature when I started going to the clinic. You know, leaflets with practical stuff like where to park and disabled access. There was a helpline number if you needed support out of hours and a section on self-help. I'm sure there was something about wearing those bands in there…'

'Can you remember what it said?'

'I may have skipped over that part.' He sounded sheepish. 'Fat lot of good an elastic band's going to do if some knob head's about to take a swing at me. Apart from flick him with it.' He clocked the look that flitted across Alex's face. 'What? I didn't know it'd turn out to be relevant.'

'It might not be,' she conceded. 'But it's worth getting Robson to explain.'

'I can run his answers by one of the practice partners, see if he's telling me any more porkies.' Coupland walked along the bank of whiteboards, circling the photograph of Asim Khan with a marker. He picked up the photo of Piers Bradley from Krispy's desk and returned it to the board beside Khan. The only photo they had of Linda Strong was taken by the press as she was led handcuffed, head dipped, into the back of a police van. Coupland moved it so that it was beside the consultant and the MP. Three people who out of the blue committed unspeakable acts. There'd been no lead up to any of them, no trigger, no reason their loved ones could think of that explained their actions. Coupland knew that criminals didn't always look a certain way, but to the public these were respectable people with responsible jobs. Pillars of the bloody community. It turned out they all suffered a weakness that eroded their confidence, but what else? It would be easy enough to close all three cases and move on. Not like there was any coming back from the crimes they'd committed, but what if there was more to it than that?

The sound of a throat clearing made them turn in Krispy's direction. 'They're for helping relieve anxiety,' he said. 'Those bands...when I got through to Strong's psychiatrist, she knew exactly what I was talking about when I asked her if Linda had one. She didn't sound too impressed either, more scathing to be honest. She told me Linda had worn one when she was admitted, she'd let her keep it as it posed no threat to her safety. In her view if it helped her get comfortable in her new surroundings then who was she to argue? Said she'd seen worse talismans over the years, strings of garlic and tin foil hats among them.'

Coupland raised a brow. 'I'm no medic but I'm with

the psychiatrist on this one. I saw the state of her after an elephant dose of knock out drops, nothing else was ever going to touch the sides, but if it gave her reassurance…' Though not enough to stop her mowing down a group of schoolchildren, Coupland reminded himself as he got to his feet. 'Let's see what Andy Robson has to say for himself.'

*

Coupland didn't bother reading anything into Robson's pleasant demeanour when he introduced the therapist to Alex as she accompanied him into the interview room. Given the man's profession he expected a calm exterior, would have been disappointed if he didn't exude composure when faced with a challenging situation.

'Seems you've hit the full house,' Coupland said as he took his seat beside Alex. 'Three serious incidents occur in one week in one city and do you know what they all have in common, or should I say who?'

Andy's smile started to spasm. He looked from Coupland then to Alex before dragging his gaze back to his former patient. 'What are you talking about?'

'Come on, Andy! Who do you think I mean? Piers Bradley, the consultant accused of killing two of his patients, had been a patient of yours since the beginning of the year.'

The blood drained from the therapist's face as quick as it would have if his throat had been cut. He saw the derision on Coupland's face.

'Which brings the body count to eight, according to my rudimentary maths.'

'Honestly, I can explain…'

'Was this some sick game you've been playing? These people clearly needed serious psychiatric help yet for some reason you patched them up with nothing more than an elastic band. Was it vanity? Greed? Or did you just not give enough of a toss about the public at large to show any duty of care?'

'Kevin…' Andy started, but Coupland flashed him a look. 'DS Coupland,' he said quickly, 'I treated all of these patients, yes, but for straightforward issues, nothing that caused any concern. When Piers was arrested for killing his patients I spoke to Dr Freeman but we agreed there probably wasn't much we could say that would add value to the investigation, it was more likely that we'd get in the way. You must be sick of so called "experts" who come forward after incidents like that.'

Coupland stared at him. 'We get oddballs posing as do-gooders,' he conceded. 'But, this was different, you were still treating each of these patients when they committed their offence, you should have come forward.'

Andy's head dropped. 'When I saw the news bulletin about Asim I wanted to conduct a case review of the files. See if there was anything we'd recorded worth taking to the police.'

'So what happened?'

'Sam said we should raise it at the next partners meeting.'

Coupland considered this, wondering why Freeman had seen fit not to mention Andy's concerns when he'd turned up at the clinic after Linda Strong's arrest. Was it simply a case of a professional covering for a fellow colleague?

'Can you tell me about the bands they're wearing round

their wrists?' Coupland asked, tapping on his phone to locate the photo he'd taken before showing it to Robson. 'I've had it confirmed that they all wore them. Can you explain their purpose?'

Robson nodded his head, grateful to be asked a question he could answer. He continued nodding as he spoke, as though it would make Coupland more agreeable. 'It's used widely in the industry as a distraction technique. One of the major issues that affect those with anxiety is the feeling that they're inside their own head, unable to experience the world around them. They become so lost in thought that they cannot seem to focus and enjoy life. The purpose of the rubber band is that when the patient snaps it against their wrist they are snapping back into reality. It's a physical reminder designed to get them to stop over-thinking.'

Alex looked as though she was writing his response down in her notebook but Coupland could see that she'd merely drawn three circles at the top of the page containing her questions. 'Do you recommend them to all your patients?' she asked.

Coupland already knew the answer to that since Andy had never suggested one would be useful to him.

'Only those presenting with anxiety. It's a useful tip in our practice guide, that's all. I don't personally dispense them to my patients.'

'I daresay you'd charge a pretty penny for them if you did,' Coupland muttered.

'Did Piers Bradley, Asim Khan and Linda Strong know each other at all?' Alex asked.

Andy shook his head. 'I've no idea. Due to patient confidentiality I would never discuss one patient with another. Whether they knew each other socially I couldn't say. I suppose it's not beyond the realms of possibility that they were acquainted, that one of them liked the support I offered and recommended the clinic to the others.'

Coupland thought about this. 'Wouldn't they tell you though? You know, as they were leaving one evening. "By the way, I told my pal the local MP how great you are"? They'd want your gratitude, wouldn't they? Isn't that how most people tick?'

Andy's head dropped as though he'd given up. 'I suppose you're right,' he admitted. 'Look, I'm not sure there's anything else I can help you with.'

Despite having the clinic in common Coupland couldn't fathom the leap that turned three people from patient to killer in the blink of an eye. Never mind grasping at straws, he was falling through the air again, scrabbling around for something to hold on to. A thought occurred to him. 'A relaxation tape was found in the CD player of the minibus Linda Strong drove into the children.' He drew his words out slowly, watching Andy wince. 'Do they come as part of the package?'

'No, there's a fee for those. We need to take into account production costs and everything.'

'Yeah, yeah…another brick in the duplex in Marbella.' He turned to Alex. 'We're in the wrong job.'

'Seems that way,' she agreed.

'Should I be getting a lawyer or something?' Andy asked, straightening himself.

'What aren't you telling us?' Coupland asked.

'Nothing!'

'Then why waste your money on legal advice when you're here voluntarily?'

'I'd like to leave, then, please.'

'Did you know Piers Bradley, Asim Khan or Linda Strong prior to treating them?' Alex asked.

Andy shook his head. 'I never met them before they were referred to me. Now I must insist that you let me go.'

Coupland didn't need to look at Alex to know she was thinking the same thing. They had no reason to arrest him other than for being the worst therapist in Salford. Or the unluckiest. Like a premier league football manager blamed because his team kept losing. Was it his fault the millionaires he managed had forgotten how to pass a ball? In the same way, could Andy be blamed for the actions of the patients passed onto him?

'So who referred them to you?' Alex asked.

'Sam triages everyone who comes into the practice,' Andy answered, rising from his chair.

Coupland's head shot up. He remembered his own assessment on his first visit to the clinic. Freeman had offered to treat him with hypnotherapy. Coupland had declined because of his own deep-seated fear of trusting others. Using his hand to indicate Andy return to his seat, Coupland stole a glance at Alex. 'Can I have a word?' he asked, rising to his feet and moving to the door before she had a chance to reply.

Outside the interview room she stared at him bug eyed as he shared his suspicions. When she saw that he was serious she put on her listening face but by the time he'd finished she was frowning. 'OK, so tell me I'm reading this wrong and you're not about to pick this Sam Freeman character up for incitement to kill using hypnosis. Are you even for *real*?'

'Derren Brown did it.'

'Did what, commit murder?'

Coupland sighed as he shook his head. 'No... He carried out a social experiment on a group of people, within in a week he'd got them robbing a bank.'

'What were they, armed robbers?'

'No, just normal folk, it was a documentary.'

'Lynn told me you don't watch documentaries unless there are animals in them.'

'Lynn doesn't know everything about me.'

'Yes she does.'

'OK, maybe she does, but on this occasion I promise you, he proved it was possible to hypnotise someone into committing a crime. At least, I think it was Derren Brown, it could have been that other fella, the one that does the street magic.'

'Derren Brown does street magic.'

'Well, whoever it was, he proved it was possible.'

'For crying out loud, Kevin, you need to do better than that when you update the boss.'

'We need to question Freeman first.'

This time it was Alex who shook her head. 'No. Do your research. As theories go it's pretty out there. You'll have to be tooled up with proof to get it past the DCI.'

Coupland's shoulder's dipped.

'Look,' reasoned Alex, 'We keep hold of Andy on one pretext or other so he can't tip Freeman off but you need to get your facts right.'

Coupland nodded, already backing away.

'Oh, and Kevin.'

'What?'

'I want it on record that I'm humouring you on this,

you know that, right? I mean, what you're suggesting is bonkers. I don't even want to be in the same room as you when you run it by DCI Mallender.'

Coupland shrugged. 'Depends what you mean by bonkers. That normal people can be persuaded to do something deviant? History is peppered with it: Rwanda, Jonestown, Kosovo. In which case everything is bonkers. And maybe that's how we have to be to keep up,' he said, turning and heading in the direction of the CID room, sounding a damn sight more confident than he felt.

CHAPTER TWENTY-TWO

Coupland telephoned Ashworth Psychiatric Hospital to ask Dr Fitzgerald to check if Linda Strong had known Sam Freeman before she started going to the clinic. 'It's important,' he stressed. 'I can always come over and ask her myself if you've got a problem…'

'What did she say to that?' Alex asked when she returned to the CID room in time to hear him make the call.

'She told me to give her an hour, tops, though she did mutter something along the lines of me going away and pleasuring myself while I waited, though I'm not sure I'd know what to do with the other fifty-five minutes…'

His next call was to Ruth Bradley to ask her the same question about Piers. 'She says her husband never mentioned anything about the therapists who treated him, so she assumes it isn't likely,' he said when he ended the call. 'Which isn't quite as reliable as hearing it from the horse's mouth, though it's as good as we're going to get.'

Coupland tried to book a video conference with Asim Khan but there was a problem with the prison's IT equipment. He swore quietly to himself, realising he hadn't ended his call properly when the person on the other end of the line could be heard saying 'Same to you an' all.' He glanced at his watch. His knowledge of hypnotherapy amounted to the square root of bugger all.

He needed to do some serious fact finding if he wanted to get DCI Mallender onside. After all, he was creating a case where none existed. 'Ashcroft,' he said, his gaze settling on the DC as he bit into a protein bar. 'Can you do me a favour?'

*

HMP Forest Bank
DC Ashcroft waited in the room set aside for visiting lawyers, his eyes fixed on the door Asim Khan would be brought in through. He'd been in a fair few prisons in his time. As a DC in the Met he'd become acquainted with the interiors of HMP Pentonville, Wormwood Scrubs, Wandsworth and Belmarsh. North or south of the country, they were pretty much all the same. Underfunded, draconian facilities rife with drugs. The remand wings were slightly better, in that the inmates awaiting trial weren't there long enough to form allegiances that would determine their treatment once properly inside. It was hard to call how a disgraced MP would be viewed. A novelty at first, Ashcroft reckoned, until those that called the shots worked out what he could do for them.

He wasn't deemed a risk to anyone, that much was clear, as the door opened and a female officer and lad young enough to be on work experience escorted Khan into the room. After closing the door behind them they remained either side of it, nodding at Khan when he looked to them for permission to join the detective.

'It's funny how quickly you become institutionalised,' he commented as he took his seat. 'Though I guess that's the point. It's the predictability of the days that make them bearable.'

'So you're coping then?'

Khan pursed his lips together, whether a deliberate act to prevent him from answering truthfully Ashcroft couldn't be sure. Khan was thinner that the last time he'd seen him, but prison food did that to you. His eyes were guarded, purple shadows under them suggesting sleep evaded him despite his bravado. Beneath a navy sweatshirt his shoulders hunched. There wasn't much call for charisma in jail, unless you had the bulk or the back up to defend it.

DS Coupland had made the call to the prison to inform them of Ashcroft's visit. Still, he thought it wise to make sure Khan understood why he was there. 'There's been a development of sorts,' he began. 'Not just in relation to your case, but two other incidents that are on our casebook.'

'What sort of development?'

'I'll tell you more in a minute, but I need to ask you if you knew the therapist that treated you for your anxiety before you started going to Brookdale House.'

'Andy Robson?'

Ashcroft shook his head. 'No, a hypnotherapist by the name of Sam Freeman.'

Khan moved his head from side to side. 'No, should I have done? I mean, it's easy not to look at someone beyond the service they perform for you but I'm fairly sure. People approach me all the time in my capacity as their MP, could it be in that context?'

'No, I was thinking in terms of when you were younger. School perhaps?'

A shrug. 'I was very quiet in those days. Not much of

a mixer. My social circle left a lot to be desired.'

'What school did you attend?'

Asim told him.

Ashcroft slipped his phone from his pocket and sent a text to DS Coupland as agreed, giving him the details.

'What's this about?' Khan asked.

'To be honest I'm not entirely certain. We're exploring the possibility that you were manipulated in some way when you were placed under hypnosis.'

'In what way?'

'That's the thing, my gaffer told me the bare bones of it but I'm none the wiser in all honesty.' It was safer all round, Ashcroft decided, to act as though he was out of the loop, the last thing he wanted was to be accused of planting ideas inside Khan's head that could be used by defence. Unless this hypnotist really was to blame, he reasoned.

Hopeful eyes stared back at him. 'Will it help my defence?' 'I don't know,' he said. 'But it may provide the answers you've been looking for – like how you got into this situation in the first place.'

'Why does it matter then? I'll still go to prison for it.'

The guards who'd brought Khan through were discussing the previous night's I'm a Celebrity, were in no hurry to return to patrolling prison landings. They weren't the only ones happy to stay put for a while. Ashcroft pulled out his notebook and scanned down the notes he'd made during the last incident briefing. 'Did Freeman give you a CD of some sort? Something to help you relax or sleep?'

A nod. 'Yes, I played it in my hotel room when I got back from the conference.'

Ashcroft swallowed. He hadn't checked the CD player when he'd attended the locus, he'd need to check the chain of evidence log to see if it had been picked up at the time. He made a mental note to phone DC Turnbull, who'd been CSM that day.

'So you think my therapist might be responsible in some way, for what I've done?' asked Khan, breaking into his thoughts.

Ashcroft regarded him. 'That's what we're trying to find out, Asim. My DS reckons it would have been an easier proposition, though, if your paths had crossed before.'

'Sorry I couldn't help.' Then, almost as an afterthought, Khan frowned. 'Now, if you'd asked me about the consultant who killed himself in Strangeways, we'd have been having a very different conversation…'

*

CID Room, Salford Precinct Station
The information on the screen was underwhelming. Derren Brown had conducted a social experiment several years before which had aired on Channel 4, Coupland had been right about that. The illusionist had assembled a group of middle managers under the guise of a motivational seminar, then attempted to convince them to steal cash during a staged armed robbery by insidiously drip-feeding the idea into their heads over time. Hardly crime of the century, and definitely not in the same league as murder, Coupland conceded. The confidence he had shown half an hour earlier was beginning to ebb.

Further research revealed that while several hypnotists

around the UK had been jailed and put on the sex offenders register for a range of sexual assaults, the only examples he found relating to convicted criminals claiming they'd been brainwashed were on the more dubious websites that looked decidedly amateur-hour. He needed expert advice, and fast. He could only think of one person who'd make time for him regardless of how heavy their own workload was. He pulled out his phone and dialled a number.

One ring. Two. Three rings. Four.

*

Roddy Lewisham had spent the morning in court and was more than happy to speak to Coupland provided he made his way to Minshull Street Crown Court. 'A coffee and a decent sandwich wouldn't go amiss either,' he instructed, adding as an afterthought, 'I've gone vegan.'

Once past the court's security Coupland looked out for Roddy amid the sea of black-cloaked rooks clutching files as they took last minute instructions from their clients. Roddy raised a hand in greeting, beckoning for Coupland to follow him into a side room beside court one.

'I figured you were joking about going vegan,' Coupland said, tossing a roast beef salad sandwich in his direction which Roddy caught one handed.

'And if I hadn't been?' the lawyer grinned, dropping his files onto the table and tucking the tails of his gown under him as he took his seat. He'd ripped into the packaging and was about to take a bite when Coupland answered.

'I'd have done the right thing and eaten yours as well, obviously.' Coupland tucked into his own corned beef and pickled gherkin bap with gusto.

'So tell me more about this theory of yours.'

Coupland had just taken another bite so chewed his mouthful as fast as he could, wiping the corners of his mouth with his finger and thumb. He took a breath. 'I think that Piers Bradley and Asim Khan…'

'The MP charged with murder?'

'Yep, the very same. I think they, and Linda Strong…' Coupland regarded Roddy as he spoke next. 'She's the teacher that…'

'I know who the bloody hell she is, I don't live in here, you know,' he said, indicating the court house. 'Even though at times it seems like it.'

'Well, anyway,' Coupland continued, more slowly this time as he felt his confidence wane. 'I think they have all been involved in some form of…' He looked around to think of the right word, something that would do his theory justice. 'Mind control?' His voice went up an octave, as though embarrassed about what Roddy might say.

'You mean coercion?'

Coupland was already shaking his head. 'More than that. They weren't consciously aware of their actions, nor were they forced into carrying them out. I think the idea to kill was literally put into their head.' Coupland waited for Roddy to form the right words to tell him he was certifiable, that the sooner he put the theory to bed the better, and they need never speak of it again.

Instead the lawyer nodded. 'It's been claimed – and proven, before,' he said, placing his half eaten sandwich on the table, hunger forgotten. He leaned back in his chair. 'Known as the Svengali defence, it's a legal strategy named after a character in a 19th century novel, and refers to a defendant who has been "a pawn of a more influential mastermind." It was used most recently in the trial of the Boston Marathon Bomber, Dzhokhar Tsarnaev. In that case, Tsarnaev's defence team claimed his older brother Tamerlan, was the principal architect of the bombings, and manipulated his impressionable brother into participating.'

A feeling washed over Coupland like an incoming tide. He wasn't sure whether it was relief or sorrow, wasn't convinced that it mattered. What did matter was that he'd found the common link in all three cases, now all he had to do was *prove* his suspicions were correct. 'It would certainly explain Piers' demeanour the last time I saw him,' said Roddy. 'He was so adamant that he was innocent when the accusations were first made. Then everything changed overnight. I mean, the golden rule of defence is that the less evidence there is the better. In Piers' case his downfall was that he was caught on tape. My heart sank when I saw it. Normally video evidence provides a clear and irrefutable picture of what happened. When Piers saw the tape he accepted his guilt.'

Coupland nodded. 'The camera never lies, or so we're led to believe. I've studied that footage over and over again, and in this case it doesn't tell anything like the real story.' He told Roddy about the footage of Asim Khan in the lift and Linda Strong in the minibus driving at the children.

Roddy tilted his head to one side as he considered this. 'It's still a question of *mens rea,* Kevin. Of criminal intent. Did the defendants know what they were doing? Did they know that it was wrong?'

'That's exactly the conversation I had with my therapist during one of our early sessions,' Coupland observed, thinking he might want to rephrase that sentence in the future.

'The point is I think they were under some form of hypnotic state when they committed those murders. I'm just not sure how I'll go about proving it.'

'That's for the lawyers to fight out, Kevin, all you need to do is to show it's a possibility.'

'And how the hell do I do that?'

Roddy reached in his pocket for his phone. Tapped on it several times, enlarging the image on screen before sliding it across the table to him. 'Professor Del Viscio is an experienced psychoanalyst. Does a lot of work around the court circuit. I'll text him and tell him to expect your call.'

Coupland copied the number onto his phone before getting to his feet.

'One thing though,' Roddy asked as Coupland turned to leave. 'Why those three? Or were they chosen at random?'

Coupland shrugged. 'Your guess is as good as mine.'

*

Ashcroft had pulled out of the car park at Forest Bank Prison when he remembered he needed to speak to DC Turnbull. He pulled into the side of the road, unscrewed the lid of a Lucozade bottle and took a sip before calling up Turnbull's number on his mobile. He hit the 'call' button.

Turnbull answered after a couple of rings, his shouty voice causing Ashcroft to hold his phone away from his ear. Most people had a telephone voice that was quieter, more genteel than their day to day voice. Turnbull's decibel level went in the opposite direction, resembled a footy supporter on match day telling their losing team where they were going wrong. Ashcroft resisted the urge to tell him in terms of Dom Joly impersonations he'd got it pretty off pat. After all, he was the one on the back foot. He told Turnbull about his conversation with Asim Khan, that the MP confirmed he'd been playing a CD in the hours leading up to Rose King's murder.

'And you thought 'oh shit' or words to that effect.' Turnbull's voice tumbled down the phone with all the elegance of a backfiring motorbike. *'I'd better telephone that pedantic old git and see if he did his job properly.'*

'That's not quite how I'd put it,' said Ashcroft. 'In truth I never even gave the CD player a second thought when I was looking round the room.'

'That's why you get all the sexy stuff and I get the dross,' said Turnbull. *'Not that I'm not complaining, I happen to be good at dross.'*

'Does that mean..?'

'It does. I removed the CD, though I didn't play it. I just logged it and bagged it and thought no more about it until I went down to the EMU to pick up the one that had been in the school minibus.'

'So you've already collected it then?'

'Yep, and they're sitting in DS Coupland's in-tray as we speak.'

'What about Piers Bradley?'

'Seems Cueball was ahead of us both on this one. Bradley's CD was on the Sarge's desk, ready and waiting.' A pause. *'You two vying for promotion or something?'*

'Why do you say that?'

'There's a rumour going round that DS Moreton's got itchy feet.

Stands to reason they'll be looking for someone to fill her shoes.'

Ashcroft grunted a non-committal reply before thanking Turnbull and ending the call. He tossed his phone on the passenger seat beside him. Back in the Met he'd been offered promotion, it was one of the reasons he'd transferred back up north. They'd wanted him for a poster boy, had plans to base him in one of the city's most notorious neighbourhoods. That wasn't how he wanted to rise through the ranks, to be some form of head office quota. He'd not felt that same culture since his transfer back to Greater Manchester. He'd settled in well since his move, though he'd done nothing about studying towards the sergeant's exam. If Turnbull's gossip was true then he'd need to get his skates on if he wanted to be in with a shout.

*

Bernard Del Viscio was Professor of Psychology and Criminology at Salford University. Roddy Lewisham had been as good as his word, so when Coupland called him on his way back to the station the academic's curiosity was already piqued. 'As luck would have it I'm delivering a lecture at the Mary Seacole Building this afternoon,' he told Coupland. 'I'm free now if you've time for a coffee. A far more interesting prospect than reading through undergraduate essays.'

Coupland feared another coffee would have him bouncing off the ceiling but given the lecture theatre was spitting distance from the station it was too good an opportunity to miss. He swung into the university staff car park and found a parking space near the building's entrance. Five minutes later he was sipping the most bitter coffee he'd ever tasted, and eyeing the glass cafetiere from which it was poured with contempt. One thing was certain, he'd never complain about the vending machine coffee at the station again.

'I can spare you twenty minutes,' Professor Del Viscio said when he'd taken his seat opposite Coupland in a quiet part of the coffee lounge. 'Obviously any information you give me will remain in confidence,' he added, barely able to contain his delight at his advice being sought. Some people collected anecdotes like others collected parking tickets. For the professor, helping the police with this enquiry would be something he'd be able to dine out on for weeks.

Coupland outlined his suspicion that three murder cases that had come across his desk had been orchestrated by a third party. 'But at the moment it's all supposition. I need to know it can actually be possible, and how the hell I can prove it.'

The professor's eyebrows had risen only slightly while he'd been listening, much to Coupland's relief. 'Well, I'm going to have to make a lot of assumptions here, but my first reaction would be: yes, anything is possible, if one party is determined – and skilled enough – and the other is susceptible to auto-suggestions.'

Coupland leaned forward in his chair. 'Let me get this right, you're saying it is possible for someone to incite a third party to murder during hypnosis?'

Prof Del Viscio studied Coupland, as though trying to assess his receptiveness. 'You're the one who came to me,' he reminded him.

'It's important, Professor,' Coupland said. 'I need something I can take back to my boss.'

The professor nodded. 'Very well. But before I give you my opinion you must remember most psychological crimes require trust – the victim must feel the perpetrator has their best interests at heart. This can only be achieved over a period of time. In the same way we understand sexual predators groom their victims, so too must those whose aim is to control the thoughts and ultimately actions of others. As I said earlier, how effective this can be depends on the individual. Brainwashing is like the meeting of two rivers. One clean and one polluted. The clean one always loses as it takes on some of the pollution.'

At last, something that Coupland could understand.

The Professor continued. 'I practised hypnotherapy for several years before I went into teaching. Some folk are completely resistant to it; others… can be too amenable for their own good.'

'So how does it work, then?'

'Do you mean how would I put someone under?'

Coupland nodded.

'It's important to make the patient feel secure, so I would explain in great detail what was going to happen, what I was going to do and say and what they may hear.'

'Hear?'

'Yes, sometimes I may refer to notes about the patient or other cases I've worked on where particular approaches have proved useful. They may hear pages rustling, my chair squeaking as I reach for a file. I would keep my voice calm; explain that their eyelids will soon feel heavy, that soon they'll want to close them and that their breathing will deepen. I describe what will happen through the body from head to toe; then I'd work my way up again.'

Coupland pulled out his notebook and pen, grateful when the professor paused while he took notes.

'After that I would get the patient to imagine places and simple events. I'd insert commands to check the degree by which it is working by lifting their hand to see if it stays unsupported when I let it go. At this point I will ask the patient to visualize a grey scale; what I'm really doing here on a practical level is removing any fear they may otherwise be experiencing.' Del Visio regarded Coupland. 'This also helps block memories and removes critical thinking so that the patients can't remember what's happened, nor are they able to resist the ideas put into their head, no matter how much they are outside their normal thought processes.

Bingo.

'So it *is* possible to make someone commit a crime?'

The professor looked thoughtful. 'There are far too many factors to just give you a straight forward yes or no, but it's not beyond the bounds of probability. Obviously it will be much harder if you take someone with an immensely solid moral compass than if you take someone who's initially prone to crime in the first place.' Coupland's shoulder's dipped. 'However, there's nothing to say that slowly, over multiple sessions, they could not be convinced that a gun is safe to shoot, for example, and that there's nothing wrong in pointing it at someone. In this example you'd have to provide them with a gun but in the cases you've described to me the killing machines were already available: The minibus in the case of the teacher, medication in the case of the consultant, and in the case of the MP, the sex worker's stocking. It's a matter of multiple, slow, small steps to get there.'

Coupland liked where this was going. Even more so when the professor shuffled his chair closer to Coupland and lowered his voice. 'It's similar to putting a moral, decent, "good" person in a nasty situation. Imagine you're being chased by someone who wants to kill you. Someone hands you a gun, can you kill them to save yourself? If you had to kill someone to save a baby, could you do it? If you put someone in an extreme enough situation they may have an "out" in their moral code allowing them to do something unspeakable.'

'They'd all been this particular therapist's patients for several months,' Coupland told him.

'Plenty of time to programme them into killing machines, then.'

'But how did it culminate into the incidents that took place?'

'It's possible they were trained to respond to a certain word or sound. Some triggers may induce sleep, or confidence, for example, and in extreme cases can signal to the patient the time has come to perform the role that was rehearsed while they were in a hypnotic state.'

'How would they hear the trigger when they are away from the clinic?'

'I have patients frightened of public speaking who by tapping a pulse point on their hand can walk onstage and deliver a rousing speech. Strategies like this, even negative strategies, can be taught so that the person can use them on their own.'

Coupland thought of the three CDs left in the in-tray on his desk. Each one belonging to Bradley, Khan and Strong respectively. 'Could the trigger take the form of a

CD they play when they are feeling low?'

'Yes, but they'd need to have been given specific instructions regarding when and where to play it.'

'Play the CD while you're waiting for the swim team to come out of the pool?' Coupland suggested, waiting for the professor to nod. Had Asim Khan been told to play his when he got in from the conference, so the fate of Rose King was sealed the moment she knocked on his door and he handed over £200? Coupland made a mental note to have Freeman's premises searched for the pre-paid phone used to call the hotel concierge, though it was likely to be long gone. If Freeman had told Piers to listen to his CD whilst on call then the patients he treated never stood a chance.

Play the CD and kill a call girl.

Murder your patients.

Plough a minibus into a group of children.

A cold shiver ran down Coupland's back. This was the bogeyman people didn't see in their dreams. It was a voice in their heads instructing them to perform the darkest of tasks.

Coupland needed to be absolutely sure he was on the right track. 'If you were asked to commit one way or another, whether grooming someone to kill in this way was possible, which way would you go?'

This time Del Visio didn't hesitate. 'It'd be yes, DS Coupland. It is absolutely possible.' The professor looked at his watch and sighed. 'I'm afraid I need to go,' he said apologetically, getting to his feet.

'You've been really helpful, Prof, I needed some form of rationale for when I took my theory to my boss.'

'I'm afraid I must confess to some self-interest DS

Coupland,' the professor smiled. 'May I ask a favour?'

'You can ask,' Coupland said, not wanting to commit himself to something that would come back to bite him.

'When you've concluded your investigation and the case has gone to trial, I'd like to write a paper on it. I'm fascinated, you see, on what compelled your suspect to target these particular people. Unless, of course, they haven't finished yet.'

Something sharp twisted in Coupland's gut as he considered the implication.

He was back in the air again, falling.

Coupland reversed out of the parking bay and swung the car round. Drove at speed along Belvedere Road. The station car park was full but rather than park across the road at Gala Bingo he left the Mondeo outside the main steps, tossing his car keys at a passing PC. 'Find a space for this and leave the keys in reception,' he called out.

'What did your last slave die of?' the officer grunted.

'Lack of oxygen,' Coupland growled back, taking the steps to the main entrance two at a time.

'You sure about this, Kevin?' DCI Mallender squinted at Coupland as though trying to work out where the 'mute' button was. Coupland hadn't paused for breath since marching into his office fifteen minutes earlier, fearful he'd forget the Professor's salient points if he waited for the DCI to catch up. He threw in Roddy Lewisham's reference to Svengali Defence to add legal weight, and that if his suspicions were right Sam Freeman was behind the multiple murders that had been happening in the city. 'Piers Bradley, Asim Khan and Linda Strong were all patients at Brookdale House, and all attended one-to-one hypnotherapy sessions with Freeman.'

'You're making this therapist out to be some sort of puppet master pulling all the strings from behind the scenes.'

'That's exactly what I'm saying, and the professor I've spoken to assures me that it isn't beyond the realms of possibility that Freeman implanted commands into all three of them whilst under hypnosis, to carry out murder by proxy.'

'OK, so you've told me how, but why were they selected?'

Coupland ran a hand over his hair. 'The team are trying to work that out boss, but we need to bring Freeman in now. We can't be sure what else this crackpot has got planned.'

'So what do you suggest?'

'The clinic needs to be closed and every patient contacted so they can be assessed.'

Mallender looked up at the ceiling. 'How many patients are registered with them? Fifty? Five hundred? You can see where I'm going with this, assuming I've got my head around any of it, and I've not made my mind up about that yet.'

'Krispy can manipulate the clinic's patient database with characteristics we do know, the task might not be as cumbersome as it sounds, and if there's an efficient way of gathering data that kid can do it. Look at the havoc that's been wreaked over the last two weeks, do you really want the press to accuse us of being caught napping if another incident comes in?'

Mallender sent Coupland a look that told him he knew damn well he was having his buttons pressed. Even so. 'Bring Freeman in,' he sighed.

*

CID Room, Salford Precinct Station

With uniforms dispatched to bring in Sam Freeman, Coupland returned to the CID room. They'd decided it was better that Alex accompany the officers to the clinic, given Coupland had been a patient there.

'A message for you Sarge,' Krispy called over as Coupland made his way over to his desk. He held up a post-it note which he proceeded to read from. 'The doc from Ashworth Hospital rang, said Linda Strong didn't know Freeman before she started going to the clinic. She says she's struggling to remember anyone right now and questions like this aren't helping.' Coupland grumbled a thanks, telling Krispy that he was to work through the clinic's patient list when Alex returned from Brookdale House with it. 'I want you to produce a shortlist of other potential targets.'

'But I'm going to need some parameters, Sarge, if you want results to flag up who might be at risk.'

'I know, son, believe me I'm working on it. All we have at the moment is that Bradley, Khan and Strong were all patients of the clinic.'

Just then his phone beeped. A voicemail from Ashcroft. Coupland's face brightened as he listened to Ashcroft's message; when it was over he phoned him straight back. 'Get your backside over to Ashworth Hospital and tell that psychiatrist what you've just told me. I want you to show Linda Strong a photo of Piers Bradley and Asim Khan, see what she has to say.'

He put the phone down and grinned at Krispy. 'We may well have just found your parameter,' he said, checking through his text messages until he found the one Ashcroft had sent earlier with the name of the school Asim Khan had attended. Arkholme Grammar. He handed his phone to Krispy. 'Khan and Bradley were in the same class at school. While we're waiting for Ashcroft to confirm Linda Strong also attended, I want you to get onto the school and ask them to pull up records for every pupil in that class. Cross check *that* against the patient register and with any luck…'

'Boom,' said Krispy. 'You'll get your shortlist.'

Coupland's desk phone rang. He snatched at it, barking his name into the receiver. The custody sergeant informed him that Alex had checked Freeman into the facilities and his presence was requested in interview room three.

'Sarge?' Coupland was at the CID room door when Krispy called out his name. He could tell by the tone of his voice that the news he had was going to be good, and Christ knew there was little enough of that going round that he could afford to ignore it. He turned, throwing a quizzical look in the junior DC's direction.

'I've been onto the school and they've promised to go through their archives. They know this is a priority and have promised to send what they can find through by close of play tonight.'

Coupland tried to hide his irritation, this was hardly breakthrough stuff.

Sensing his impatience Krispy got to the point. 'While I was speaking to the secretary on the phone, I looked up the clinic's website online. I wanted to download Freeman's photo to put on our white board. There was a group photo on the home page with Freeman in the centre. Only the more I looked at it the more it got me thinking about an action I'd been given during the investigation into Rose King's murder. I'm sure you'd want to see this, Sarge, before you go down to the interview suite…'

Intrigued, Coupland waited while Krispy tapped on his keyboard before leaning in close to see what the DC was pointing at. Closer still, in case he was seeing things. When Coupland turned to look at Krispy his grin was so wide his face ached.

CHAPTER TWENTY-THREE

Sam Freeman smiled as Coupland took his seat beside Alex. He noticed the therapist wore her hair down, In the clinic she tied it up off her face in a severe knot which in his view aged her. The curls hanging loose around her face softened her features, made her look younger than he'd originally thought. She gave him a knowing smile as though she was able to read his mind. Then again, Coupland reasoned, he wouldn't put anything past her.

'It's interesting to see you on your turf for a change, DS Coupland. Though I can't say I'm happy about the circumstances.'

'I'm pretty sure your victims aren't entirely happy either, being locked up for something you made them do. Even more tragic for the one who couldn't hack it any longer…'

Freeman turned to look at her lawyer, all traces of humour gone. Her voice took on a sour tone as she jerked a thumb in Coupland's direction. 'Two weeks ago he wasn't fit to be in a police station and now he's making wild accusations—'

'—Not so wild!' said Coupland, savouring the information that he'd just become party to, deciding, for the time being, to keep it close to his chest.

'You know,' he continued, smiling. 'When it boils down to it my job is all about "Fess ups or Fuck ups".'

'Sorry?'

'It's how most crimes are solved at the end of the day. Confessions or errors. Some folk can't stand the guilt burning away at them like acid. Others are hard-faced and try to front it out. They think they're a cut above everyone else in the intelligence stakes, only that's when they fuck up. They say pride comes before a fall...'

Freeman's smile was more confident than Coupland would have liked. Maybe she played poker in her spare time, when she wasn't sticking pins in people.

'So it's a good job you screwed up then,' Coupland prodded.

'I have no idea what you're talking about,' she said, starting to look a little less smug.

'Let me help you out then. Piers Bradley. Asim Khan. Linda Strong. All clients of yours. All charged with murder. Yet you never saw fit to inform us you'd been treating them, even when your colleague sought your advice about coming forward.'

'That doesn't mean anything!'

'Maybe not,' Coupland conceded. 'But this does.'

He placed the iPad he'd brought with him in the centre of the table. 'One of my DCs contacted the phone carrier to find out where and when the phone used to book Asim Khan's escort had been purchased. He went round to the shop when they told him they had CCTV. At the time he'd been on the lookout for a well-dressed Asian man, had paid no attention to the attractive brunette waiting at the counter. Am I allowed to say that?' he asked, turning to Freeman's solicitor for approval. 'Or is it one of those contraband words we're not allowed to use anymore? I mean, I only have eyes for my missus, I wouldn't notice an attractive woman if she fell down with the rain but sometimes you've got to call it as it is. As I was saying, my DC didn't have cause to think anything was amiss until he looked at the clinic's website this afternoon and saw your photo…' He stared at Freeman. 'And realised you were the woman on the CCTV.' Coupland regarded the therapist. 'There's no denying it's you, is there?'

For the first time Freeman's smile slipped. 'Now, for the purposes of the tape can you tell me why you'd be buying a pre-paid phone from a shop in the opposite end of town from where you live and work? My DC checked, you'll have had to pass two other mobile phone providers to reach that one. Bit odd, don't you think?' Coupland kept his smile in check, watching, waiting.

Freeman leaned back in her chair and sighed.

'I'm afraid I'm going to have to hurry you,' he said eventually. Freeman lifted her gaze until she made eye contact with Coupland once more. Kept on staring. 'Nothing to say? Then I'm afraid I'm going to pass it over to the other team…' He opened the iPad and turned it so Freeman and her solicitor could see the screen. He played the footage Krispy had shown him of her purchasing the phone. 'Just in case you were in any doubt, this picture shows you buying the phone we now know was used to text the concierge at the Lowry Hotel claiming to be Asim Khan, requesting a sex worker to go up to his room. By doing this you sent a woman to her death and the man charged with killing her to the best part of his life in jail.'

Freeman remained silent, her gaze boring into Coupland until he broke eye contact in case she was doing a number on him too. It hadn't gone unnoticed that she'd stopped protesting. For want of something to do he held out his hands as he counted off the consequences of Freeman's handiwork: 'You are responsible for Rose King's murder, as well as the deaths of a mother and three school children, not to mention two patients that died at the hands of a respected doctor who then took his own life.' Coupland held up both hands and for the purpose of the digital recorder said: That's eight lives lost, two lives ruined, not to mention the families…' He ran his hands over his face, letting them drop onto the table like discarded props. 'The last few days have been a steep learning curve for me. I didn't think what you've done was possible. The damage you've caused… what you've made other people do… it beggars belief.'

Freeman's lawyer finally sprang into life. 'DS Coupland, I'm afraid I must interrupt on behalf of my client. I've heard a great deal of rhetoric while we've been sitting here, yet nothing of any substance.'

'Rhetoric, eh?' He cast a glance in Alex's direction. 'No one's ever accused me of that before. Bluff and bullshit on the other hand, there's plenty folk think I'm full of that.'

'Why doesn't that surprise me,' muttered the lawyer.

'I'll tell you why,' Coupland said. 'Even though I reckon *your* question was rhetorical…' He looked at the recorder and wondered how much of his comments he'd be bollocked for when DCI Mallender played it back. 'It seems to me you've worked out that this isn't a fishing exercise, that I've caught your client hook, line and sinker. I have it on good authority – in fact the highest authority in this field – that your client planted words and thoughts – even images too…' he added, thinking of the staged way Rose King had dressed for her meeting with Khan, the kind of 'call girl' look favoured by TV producers rather than how the sex workers who walked the streets of any city really looked, '...into the minds of three patients who'd attended your client's clinic in good faith.'

Beside him Alex shifted in her seat. He hadn't needed to tell her Professor Del Viscio had peppered his statements with cautionary words like 'Not beyond the bounds of probability'; Alex knew from experience how careful academics were. Besides, Coupland only had minutes to brief him before he sought his advice. When it came to submitting the evidence to the CPS the professor would need to elaborate a lot more to corroborate Coupland's theory. But for now he had enough information to sound as though he knew what he was talking about.

Freeman's hands during this time had been in her lap; she moved them now, placing them flat on the table between them. Coupland made a point of meeting her gaze and holding it. 'You need to talk to me, Sam. Tell me if anyone else is in danger.'

Alex spoke up next: 'You'll be punished for what you've done, there's no getting away from that. But speaking up now, if it means lives can be saved, may make the difference between the type of prison you are sent to, or where it's located. Wouldn't you rather your loved ones came to visit you as often as they could rather than not seeing you for months on end?'

Freeman barely acknowledged that Alex had spoken. Instead she turned in her seat so that she was addressing her lawyer. 'I'd like a break now,' she said.

*

Ashcroft sat in his car in the car park at Ashworth Psychiatric Hospital. He'd telephoned ahead to give them notice of his visit but was told Linda Strong's visitors were by Dr Fitzgerald's approval only. He had no option but to sit tight and wait. He'd picked up a sandwich on the way over, a tuna mayo with more mayo than he'd bargained for. He bit into it cautiously, a serviette positioned to catch the worst of the drops. He was halfway though it when his phone rang. He grabbed it, hitting the answer button then waited. Linda Strong's psychiatrist had given clearance that he could speak with her patient.

*

The woman staring back at Ashcroft was older than he'd imagined but then trauma could do that. It didn't matter that children had been killed by her own hand; if DS Coupland's theory was right, Linda Strong was a victim too. He tried to summon some compassion, decided faking it was better than nothing.

'How are you?' he asked, regretting his question when her eyes filled with tears.

'I want to go home but they keep telling me I'm not allowed to leave.' She sniffed several times, dabbing her runny nose with her sleeve.

Ashcroft patted his pockets for a tissue, found a spare paper serviette and handed it to her. 'Look, something's come up that we need to check out. It might help your defence, though don't quote me on that.'

He pulled out his phone, tapped onto the photo icon and selected Asim Khan's photograph. 'Do you know this man?' he asked. A nod. 'Where do you know him from?'

'We were at school together.' The same response Khan had given when Ashcroft had shown him Linda's photograph. When Khan had told him he knew Piers

Bradley from school Ashcroft asked him if he also knew Linda Strong. When he asked why, Ashcroft had to remind himself that Khan had been incarcerated since Rose King's murder, wouldn't have known that Strong had made headline news for the same horrifying reasons he had.

'Linda, do you remember Piers Bradley from school too?'

Another nod, albeit slower.

Ashcroft composed a text to DS Coupland, confirming Linda knew both men from school, where they'd been in the same class. He hit send, glancing up from his screen to see her looking at him expectantly, as though hoping he could take her back in time and rewind what she'd done. 'Did you keep in touch with them after you'd left school?'

'Not really, we all went away to university, I taught abroad for several years before I returned to Salford. I'd heard Asim had gone into politics, and Piers was always destined to go into medicine, there was no reason for our paths to cross other than by chance.'

'Yet they did, when you all attended Brookdale House for outpatient treatment.'

'But I had no idea…'

'So tell me, how did you hear about the clinic?'

A shrug. 'It was an advert that popped up on social media. I'd been searching for help to give up smoking and the claims the clinic made were really promising.' She held out her nicotine stained hands. 'I wanted to look good for my daughter's wedding photos. I was more decrepit old chain smoker than mother of the bride, and I wanted that to change.'

'So what did you do?'

'I gave the number on the ad a call and was invited for an assessment…'

*

Coupland was in the CID room, nursing a coffee while he paced the floor. 'If we can make this stick Freeman's facing multiple life sentences, why is she so calm?'

Alex considered this as she sipped at a concoction of apple juice and ginger she'd started bringing into work with her.

'How can you drink that stuff?' asked Coupland. 'It looks like a urine sample taken from someone with an unpleasant infection.'

'Want to try it?' she smiled, offering him her glass. Coupland wrinkled his nose and turned his head away. 'And there's my reason,' she grinned. 'None of you lot'll pilfer this out of the fridge any time soon.'

Hardly surprising, Coupland thought, taking a sip of his own tepid latte.

'Maybe she's calm because she's achieved what she set out to do?' Alex observed.

'Which was what? Prove how clever she is? Not sure I'm buying that.'

Coupland's mobile bleeped signalling an incoming text. It was Ashcroft. Coupland scrolled down the message, nodding when he reached the end. 'Linda Strong confirms knowing the other two from school,' he informed Alex. 'Yet none of them knew Sam Freeman before they started attending the clinic for treatment.'

They considered this. 'So why did she choose them?'

'I don't believe there isn't a connection.'

Coupland looked over at Krispy. 'That school secretary got back to you yet?'

'She's emailed through a photocopy of the school roll for the years Asim Khan attended. I've entered the pupil names onto the database I created. I was just going to upload the patient contact details and see if we have any matches.'

Coupland looked at him. 'Well don't let me stop you.'

Krispy tapped several keys on his keyboard before hitting the 'submit' button.

Alex looked up from her desk. 'What about female pupils? Some of them may have married, or divorced and remarried even.'

Krispy was already ahead of her. 'The clinic's patient database includes their marital status, and maiden name. I've added a date of birth field into my parameters as a safety measure to double check they're the same person.'

Coupland grunted his approval. He moved to Krispy's desk, waiting for the database to spew out its results. They studied the screen together though Coupland wasn't entirely sure what he was looking at.

Krispy's face fell. 'The only patients who attended this school are the three we already know about.'

'What about Sam Freeman?' demanded Coupland.

'None of them knew her prior to treatment,' Alex reminded him.

'Maybe they just didn't recognise her. Make up and a change of hairstyle for a start…' Not to mention a change in perception, Coupland thought, remembering Khan's comment about not really looking at people who provide a service.

Coupland rang through to the custody desk to get

Freeman's date of birth, which she had provided when she'd been booked in earlier. He gave Krispy the date. 'Run it through your database to see if it matches with any of the female pupils in Asim's class.' He held his breath, willing them to get the break they needed.

Krispy's smile told him all he needed to know. 'There's a name coming up, Sarge.' They waited. Eyes fixed on the screen as it churned out its results: Samantha Riding.

'Get back onto the school secretary, I want a photo of this kid, pronto,' demanded Coupland. Finally they were getting somewhere.

Coupland's phone rang. It was Ashcroft. *Linda Strong saw an advert for the clinic, Sarge, it came up on her social media feed. She clicked on it to book an appointment and hey presto. The rest, as they say, is history. I'm guessing that's how the others were drawn in.*

'Listen up, Freeman did go to school with them. Her maiden name is Riding. Krispy's going to send a class photo through to you when it comes from the school. Stay with her until you get it. See if it jogs a memory when you show it to her.'

*

Ashcroft turned to Linda Strong. 'Does the name Samantha Riding mean anything to you?'

Linda's eye twitched in a way that told him more than any direct answer would. 'It's Freeman's maiden name. We've reason to believe you, Piers and Asim were targeted because you were at school together. Is there anything you can tell me about the time you were there?'

Ashcroft's phone bleeped. A text from Krispy with a photo attached. He handed his mobile to Linda for her to take a look. 'You remember her then,' he said, reaching to grab the phone as it slipped from her fingers, her hands flying to her mouth to stifle a cry.

THEN

CHAPTER TWENTY-FOUR

Arkholme Grammar School 1990

'Hippo!'

'Chubby Bunny!'

'Whale!'

She huddled in the changing room after PE, knowing what came next, her heart filled with dread. There was an order to their taunting, a regularity she could set her watch to. Quite frankly double games wouldn't be the same without it. Her life had become punctuated by goading and threats. A sentence she had to endure. She'd forged another note excusing her from showering but the PE teacher had torn it up in front of everyone while telling her not to be so bloody sensitive. 'Strip off like everyone else. There are no special rules for you, Samantha Riding, you're no different.' If that was true then why did the others call her names?

'Hey, Porky!'

'Lard arse!'

The taunts were worse when she was in the shower because there was nowhere to hide. Every inch of her on display. Linda Mills stood in front of her, eyes narrowed into mean little slits. She pointed at the parts that wobbled and bounced, at the dimples and stretch marks, the folds and chafed skin.

'Leave me alone! Don't come near me, I mean it!'

Her parents kept telling her to stick up for herself,

that bullies don't like confrontation. Her words made the spectators they'd attracted fall about laughing.

'The only fight you'd win is on a see-saw,' Linda laughed, causing the others to laugh too.

She tried to push her way past them but they had formed a circle around her. Poking, prodding, punching.

Afterwards, when they'd finished and the changing room was quiet once more, she got to her feet. She washed away the blood from her nose and grabbed a towel, pulling it around her as she headed to where she'd left her clothes, but they were no longer there.

'Here,' the PE teacher said irritably, appearing in the doorway now the furore had died down. She handed her a tracksuit from the lost property box. The same tracksuit her mother had been washing and returning every week for the past six months. 'They'll grow tired of it,' she kept telling her. 'It'll pass.'

But it never did.

*

'I'll walk you home.' Asim Khan was the only Asian boy in their school. He was kind to her, kept her spirits up when all she felt like doing was crawling under a stone. He accompanied her on this weekly walk of shame, helping her find her clothing which had been scattered around the recreation park beside the school. Asim understood what it was like to be different. 'If I had my way I'd make picking on people illegal,' he said.

'You going to be the next prime minister then, are you?' she'd laugh.

Khan grinned. 'You never know…'

'Hey, Mowgli, what are you doing with the Weeble?'

Neither had noticed the sporty-looking boy who'd run up behind them from the gymnasium. Piers Bradley was a straight A student. It was his prowess on the athletic track that stopped him being treated like a nerd; that and his smart mouth. 'Hey, I'm talking to you.'

'Keep walking, Asim,' she said to her friend but he'd already stopped. 'You can come to mine. Mum'll make us something to eat.'

Bradley sniggered behind them. 'What's she gonna make you, an all-day buffet?' He sprinted the last couple of steps until he was beside Asim. 'Come on mate, bin her, or do you like 'em supersized? Look at her, she's the reason double doors were invented.'

It was the word mate that did it. That irresistible suggestion they could be friends, as long as he made the right choice.

'Come on, Asim,' she urged but he wouldn't budge.

The look he gave her made something inside her shrivel. 'Why would I want to be seen with you?' he jeered. 'Tubster! You're so fat the only letters in the alphabet you know are KFC.'

A crowd had formed behind them. More sporty types, looking at her and laughing.

'I thought you were my friend,' she whispered, head bowed.

'Why would I be friends with you? I felt sorry for you, that's all.'

A familiar face pushed her way through the crowd that had formed. 'What are you still doing here?' shrieked Linda. 'No one likes you. Or are you looking for trouble?' She lunged at her then, causing her to fall backwards awkwardly, landing in a heap at their feet. A pain shot up her leg as though she'd trodden on a live cable. She curled up in a ball, wrapping her hands around her head in readiness for the kicks and blows to come…

NOW

CHAPTER TWENTY-FIVE

Ashworth Psychiatric Hospital

Ashcroft picked his phone up from the floor and examined it.

'I'm sorry,' Linda muttered. 'Have I broken it?'

'It's fine, I'm more interested in your reaction when you saw this girl.'

'That's really Sam Freeman?'

Ashcroft nodded.

'I thought she was dead.'

'Why do you say that?'

'She stopped coming to school. A rumour went round saying she'd run away or killed herself. We weren't very nice to her, you see…'

'And by "we" you mean…'

'Well, Piers, then latterly Asim, but I suppose it was really down to me…'

*

Interview Room, Salford Precinct Station

'…They were vicious bastards!' said Freeman, her mouth twisting with hatred. 'They made my life a living hell.'

When Coupland and Alex returned to the interview room they'd anticipated showing the class photo to Freeman and watching her crack. Instead, she'd blindsided them by immediately admitting her guilt. She stared at the photograph Coupland placed on the table in front of her, stabbing a finger at a skinny girl standing in the second row. She carried more pounds now but she was still recognisable. Linda Strong. Or rather, Linda Mills as she used to be called. 'She started it all, made some comment in the changing room one day that had the others splitting their sides. She must have picked up on it, enjoyed the feeling making others laugh gave her, as from then on she didn't stop.'

'What about the others?'

'Piers? He was like her lap dog. Looking back I reckon he must have had feelings for her, all the effort he put into running me down whenever he clapped eyes on me. Treating me as their punch bag was the one thing they had in common.'

'And Khan?' Coupland prompted.

'Asim.' She made his name sound like something vile. 'He was an outsider like me, yet he was quick to stick the knife in when he had a chance of joining their group.'

Coupland pointed to an unhappy-looking obese girl at the end of the second row. Regulation National Health glasses perched on a football shaped face. 'They bullied you because you were overweight?'

Freeman looked at him as though he was stupid. 'They bullied me because to them I was less than human.'

Coupland knew what it was like to live under constant threat. Even when it was behind you, the feeling of never being good enough remained. It seeped into the present, filling spaces with anger and regret. But even so.

'I can see you don't understand, DS Coupland. "Sticks and stones can break my bones…" and all that, but words *can* break your spirit. I'm nothing like the person I could have been. They made me feel ashamed about how I looked. About being me. I stopped going to school. In the end my parents moved so I could start afresh somewhere else. I worked hard and passed my exams, went to evening classes. I slimmed down, and once I was working I could afford to have my hair styled and coloured, swapped my glasses for contact lenses, I became a different person.'

'So wasn't that a good thing?' Coupland asked.

'It showed that you were resilient. A survivor,' Alex added.

Freeman laughed. 'My divorce suggests otherwise. I'm afraid my ex-husband found me just as needy and insecure as I'd been as a teenager. He couldn't cope with my mood swings and I didn't blame him. When he left me I went for counselling and it really helped. So much so that I decided to retrain as a therapist, help others to overcome the feelings I'd once had. Then one day I turned on the TV at home and Piers' face flashed up on the local news announcing that he'd been recognised for his services to medicine in the honours list, and I couldn't understand how such a nasty person could be rewarded like that. What the hell happened to Karma?'

Coupland pursed his lips. If he'd known her then he'd have told her there was no such thing. That the world worked for you or against you, whatever your deed.

'I already knew Asim was an MP. I had to endure that stupid cardboard cut-out of his self-satisfied face every time I walked past his constituency office. It was no surprise when I heard he'd gone into politics. I'd already seen close at hand what a turncoat he could be. Then I started to wonder how life had turned out for Linda, so I looked her up online. I couldn't believe she'd gone into teaching! She, of all people, was responsible for the well-being of children.'

'Maybe she'd changed. Maybe her becoming a teacher was her way of making up for the way she treated you. Perhaps she was a better teacher because of it.'

'So that makes it alright?'

'I didn't say that. Maybe she reckoned there was nothing she could do to make it up to you.'

'At this rate you'll be telling me Piers became an anaesthetist in an attempt to assuage the pain he caused me all those years ago.'

Coupland hadn't thought of it like that, but it was possible. The mind worked in mysterious ways.

It seemed to Coupland that Freeman was looking for absolution. That need for approval that marked out the victim from their bully. She jabbed the table with her index finger. 'What victim doesn't wish harm on their tormentor? To hope that on some level ill will befall them to equalise their pain?'

Coupland thought of his father. The number of times he'd wished the old bastard didn't made it back from his shift. What was different, he supposed, was that he outgrew his old man. The threat he'd once been ceased to exist.

'All I wanted was for it to stop. I used to wish I was invisible. To be one of the fortunate ones who pass through life unnoticed, free to be themselves without judgement or ridicule. I never had the luxury of being myself. If I was rude I'd be a rude fat cow. If I ate in a restaurant I was a greedy fat cow, and if I dared to look happy? Well, I'd no right to be. My bullies made sure of that.'

'The truth was, I resented the fact that life had turned out so well for them. They were at the top of their game, commanding respect from their peers, adulation even.'

Coupland shook his head as though he was hearing things. 'So you thought murder was the answer? I see why you might have wanted to harm your tormentors, but using them to murder people who hadn't hurt you in any way? It doesn't make sense.'

'I wanted them to be loathed, the same way I'd been loathed at school.'

'Well, you got that bit right.' Coupland was shocked by her lack of remorse, as though the pain and suffering she'd caused was a small price to pay as long as she got her own back.

'I started following them online. Watching their perfect lives fuelled my anger but it was addictive. I wanted to see them in the flesh, see if they'd recognise me, and if they did, what their reaction would be. I saw in Linda's posts on Facebook she was a smoker, that she was trying to quit for her daughter's wedding. I had no idea whether Piers and Asim had issues they'd need help with but you don't get to our age without some form of neuroses.'

Coupland couldn't disagree with that.

'I put out a small number of ads targeting their demographic: middle-aged professionals living in this area. It was easy really, the adverts stated how the clinic could help break bad habits, deal with phobias and stress, it was similar to our normal advertising copy, I just wanted to be certain it reached them too.'

Coupland could see why they'd be drawn to respond; after all, it had been the claims made on the clinic's website for treating anger that had compelled him to make an appointment. 'So what happened then?'

'Linda responded first. I booked her in and then waited. I remember feeling the old fear rushing back as I anticipated seeing her face to face after all these years. I wanted her to recognise me. To see how good I looked, to see how far I'd come, but she didn't give me a second glance. It was all about her, that whinnying voice droning on and on. Every time she spoke all I could hear were the names she used to call me. The prods and the pokes, the trips and the kicks. It dawned on me that I could get my own back. Make her the centre of attention for all the wrong reasons. I wanted her to feel the way she used to make me feel.' She leaned back once more in her chair and smiled. 'I told her a dozen sessions should do it, that she'd feel like a different woman in no time.'

'And the others?'

'Talk about a stroke of luck! Piers needed to overcome his fear of flying and Asim, dear Asim, was unable to cope with the demands of his job. All they cared about was discretion. God forbid anyone should think they were flawed. It's funny how we don't really see people, isn't it? Like we haven't got the time, or the energy, to look any deeper than the image they present to us.'

'So they came to see you every week?'

'Yes, but I made sure their appointments didn't overlap. I wanted to take advantage of the fact they were oblivious to who I was. Bumping into each other might have made them suspicious.'

Coupland considered this. 'How did you know it would work?'

A shrug. 'I didn't. All I knew was deep down they had the capacity to be cruel. It's funny isn't it? How people are willing to admit they were bullied, some are so traumatised they are defined by it. But who owns up to *being* a bully? No one ever puts their hand up and admits they were a mean little shit, that they persecuted someone to the point they considered ending their life? Odd how *those* memories fade… But I knew what this trio were capable of. I knew they had the capacity to wound others, if I pushed them hard enough. They would sit in front of me, limp, like the impotent imbeciles they really were. Once they were under hypnosis I repeated statements and affirmations telling them what I wanted them to do. By now I was well aware of their work schedules; after all, they had to plan appointments with me around their diaries. I knew the dates of Asim's conference, the swimming galas Linda drove her pupils to and when Piers was on call.'

'And the CDs you gave them, they reinforced this message?'

Freeman laughed. 'The CDs were blank, DS Coupland. The actions I wanted them to carry out were already implanted in their subconscious. Playing the CD gave them the time and space needed to bring my commands to the front of their mind, that's all. I reinforced these triggers week after week, reminding them of what needed to be done.'

Coupland pictured them snapping the elastic band on each of their wrists before setting about Freeman's game plan: throttling a sex worker, overdosing two patients, obliterating a group of children. He shifted back in his seat. 'Arranging to send a girl to Khan's room dressed like a TV prostitute was a visual trigger. The other two were just a matter of time…'

Freeman smiled, unlike her lawyer who threw

Coupland a stony look. 'Are you going to charge my client now, DS Coupland?'

Coupland regarded him. 'Oh, we're going to charge her alright, but I want her to answer my original question first.'

The lawyer's brow creased but Coupland didn't have to look at Freeman to know her smile was still in place. It wasn't a half moon smile signifying pleasure, more an enigmatic one, the kind that hinted she knew something that he didn't. 'What my colleague said to you earlier is right. Helping us now would be looked on favourably in court.'

Freeman said nothing.

'I know you're holding something back,' he added, wondering if they should just warn everyone on the clinic's patient list anyway. But warn them of what? Evil thoughts that won't go away? A temptation to kill and maim? Freeman hadn't mentioned anyone else who'd tormented her at school, and none of the other patients on the clinic's list had attended Freeman's school. But still.

'I'm afraid it's my turn to hurry you...' Freeman's lawyer smirked, causing Coupland's head to fill with its own malicious thoughts.

He fantasised for a few seconds about the CCTV blind spot in the station car park where the prick had parked his car, before pushing himself to his feet. 'You do the honours,' he said to Alex. 'I'm done.'

*

DCI Mallender patted Coupland's back when he told him Freeman had all but rolled over and confessed. The relief on his face suggested Mallender had more reservations than he'd admitted to when Coupland had come knocking with his theory. 'What a way to mark your return to work. The Super will be cock-a-hoop.'

Try as he might, Coupland couldn't feel quite as ecstatic as the boss reckoned he should be. 'She's been bypassed by the empathy gene. Makes you wonder whether she was born that way, or shaped by her experience.'

In truth very few psychopaths committed murder. They were more likely to be found in important political roles or the CEO of a large company. When they did kill, however, they did it with cruelty.

Mallender batted away Coupland's concerns. 'Doesn't matter either way. She'll pay the price for what she's done. You've made sure of that.'

As Coupland acknowledged the DCI's praise, a feeling came over him that he had overlooked something relevant. That something crucial had presented itself but he'd failed to interpret it.

*

The desk sergeant held up a set of car keys and jingled them in Coupland's direction as he walked through reception. 'I believe these are yours,' he said, tossing them towards Coupland who caught them one handed.

'Did he say where he'd parked it?' Coupland called over, picturing the stroppy PC he'd handed them to hours earlier. The desk sergeant widened his arms in a 'fucked if I know' gesture, his attention turning to the ringing phone on his desk.

Coupland stepped outside, turning up the collar of his jacket as he scanned the public car park before heading towards the section reserved for staff and police vehicles.

He circled the perimeter, pressing his key fob on and off several times making the car's lights flash until he could see it. He found it abandoned on a pavement, having been driven up the kerb with as much care as a joyrider would take. Several pigeons who nested in the adjacent shopping centre had claimed it as their toilet, peppering the bonnet with their shit. Coupland eyed the remnants of a sandwich scattered on the car's roof and muttered something foul.

CHAPTER TWENTY-SIX

Coupland woke with a start. He'd had that falling dream again, had to stretch out gingerly to check he was still in his bed. The side where Lynn should have been was cold. He checked the time on his phone, knew fine well sleep if it came would be pointless; his alarm was set to go off in less than half an hour. The falling dream no longer bothered him; it was preferable to the ones that forced their way into his subconscious, unbidden. The kaleidoscope of victims that kept him awake. The roll call of killers. The ones on either side of that fence yet to be discovered. Little wonder he felt out of sorts.

He showered for longer than normal, his mind working overtime as he contemplated the events of the last two weeks. Multiple murders inflicted by three killers who in reality were no more than puppets. An anaesthetist, a teacher and an MP. It was like one of those bad jokes now considered inappropriate: an Englishman, Irishman and a Scotsman walk into a bar... Three professionals who acted out of character. So out of character in fact the community had been left reeling, no wonder the press were wetting themselves with the material they'd been given: 'Gay Muslim', 'Dr Death' and 'Teacher from Hell'. Coupland wondered what the punchline would be if *they* all walked into a bar. He stepped out of the shower and dried himself. Pausing when it occurred to him why he was feeling so maudlin.

Today was his birthday. He felt no elation, though. His mother was dead. Any hopes he'd had of hearing her joke what a bugger he'd been to give birth to or how untidy he was as a child had been obliterated. All he had left of her were memories that he doubted bore much resemblance to the truth. Besides, there was no point making a fuss, drawing attention to the fact he was no longer in his prime. He dry-swallowed a blood pressure tablet as he stared at his reflection in the bathroom mirror, caught the gleam of silver in the stubble on his chin, which quite frankly was the icing on a very shitty cake. He was forty-three and felt every fucking minute of it.

He supposed there was a point in most men's lives, if the locker room banter was anything to go by, where they pondered the mark they'd made on the world. The change they'd brought about. For Coupland it was a no-brainer. Family came first. He lived by a simple rule: you were either inside his tent pissing out or outside his tent pissing in. It's what drove him to do his job. To protect the public and the people they cared about. To bring those that put that under jeopardy to justice. Coupland didn't have an academic bone in his body. He would never find the cure for cancer or eradicate poverty but he understood the fear people carried in their hearts because he felt it too. He gave himself the beady eye. He wasn't ready for the knacker's yard yet but his prime was behind him. How much longer could he hold his own with gobshites or chase down suspects who absconded?

He was padding downstairs when he clapped his eyes on the 'Happy Birthday' banner that had been placed on the living room wall. A pile of cards and presents had been left on the coffee table. The girls liked to make a fuss on his birthday. From a young age Amy had this thing about quantity, would wrap up every item they'd bought him individually: five pairs of socks and pants would take forever to open but he'd put on his curious face and play along, winking at Lynn who'd save her special present for later.

The floorboard creaking overhead signalled Amy was pacing around with Tonto. Lynn wouldn't be back till later and he needed to get a move on. He knew damn well Sam Freeman was holding something back. Yesterday had been a game to her, a show and tell of the highest order. What was going to be her big reveal? He closed the living room door quietly. The presents would keep.

'Jaxxon's got something for you, Dad,' Amy said, appearing in the hallway with his grumpy grandson in one hand and a crumpled paper bag in the other.

'Looks like he wrapped it too,' Coupland said, staring wide eyed at the grumpster until he started smiling. Coupland took the parcel and made a show of opening it, his face already forming a look of mock surprise. It took a few moments to realise what he was looking at. A metal Sheriff's badge, embossed with an image of a horse and rider at the top and the words 'Lone Ranger' across the middle.

Coupland held it up to inspect it, turning it over in his hands like he'd been asked to give it a valuation. 'Nice,' he said, pinning it onto his jacket lapel.

Tonto threw his arms out as though he'd changed his mind and was claiming the gift for himself. 'Not so fast,' Coupland said, scooping him out of Amy's arms and lifting him into the air, whooshing him around while making aeroplane noises.

'You'll wind him up, Dad.'

'I don't care, it's my birthday.'

'I'll let you change his nappy then while I make you a birthday cuppa.'

'I suppose I walked into that,' Coupland grumbled, reckoning another ten minutes wouldn't make any difference.

His phone rang. He snaked one arm tight around Tonto's middle while he retrieved it from his pocket and hit the reply icon.

'Is that Kevin?'

He grunted a yes and waited.

'I'm calling to make you aware of the rising cost of funerals…'

Jesus wept. If that didn't put the cold into cold calling he didn't know what did. Coupland told the caller what he could do with his funeral plan, grateful Tonto was too young to understand or repeat what he was saying. He pocketed his phone, placed a hand on Tonto's back to feel his rhythmic breathing. Was it wrong to think of the future when he held him in his arms? Right now this baby belonged to them, but in time he'd have to navigate the school playground, learn to find his place amongst others.

'Maybe I should buy him a punch bag,' Coupland said when he joined Amy in the kitchen. 'So he knows how to handle himself…'

Amy had been stirring milk into their coffees; she put the teaspoon down before turning to face him. 'Yeah, because a sharp right hook will go down really well in nursery.'

'Kids need to know how to handle themselves.'

'He's a baby, Dad.'

Coupland pictured Tonto being cornered in the

playground. What he'd do if that happened...

'Ah, Jesus, I need to go,' he said, handing him back to Amy while reaching for his car keys.

*

CID Room, Salford Precinct Station
The mood in the CID room was light-hearted. Word had spread that the person responsible for the killing spree that had plagued the city over the past two weeks was in custody. As shifts overlapped, officers piled in to hear how Sam Freeman had manipulated three outwardly intelligent people into carrying out unspeakable acts. They heard how Bradley, Khan and Strong had been groomed for several months, how every time they met with her they'd unwittingly lowered their defences and let her in.

Coupland caught Alex's eye as he hovered in the doorway. One look at his troubled face and she was on her feet.

'What's up?'

'I want another crack at Freeman. I think her next move is going to involve her son.' He remembered the photo of the sullen faced boy hanging on his mother's office wall.

From a desk nearby, Ashcroft heard their exchange. 'Do you want me to bring him in Sarge, if you think he's in danger?'

Coupland nodded, although if Freeman's previous actions were anything to go by the word 'danger' didn't touch the sides.

The custody officer looked up as Coupland entered the booking-in area. 'If this is an early morning call you've left it too late. Our guests enjoyed breakfast in their rooms an hour ago. Their carriage to court will be arriving in five minutes.'

'I need to speak to Freeman,' Coupland told him. 'I've squared it with the boss.'

'I've not had a call to say as much,' the officer said.

Coupland paused by the desk, rammed his hands in his pockets as though he had all the time in the world. He nodded at the phone on the end of the counter top. 'Fill your boots. He's just gone into a briefing with the Super but I'm sure he'll be pleased to take your call. You know, admitting in front of Curtis that he's been slipshod when it comes to procedure. I reckon he'll thank you for that, in time.'

The custody officer shoved a fat finger into the collar of his shirt as though overcome with heat. He eyed Coupland's sheriff's badge but rightly decided now wasn't the time to comment on it. 'Five minutes,' he said. 'Any longer and I'll bypass Mallender and ring the Super himself.'

He pushed the door release button enabling Coupland and Alex to pass through the security door into the corridor of cells. Alex held the door open whilst the officer reached for his keys, making sure it clicked shut once he'd passed though. They followed him until they located the right cell, stood back while he opened the door. Freeman was sitting on her cell bed, looking as fresh as it was possible to look when you'd spent the night on a mattress less than one inch thick.

Coupland got straight to the point. 'When we first met you told me your son was having problems at college. You said you'd been helping him. Is he being bullied too?

And if so, what the hell have you got planned?'

The hypnotherapist's smile was slow but confident. As though she'd known all along this moment would come and she wasn't in the least bit fazed by it. 'All you want to do as a parent is keep your child safe. Keep them away from violence and prejudice and sarcasm. Then one day you realise you can't, and you start to live in fear of them experiencing the things that damaged you. History mustn't be allowed to repeat itself.'

Coupland felt the first trickle of unease. 'What have you done?'

Freeman pushed herself to her feet. Her movements were slow and it was only as she started walking around that Coupland noticed her limp.

'Piers stamped on my knee,' she said, anticipating his question. 'The day he turned Asim against me. As if humiliating me wasn't enough. It was Linda that pushed me over. Held me down so that I couldn't defend myself. A surgeon put pins in it, but it still plays up every now and again.'

Coupland tried not to let his frustration show. 'What about your son? Has he been getting a hard time too?'

Freeman began to whisper to herself. 'They think they're so much better than him. These self-absorbed celebrity-obsessed wannabees have the gall to treat him like a leper because in their view he's a geek. He's always found it hard to mix, prefers his computer games to going out. What harm is he doing?'

'What did they do?' Alex asked.

'It was small things at first. Ignoring him when he spoke to them. Then they started posting cruel comments on his Facebook page. There's a girl, she was friendly with him for a while, or so he thought, turns out she'd only befriended him so she could get her hands on his mobile number. That's when they stepped it up a notch, sending him texts saying he was a waste of breath.' She looked at Coupland then, her smile gone. 'He was sat in the bath with his wrists cut when I found him. I wrapped towels around his arms and dialled 999. I'd only gone home early because I had a migraine. If I hadn't…'

The custody sergeant cleared his throat. 'She's due in court—'

'—She's going nowhere.' Coupland cut him off midsentence, indicating they be left alone. Coupland was aware of the look the officer threw in his direction but that only mattered if he gave a fuck.

He focussed his attention on Freeman. 'I won't pretend to imagine what you went through,' he told her, trying not to think how he'd feel if it was Amy or her boy.

'What's your son's name?' Alex asked.

'Shaun.'

'It's not too late to stop whatever it is you've got planned. Surely you don't want Shaun living with the same terrible guilt as the others?'

When Freeman spoke next there was a tremor in her voice that hadn't been there before. 'He told me that he doesn't want to live! They've made him feel worthless. Two weeks off college and not one person came to see him. Not one card. Some things can't be fixed once they're broken, DS Coupland.'

She smiled then, but her eyes were like stone. 'But that doesn't mean he can't make them pay, while he still can…'

CHAPTER TWENTY-SEVEN

*H*e's floating on air. Either that or his feet are on castors. Like he's gliding. Yeah, he feels like he's gliding. He's moving despite not making any effort. As though someone's pulling him along, like a puppet on a string. Everyone stares at him. He touches his face self-consciously, pats down the calf lick in his hair that he's hated since he was a child. He isn't used to being the centre of attention, unless being the butt of everyone's jokes counts. They aren't laughing now though. The dining hall falls silent as word gets around and people turn to look at him. Some smart Alec's bound to get their phone out, start filming him for posterity. He shrugs. Not as though it's the first time stuff has been posted about him online.

His body feels light. Lighter than it has for years. As though the burden he carries has evaporated like morning dew. So many wide eyes, gawping. For the first time in his life he's in control. He calls the shots. He feels like that guy in that advert for Money Supermarket. Finally things are going his way. People like him don't get to feel this good. It's one of the rules of life that aren't written down but are there nonetheless. Some people lead charmed lives. Others have to make do with large helpings of misery. Life isn't fair.

His phone buzzes in his pocket. He doesn't bother answering it. Whoever it is will leave him a message. They always do:

Ugly prick.

Hope you die.

Loser.

A slow smile spreads across his face.

He isn't a loser now.

His eyes scan the diners and those waiting to be served. No one has moved since he walked in. Instead, they stand rooted to the spot, as though the sight of him has turned them to stone. He throws a quizzical look in the direction of someone he knows but the boy looks alarmed, starts backing away. Even the ones who've never caused him any harm start backing away, their faces serious. It's the silence that alerts everyone. The usual lunchtime din, replaced by a collective gasp. It takes several seconds for onlookers to understand what they are seeing, to realise that their eyes aren't deceiving them. A girl screams as she points towards him. Several more follow the trajectory of her finger and begin screaming too. He wonders what the hell the fuss is about. Until he looks down and sees that he's holding a gun.

CHAPTER TWENTY-EIGHT

'You OK Sarge?' Krispy asked, eyeing Coupland as he stomped into the CID room.

'Tell me where Freeman's son goes to college and I'll be cock-a-bloody-hoop. Turns out he's been a victim of bullying too.'

Freeman had said all she wanted to say on the matter, had no intention of making Coupland's job easier by cooperating with him. It was up to them to fill in the missing blanks.

Krispy slipped on his phone's headset, started dialling the numbers that he'd called up on screen. Several local colleges had merged into a 'super college' a couple of years back, though he'd still need to make separate calls to each campus to locate where Shaun Freeman was enrolled.

'How come you're in so early, anyway?'

Krispy tugged self-consciously at creased shirt sleeves. 'I haven't actually been home, Sarge,' he admitted, running his hands over the boyish bum fluff on his chin. 'The IT specialist got in touch to say he was held up with another job but could talk me through a system repair if I was willing to stay on.'

'Stay on? More like move in... did it work?'

Krispy moved his head from side to side. 'Nothing's changed, as far as I can see, other than that's several hours of my life I'll not get back. Oh, hang on,' he said, pointing to his headpiece he indicated his call was being answered. He explained to the switchboard operator the information he needed, waited to be put through to Student Services at City College then repeated his request, coming back with replies Coupland would have been proud of when Data Protection raised its head.

He'd been put on hold for the third time when Coupland jingled his car keys to get his attention. 'I'll take a drive over to the sixth form college and see if I can make headway face to face. Call me if you get a result.'

Krispy gave him the thumbs up.

Coupland had crossed the junction at Langworthy Road when his phone rang. He hit the hands-free button and barked his name.

'Sarge?' It was Ashcroft. *'There's no answer at Freeman's home. I tried accessing Shaun's Facebook profile but it looks as though it's been closed down.'*

Little wonder. 'He's been bullied at college,' Coupland said. 'I reckon he might be on some sort of suicide mission. Krispy's ringing round, finding out which college he goes to. I'm heading out to Pendleton, see if I can cut through some of the red tape face to face. Besides, I want the names of the kids who've been giving him a hard time. Something the student service team may be less than happy to give up over the phone.'

'I'm close by Eccles College, Sarge, want me to call in there while I'm passing?'

Coupland grunted a yes. 'But make sure you keep Krispy in the loop,' he said, pushing the button to end the call.

Coupland made a sharp left into Dronfield Road, leaving his car as close to the main building as he was physically able. 'I'll be two minutes!' he called out to the security guard who started to approach him. He marched to the reception desk, pushed his warrant card under the nose of the receptionist busy texting on her phone. 'I'm Detective Sergeant Coupland and I don't have time to piss about…'

It took closer to five minutes to get the information. The security guard looked put out when Coupland returned to his car. 'You need to get this thing washed mate.' He wrinkled his nose as he pointed to the pigeon droppings on the Mondeo's roof. 'It's a bloody health hazard.'

Coupland could think of worse ones, but now wasn't the time to play Murder Squad Top Trumps. Once in his car he checked in with Krispy: 'Nada. No one by the name of Shaun Freeman is enrolled at Pendleton College. Any luck your end?'

'He's not at City College, and DC Ashcroft rang to say he's not at Eccles either. There's a couple more to call before I widen the area out,' he said. A pause.

'What is it?'

'Hang on a minute, Sarge.'

Coupland heard Krispy's breathing as he tapped something into his keyboard.

'Come on, son,' he prompted, patience wasn't one of his strong points.

'After you left I tried searching IPOS for 'college related incidents', just to see if the database was working yet, but it kept throwing up an error message. Only it appears to be up and running again, now. I've just typed in the exact same search request and it's started churning out data.'

Coupland waited.

'Uniforms attended a disturbance last month at the Metropolitan College in Walkden. No injuries were reported. The matter was to be dealt with internally by the principal.'

'Does it say what the disturbance was about?'

'Hang on, Sarge.' A pause while Krispy skim read the report. *'Yeah, something to do with offensive messages sent to a mobile belonging to Shaun Freeman...'*

Coupland felt his pulse racing. 'You need to get hold of DCI Mallender. Tell him to call the principal and get him to shut the college down. Tell him I'm on my way there.'

Another pause. *'What if DCI Mallender asks for a reason?'*

'Tell him that Shaun's been bullied by kids at the college. That he's suicidal and desperate. That with his mother's track record he's capable of anything. If he sounds like he's dithering mention how many attempts it took for you to get the information we needed from IPOS.' Mallender would work out the subtext: better to go in gung-ho than spend the next five years dealing with a lawsuit because our response wasn't quick enough due to dodgy IT.

Coupland ended the call and put his foot down.

CHAPTER TWENTY-NINE

Coupland thundered north on Langworthy Road with one eye on the dashboard clock. The college was no more than ten minutes away. By the time he arrived Mallender would have spoken to the principal and it would simply be a case of helping him evacuate the students until Shaun Freeman had been apprehended. Assuming he was there of course. That he hadn't decided to sack the day off and spend it window shopping in the Arndale Centre.

His phone rang. DCI Mallender's name came up on the hands-free screen.

'Boss,' Coupland said as he hammered the Mondeo across a roundabout, turning left into Broad Street before joining the East Lancs Road. 'I'm guessing you've spoken to the princi—'

Mallender cut him off mid-sentence. '*—Kevin, listen to me, a report's come in that someone holding a gun was seen entering the Metropolitan College. A tactical unit has been mobilised and I've put in a request for a negotiator.*'

Coupland couldn't believe his ears. 'We can't wait for a negotiator! Besides, this kid isn't in his own head. He's in someone else's.'

'*What are you going to do?*'

The college was no more than half a mile away. 'Doesn't look like I've got much choice,' Coupland said, putting his foot to the floor.

A hard right and he was on Walkden Road, his foot pumping the accelerator. A line of stationary vehicles appeared in front of him as the college came into sight. Nothing moved despite him pressing his hand down on the horn, gesturing wildly for the cars in front to get out of his way. No one budged. There was nowhere they could budge to, given the row of bollards blocking one lane and the temporary ramp across the other.

Fucking roadworks.

*

It's like he is outside of his body, watching himself.

He's on a movie set. A Western. The lead actor whose character is about to teach those who've wronged him a lesson. All he is waiting for is the director to shout 'Action!' Or maybe there'll be some other signal. Either way he knows that when the moment comes he'll be the victor, for he is the defender of the weak. People will look on this day and know it was the day that everything changed. The day the vulnerable took stock and hit back. He puffs up his chest. He's unstoppable. A God-Damned superhero!

He stares down at the gun in his hand. The people around him hold their breath as they cower behind furniture. The stench of their fear invades his nostrils. He watches them as though looking through someone else's eyes.

Then he sees her. The one person he thought was his friend. The one who passed his mobile number onto the rest of his tutor group. The one who called him a loser.

She cowers as he moves towards her and drags her to her feet.

*

Coupland could still hear the horns blaring from the main road where he'd abandoned the Mondeo and started to run.

Jesus wept…

He heard sirens in the distance. Back up. Armed response. How long until they got here? How long could he keep this up? His legs felt like lead. His chest thumped.

Nearly there.

He sidestepped students as they ran down the steps of the main college building. They were being directed away from the canteen by security staff. Men in high viz tabards clearly out of their depth.

Some students were sobbing. A helicopter overhead drowned out their crying.

Other staff members began to emerge from the building. One woman wrapped her arms around the shoulders of a boy who was hyperventilating, helping him count his breaths. 'One, two, three,' she said over and over. 'One. Two. Three.'

Coupland scanned the scene in front of him for any obvious signs of danger. Checked the building's angles and vantage points.

Then he ran into the building.

He didn't need signposts to see where he should go. He followed the sound of screaming, saw the fear on the faces of the students as they barged past him in the other direction.

He pushed through a set of double doors, taking in the scene that greeted him:

A girl knelt in the centre of the room. Shaun Freeman aiming a gun at her head.

Any minute now the tactical unit would surround the building while awaiting orders to storm inside. Emergency vehicles would already be taking up position around the perimeter of the campus, parking on the driveways of the houses nearby as they waited. Coupland drew in a breath as he readied himself. Moments like this, when a gunman felt cornered, could only end one way.

Shaun grew still as he turned his attention to the sweaty man in the creased suit.

The boy's eyes were distant, like someone in a trance. He smiled but it was sleepy. Coupland studied the gun in Shaun's hand. A Glock 17. Weapons like these could be bought from most street corners if you knew where to go. Cheap. Untraceable. Deadly. He had no doubt Freeman had purchased it on behalf of her son. Had probably had it for weeks, getting him used to the feel of it while he was under hypnosis.

'I know that none of this is your doing,' Coupland said, moving towards him slowly, arm outstretched. 'I'm a detective. I've spoken to your mother. She told me what you've been through, that she's programmed you to take revenge. Trust me, there's another way. This isn't the answer.'

He studied Shaun's face, looking for something, anything to suggest his words were getting through. 'Can you hear me? Do you understand what I'm saying?'

The boy looked distracted, as though unable to distinguish between reality and the parallel universe he'd been jettisoned to. He was both the actor and the audience, united as one. He nodded slowly. 'Please don't be cross with me,' he said.

Coupland heard the heavy breathing of the students around them. He wondered, as they huddled under the canteen's tables, what they'd remember of this day. He hoped to Christ they remembered nothing. 'Give me your gun, Shaun. We can go somewhere and talk about what's going on.'

Shaun frowned, as if he was trying to see something that was out of focus. He looked from Coupland to the gun in his hands, his face clearing as though he'd solved a puzzle that had been bugging him. In that moment the shadow he was under lifted. When he looked at the detective his eyes were clear.

Coupland had long since learned that no matter how well you organized your life, made plans, you were always at the mercy of chaos. Stepping into the road the moment a driver reached across the passenger seat to answer their phone. The thud in your chest when the doctor asked you to take a seat. Coupland eyeballed Shaun and felt the shiver of intuition. He knew damn well how this would pan out.

'This isn't the way,' he repeated, stepping in front of the girl.

Shaun locked eyes with Coupland. 'You shouldn't have done that. It means I'm going to have to shoot you too.'

'You shoot me and you'll go straight to jail. You shoot her you'll go straight to jail. What was the point of working hard for your grades if you're going to blow it all away?'

A blink.

'Look, I know this isn't your doing. You've been set up. You've been fed lies, which is why you're acting out of character. It's not too late to walk away from this and get on with your life.'

'Why should I believe you?'

'Because people can turn their lives around. Don't let this be the thing that everyone remembers you for.'

'They think I'm a loser.'

'Better that than a killer.'

Shaun jerked the hand holding the gun towards his target. '*She* thinks I'm a loser.'

'No she doesn't,' said Coupland, turning to eyeball her, all the while nodding his head to encourage her to play along.

He saw it then. The glint of steel in her eye that told him she had no intention of doing the right thing. Her friends were watching and she intended to give them the performance of a lifetime.

She curled her lip. 'Fuckwit,' she snarled.

Shaun moved his head and stared at her with empty eyes. Saliva dribbled from the corner of his mouth. He raised the arm holding the gun and pulled the trigger.

If Coupland divided people up into those worth saving and those he'd let rot, this stupid girl would be top of the pile he didn't give a fuck about. With her mean face and cruel mouth would the world really miss her? Would she go on to feed starving children or batter her baby? Sometimes it was better not to know.

He took a breath and stepped into the unknown.

He felt the burst of fire from the barrel of the gun, felt himself pivot backwards before he realised that the bullet had struck. He spread his arms out wide, made a grabbing motion with his hands but there was nothing to cling onto, nothing but the air as it whooshed through his fingers.

He was falling.

He clutched at his chest as his head slammed into the ground. He wasn't a religious man. Bad things happened to too many good people for there to be a god he wanted to believe in. But he wondered in that fleeting moment, if his life ended today, whether his mother would be waiting for him on the other side.

CHAPTER THIRTY

Emergency Department, Salford Royal Hospital

Coupland opened his eyes. Blinked them rapidly for several seconds until he got rid of the stars that kept forming.

'Well I can't be dead,' he said as a male nurse in scrubs flashed a torch into his eyes. 'Because you look nothing like a bloody angel.'

The nurse said something out of earshot before stepping back to make room for the tired-looking junior doctor who peeped through the cubicle curtain before drawing it back.

Confused, Coupland wriggled his fingers and toes. Lifted a hand to where the bullet had made contact. The doctor smiled. 'Do you believe in luck, DS Coupland?'

'Not a shred of it,' Coupland answered, wincing as he shook his head.

'Well someone was looking out for you today. Nothing more than a slight concussion,' the doctor added, holding up a piece of metal bent and twisted out of shape. Coupland stared at what was left of his birthday present. The Sheriff's badge Tonto had given him that morning.

He reached out. 'Can I keep it?'

'If I were you I'd never want to let it out of my sight,' the doctor said, placing the badge in his hand.

'So the rumours are true, then,' Alex observed as she stepped into the cubicle. 'The message from control said an officer had been shot then five minutes later it said the officer in question was being taken to hospital as a precaution.'

Coupland showed Alex the badge. The lapel where he'd jokingly fastened it that morning.

'Jesus, Kevin, an inch either way…'

Coupland didn't dare think about the consequences. It was that lack of thought that kept him doing his job.

Something occurred to him. 'I abandoned my car round the corner from the college…'

'Doesn't matter,' she said, reaching for her bag to retrieve her phone. 'I'll get on to Traffic, get someone to pick it up for you.'

'No need,' Coupland told her. 'There's a PC owes me a favour, I'll ring the desk sergeant, get him to pass on a message.'

Everyone made mistakes. It was only right he gave the truculent knobhead who'd turned the Mondeo's roof into the bottom of a bird cage the chance to redeem himself. Nothing a wash and wax wouldn't sort out. And an apology too, if he really wanted to bury the hatchet.

Alex looked uncomfortable.

'What happened to Shaun?' Coupland asked her.

'Armed response arrived at the scene and heard a gunshot; they had no choice but to open fire.'

'Shit.'

'He's alive, he's in theatre now. His injuries aren't thought to be life threatening. We've informed his mother.' Alex started to shake her head. 'What the hell was she thinking?'

'It never pays to go down that rabbit hole,' said Coupland. 'Be grateful you don't understand.'

It would be down to the lawyers to provide mitigating arguments for Asim Khan and Linda Strong. He doubted the evidence he'd uncovered would be enough to spare them custodial sentences, but it might reduce the time they served, make their return to society a little less traumatic. As for Freeman, he reckoned a nice one-bedroomed unit in a certain Liverpool high security hospital was already being prepared for her.

'There's some good news…' Alex told him.

'I'll be the judge of that,' said Coupland. 'Go on, I'm all ears.'

'Both pupils who had to be cut from the minibus have responded well to surgery and been moved onto a general ward. They're going to survive this, Kevin.'

As good news went he'd take it. He caught a look that flashed across Alex's face. 'So why the pained expression? Either you've got indigestion or you're about to tell me that slippery pole is beckoning…'

A tut. 'I hate it when you do that.'

'Do what?'

'Try and second guess me when I'm about to tell you something.'

'Am I right?'

A pause.

'Well?'

'On this occasion, maybe…'

'So, go on, tell Uncle Kevin all about it…'

'The Chief Constable's setting up a new taskforce. In response to Operation Naseby.'

Attempts to dismantle the network responsible for bringing in drugs and trafficked sex workers were showing early signs of success, but the industry was a lucrative one; there was always someone ready to step into a patch made vacant when a gang was sent to jail. Turf wars were on the rise, and long running feuds were erupting in 'tit-for-tat' violence. The unwritten code of not harming women, children and innocent family members no longer applied. 'This unit has been formed as a response to the number of family members being targeted. My role will be one of safeguarding.'

'Keeping threatened family members safe?'

'Partly. It's also about identifying youngsters at risk of being drawn into organised crime – and steering them away from that lifestyle.'

'What? By buying them a one way ticket to Kansas?' He thought of his own, failed attempt to help Liam Roberts start afresh. How things might have turned out differently if the arsonist had been helped sooner.

'We'd be working with kids, show them how to cope with stress and manage their anger.' She levelled her gaze at him. 'You know the sort of thing, divert them into sport. Give them something positive to do so they aren't enticed into drug running.'

Coupland's sigh went down to the soles of his shoes. He had the greatest respect for Alex, he really did. But at times… 'You know they won't have the budget to do anything meaningful, don't you? A monthly meeting with youth workers and a few printed leaflets at best. You'll spend the rest of your time parked outside some toerag's house so his missus can take the kids to school.'

'Christ, Kevin, what would you do that's so revolutionary?'

'No revolution needed. We throw all our resources

into stopping the drugs coming in, full stop. Four million pounds' worth was seized in Salford last year and you know damn well amounts like that aren't brought in shoved up anyone's backside. We should be stopping and searching every lorry that crosses our border but we don't. Until we do, this problem will never go away.'

'Rant over?'

He smiled. 'Just telling it like it is.'

'I can't change the world, Kevin, but if I can make a small difference in this city, isn't it worth it?'

'Just don't get shot.'

'Said the man who stepped into the path of a bullet this afternoon... Besides, it's a safeguarding unit.'

'Yeah, yeah. I give it a month tops, then you'll be back to being target practice like everyone else.'

They were interrupted by an angry yell and wailing that could only signify one thing.

'Please tell me the boss didn't call Lynn.'

Alex didn't have time to reply. Lynn, Amy and a ferocious looking Tonto stormed through the cubicle curtain into his line of vision.

'Oh, he told me alright, and sent a police escort to get us here! Though they turned the blues and twos off when they heard you weren't on death's door.'

'I'll leave you to it. I've got a boot full of CSI suits I'm taking over to Ben's school. Might as well start 'em young,' said Alex, tiptoeing round Lynn who was in no mood for small talk.

Tonto was doing his angry octopus impression, arms and legs flailing as he pushed away from Amy so he could glare at his grandad. Coupland looked at the three people in the world he'd gladly take a bullet for. The fright they must have had. 'Give him here,' he grumbled, readying himself for their anger.

THE END

AUTHOR NOTES

I am always fascinated by the things I discover when carrying out research into each book. The facts that made my eyes water this time around include:

Approximately £13,000,000 was paid in wages to officers suspended by 29 UK police forces between 2013 and 2018. (Source Freedom of Information data provided to BBC for their Inside Out programme aired 28 January 2019)

It costs £290,000 per year to keep someone in Ashworth Hospital. (The National High Secure Services Strategic Commissioning Plan 2010-2015)

1 in 6 children experience some form of bullying (Department for Education: Bullying in England, April 2013 to March 2018 – Analysis on 10-15 year olds from the Crime Survey for England and Wales)

And finally, an article in the Manchester Evening News, 5 February 2020, provided me with the gem of a background story: *"GMP have declared a 'critical incident' after a failed upgrade of their troubled IOPS IT system left officers recording incidents on paper."*

ABOUT THE AUTHOR

Emma writes full time from her home in East Lothian. When she isn't writing she can be seen walking her rescue dog Star along the beach or frequenting bars of ill repute where many a loose lip has provided the nugget of a storyline. Find out more about the author and her other books at: https://www.emmasalisbury.com

Have you tried my Davy Johnson gangland series? Why not try the first chapter of TRUTH LIES WAITING…

CHAPTER 1

It's funny how the do-gooding public think prison is the answer, like a magic wand that wipes your criminal scorecard clean. Only it isn't like that, the problems you leave behind are still waiting for you when you step back out into the daylight, except now they're much bigger, and this time you don't have as many choices. I was one of the lucky ones, moved back into my family home and into a job that paid decent money. I should send a shout out to my probation officer; she came up trumps, getting me in at Swanson's rather than pretend work on a poxy job creation scheme. OK, packing cardboard boxes is boring as Hell, but you can have a laugh with the guys on the shop floor and turn the radio up when you run out of things to say.

Even so, only one day in the job and already things started going pear-shaped. I was heading towards the bus-stop at the end of my shift when a small boy riding a BMX bike mounted the pavement, circling round me a couple of times like a playground bully eyeing his victim. Close up he was older than I'd first thought, maybe thirteen or so, with shaved blond hair and a forehead that was way too wide for the rest of his face. His eyes were sunken and further apart than was right and a mouth that hung open as though his lips were too heavy for his jaw.

'You Davy?' It came out as a statement rather than a question, but I nodded anyway.

'Gotta message f'ya.' The kid had a nasal whine, the kind that'd get on your nerves if you had to listen to it all the time. I wasn't worried by the sight of him though; a boy on a bike makes a bee-line for you and says they've got a message; it's not that big a deal round here. As far as I know, Hallmark and Interflora don't stock *'Glad you're out of chokey'* gifts and where I'm from your first stretch inside is a rite of passage. News of my release is bound to have got around.

'Mickey's givin' ye till the end o' the week to make your first payment.'

I nodded in agreement, his terms seemed reasonable; he was hardly going to write off my loan because of my spell inside.

'Said to tell ye he's adjusted the figures.'

Ah. Bike Boy's voice was beginning to grate but he had my full attention. 'Said something 'bout the credit crunch an' compound interest, or was it compound fractures?' the boy stated maliciously, 'Either way he said I wasn't tae worry if I forgot the gist, so long as I told ye how much yer payment has gone up tae.'

I had a feeling I wasn't going to like this. Bike Boy paused for effect, as though I was an X Factor contestant about to learn my fate: whether I was to stay in the competition or return to the life I'd been badmouthing every week.

'Two hundred quid,' he said firmly

I was confused. That was the amount of my original loan. I'd been due to pay it off fifty pounds a week until Mickey got bored but now he seemed to be giving me the chance to pay off the debt in full. It'd be a stretch, after tax I'll be clearing two fifty a week, but it'd be worth it.

Bike Boy smiled, not altogether unkindly but there was a glimmer of pleasure there, even so.

'Two hundred a week until further notice,' he clarified matter of factly.

'Yer havin' a laugh!' I began to object but the kid was already peddling away, job done. I know my spell inside meant Mickey'd had to wait for his money but this was some penalty. After bus fares and board I'd be working for nothing.

And so this morning I'm trying to manage my expectations. To start my day as I mean to go on. Good things don't happen to Davy Johnson, never have done, never will. I'm your original walking talking magnet for bucket loads of shit but today I'm going to look on the bright side; the sun is shining, I have a pack of smokes in my pocket and I have a job. I take a cigarette from the pack and light it, drawing down hard, enjoying the sensation of the nicotine inflating my lungs. Is it so wrong to be drawn to something that really isn't good for you?

The sun's rays beam down steadily and I roll my overalls to my waist before lying back on the wooden bench, savouring each lungful of smoke. My upper body tingles; already the skin on my chest is beginning to turn pink. Be good to get some colour, get rid of the grey pallor that is the trademark of a stretch inside. I close my eyes, lifting my cigarette for a final drag before returning to the pallet of cartons waiting for me. All I need to top the day off is a nice cold beer and I promise myself one at the end of the shift with a couple of guys from the shop floor if they're up for it.

A cold chill across my stomach makes my eye lids snap open. There, in my eye line, blocking out the sun like a spiteful raincloud, stands a familiar but unfriendly face. Police Constable MacIntyre arrested me six months ago and here he is larger than life staring down at me as though I'm a giant turd.

I look past MacIntyre to the squad car parked by the factory gates and the officer in the passenger seat picking his nose while scrolling through messages on a mobile. I don't think they're supposed to use their phones on duty but I know better than to air unasked for views.

Instead, I push myself to a sitting position, pulling my overalls up over my shoulders whilst checking across the factory yard to see if my visitors can be seen from the main building. Candy Staton, the boss's PA has her back to the canteen window while she busies herself getting drinks for the managers. Petite with long shiny hair tied back in a ponytail, she is the prettiest girl I've set eyes on in a long while. She smiled at me on my first day here even though she must have seen my personnel file. I wonder what she'll make of the new guy not yet a week in and bringing police to the door.

'Heard they'd let ye oot.' PC MacIntyre is a prize prick with eyes that tell you he likes a drink almost as much as he loves a ruck. Thick-set arms protruding from a dumpy body, his Kevlar vest provides an illusion of muscle. 'Thought I'd come see for myself.'

I say nothing. I learned long ago not to rise to the bait; that smart mouth answers got me locked up for the night. Instead, I stare at the man's forehead as though looking for his third eye. 'What's this… fancy dress?' MacIntyre smirks at my overalls and work boots while at the same time taking a step closer, all the better to intimidate.

Slowly I push myself up from the bench, making us

equal in height though we both knew which man has the upper hand. Over the officer's shoulder I can see Candy pause by the window, watching us.

'Look,' I reason, arms outstretched to let MacIntyre know he'll get no trouble from me, 'I need to get back, we only get ten minutes for a break.'

The officer sniggers as though this is the funniest thing he's heard in ages. '"We only get ten minutes for a break!"' he mimics. 'Who ye trying tae kid, son? Work's no' good enough fe the likes o' you,' he snipes, 'I know for a fact ye'll no' last the shift.'

Not for the first time I wonder whether there is a section in the police training manual called *Easy Steps to Provoking and Needling,* only this is a skill MacIntyre really works hard at. Each meeting is like an Olympic pissing contest except there can only ever be one winner. I stay silent, yet still there's only a slim chance of me coming through unscathed.

'What they got ye doing then, sweeping the floor?' MacIntyre smiles but his eyes are cold and hard.

'Packing boxes,' I mutter, wondering if this simple answer can incriminate me in some way, although for what, I can't imagine.

MacIntyre nods as though he already knows this answer and I've merely been sitting some kind of test. 'Ye don't have to be Einstein then, eh?' he smirks. I shrug, I've been told I was thick by every teacher in school, if this insult is intended to wind me up he's way off beam; you can't be offended by a fact.

'Then again, with your pedigree…' MacIntyre taunts. Here it comes, the bit about my Dad being an alkie and handy with his fists, especially where Mum was concerned.

How come his jibes always end up with my Dad? He was a wrong 'un so I'm destined to be one too, is that it?

'I mean,' MacIntyre grins as though he's second guessed my thoughts and has deliberately chosen to change tack, 'what with ye mum being on the game and all, not exactly going tae come across many great male role models, are ye?'

I keep my mouth clamped shut but it's getting really hard not to rise to his bait. Digs about me or my old man I can cope with, but there's not a soul on this earth who'll get away with saying anything bad about Mum. She put food on the table every day of my childhood, made sure I had decent clothes and a roof over our heads. In fact life improved once Dad was no longer around and Mum was grateful to have a job that meant she was there for me when I'd been small. *Ye gotta roll with the punches, Son,* was the way she explained it, *ye have to deal with the hand ye've been dealt.* It wasn't her fault I'd got in with a bad crowd. Yes, my bravado cost me a stint inside, but it was a mistake I had no intention of repeating.

'Cat got your tongue?' MacIntyre's sly little eyes follow my gaze toward the office window and Candy, a knowing look flitting across his face. 'Way out of your league, Sunshine,' he smirks, nodding in her direction. 'Especially when she hears about your pedigree.'

'Go fuck yersel'.' The words shoot out before I can stop them and in that moment I know how the rest of the day will pan out. Even at that point, there is little I can do to change the pattern of events. PC MacIntyre's eyes light up like a child on Christmas morning, 'What did ye say, ye lanky streak o' piss?'

'Ye heard me.' I say, in for a penny, in for a pound. I

pull myself up to my full height, which I know will look to the copper in the car like I'm squaring up but by now I no longer give a shit. I turn towards the wedged open fire exit I'd emerged from fifteen minutes earlier. The prefab building which has been my place of work for two whole days had offered endless possibilities; even the vain hope that Candy Staton would notice my existence. I look back to the canteen window; she's noticed me now, right enough, but for all the wrong reasons.

I turn to MacIntyre. 'They're expecting me,' I say simply.

'They're expecting ye to fuck up,' he says scornfully. 'Why don't you do everyone a favour and crawl back under your stone?'

Ignoring him, I walk towards the open factory door; I figure putting some space between us might stop him feeling the need to intimidate.

'Not so fast, pal,' he warns, putting his hand on my chest to prevent me from moving but I brush it aside; the sooner I get back indoors the better. A crowd has gathered beside Candy at the canteen window, watching as MacIntyre's bulk blocks the entrance into the building, a smile plastered across his face.

Want to read the rest? Click on the link below to download from Amazon today:

http://amzn.to/1KIrodZ

Printed in Great Britain
by Amazon